true

colors

MELISSA PEARL

masks #1

true colors

masks #1

MELISSA PEARL
love ultimately wins ... as you can *imagine*

True Colors, Book I, The Masks Series by Melissa Pearl
1st Edition published by Evatopia Press
2nd Edition published by Melissa Pearl Author 2018

www.melissapearlauthor.com

ISBN: 1721536132
ISBN-13: 978-1721536139

For Sharyn
The lady who's always looking out for everyone else.
You are a good soul, my friend.

xxx

one

A single moment in time can change everything. The night a stranger's hand touched mine, I was thrown into a new reality I never could have imagined.
And to think that only a few hours earlier, I had no idea it was coming...

****

Okay, Chase just took my shirt off. Whipped it over my head and I let him.

Did I want to let him?

Yes, yes, I definitely did. His naked chest pressed

against my stomach felt divine. I ran my hand over his sinewy shoulders as his lips skimmed my collarbone, his tongue trailing a path down to the edge of my bra.

Was he going to take it off?

My insides clenched at the idea. No guy had ever touched me that way before. And I did want Chase to— at least I think I did.

I wondered how long it would take him to figure out how non-existent my breasts were. My brother, Toby, always teased me, saying if you took me into the ocean, you could surf me to shore because I was so flat and skinny.

What if Chase thought the same thing? Would he still want me?

I ran my fingers through Chase's fine brown hair as his mouth worked back up my neck and his arm slid beneath my back.

Surely he'd worked it out by now. If he didn't like skinny girls, he wouldn't have even gone for me, right? And with his body melded to mine, I could definitely tell he was into me...if you know what I mean.

When I'd invited Chase into my empty house and closed my bedroom door with a definitive click, I'd made my intentions very clear. A playful smile had danced across his lips as he'd pulled me against him and firmly kissed me. Next thing I knew we were on my bed and his shirt was on the floor.

Chase's fingers fidgeted with the clasp of my bra. I leaned into him, eager for his touch, but also wrestling with the small part of me that wanted to squish my back onto the bed so he couldn't. I don't know why I suddenly felt so vulnerable. We'd been dating for a couple of months. Chase was more than ready. He'd been hinting at doing it for weeks. I should go for it. I should let him.

I was an eighteen-year-old virgin. It was about time I experienced sex. I was ready. At least I thought I was.

"Caitlyn, are you home?" My insides went ice cold as I heard my mom's voice. And then to make matters worse, she only knocked once before pushing the door open. "Oh!"

Chase leaped off me, adjusting his pants and trying to swivel away so she couldn't see how excited he was. He ran a hand through his mussed up locks and sort of grinned. "Hey, Mrs. Davis."

She didn't say a word, just folded her arms across her pristine white blouse and glared at him.

I scrambled for my shirt, crumpled on the floor beside Chase's. I flung his cotton T-shirt at him. He caught it with a mumbled thank you and pulled it on.

My face was on fire. My heart was thrumming erratically as I slid my shirt on and tugged it over my exposed naval. Mom was eyeballing me big time, but I couldn't look at her.

Chase snatched up his backpack and slung it over his shoulder. "Well, I should go, because...um, well I...I have um...homework."

Yeah, right! Chase never had homework. Or if he

did, I never saw him doing it, like ever.

Mom must have known that too, because her doubtful glare was almost comical. Almost.

"Of course you do." Cynicism dripped off every syllable as she kept eyeing my boyfriend with those hard, brown eyes. They were usually soft and warm like chocolate, but not then. In that particular moment they looked like burnt umber—irate and seething. She never really liked Chase and this was so not helping.

Chase's confident facade buckled beneath her gaze. Slightly flustered, he turned to me, his eyes rounding with a 'what the hell is her problem' kind of look.

I shrugged and forced a smile, trying not to let the full humiliation of the moment sink in.

"I'll see ya, Caitlyn." Chase gave me a short wave before awkwardly squeezing past my mother. Her glare followed him out the door before slowly tracing back to me.

My cheeks were raging with a hot blush as my gaze hit the floor. I never knew the carpet could be quite so interesting. After what felt like a century of stony silence, I finally gave in and glanced up. Mom's dark eyes chastised me. I wasn't quite sure how to react. I'd never been caught doing anything too naughty before—the odd misdemeanour, but nothing to get in a flap about. This however...well, in Mom's book, I was pretty sure this would be classed as unacceptable. I folded my arms to mirror her and went for a nonchalant shrug, my usual defence to any form of conflict.

She opened her mouth to respond, her hot words ready to scald me, but she thought better of it. Pressing her lips together, she narrowed her eyes. She was obviously too pissed to talk it out. I knew it would come later—so not cool—but I had no problem with her procrastination. Mom was the silent type. She liked to let things simmer until she could articulate her irritation without hurting anyone's feelings. In spite of being busted, I felt lucky on that count.

She grabbed the doorknob, her terse words only just audible, "I'm guessing you have homework too. You might want to get that done before dinner."

Again with the raised eyebrows.

I stifled a groan and rose from my bed. I was tempted to turn and straighten the covers, but decided against it. I knew it would make my mother happy, but it would also make me look guilty and I wasn't sure I wanted to feel that way. I was eighteen! I could have sex with my boyfriend if I wanted to.

Crossing to my desk, I avoided eye contact and took a seat, not looking at my door until I heard it click shut. With a little huff, I dropped my head into my hands and begged the bedroom floor to open up and swallow me whole.

****

The thing about my parents is, they're kind of old. I mean they're not ancient, but compared to the rest of my friends' parents, they may as well be dusted off and displayed in a museum. I mean they've got five grandchildren already.

You see they were done with their family. Two boys. Two girls. The perfect set. And then my unplanned-self came along. To say I was an unexpected surprise is a major understatement. Mom was like forty-four when she found out she was pregnant with me and I think it took her and Dad a long time to deal with it. Toby, the 'baby' of the family was nearly fourteen when I came along. So I've kind of been raised as an only child. It doesn't bother me too much, until afternoons like this when all the heat is on me. There are no siblings to throw the attention to, because I'm the only one still at home.

I slumped down the stairs after Mom's dinner call.

We'd lived in this house since Toby was one. That's like thirty years. I wasn't complaining or anything. The Pacific Palisades is the nicest part of L.A., in my opinion. The beach is ten minutes away. That is something vitally important to my whole family. We've all grown up in and around the water.

I ran my hand along the hallway wall, the way I always did when I headed to the dining room. It was like this little tunnel before popping out into an expansive open planned area. It didn't used to be like that. When Toby moved to San Diego ten years ago, my parents decided to go ahead with the big renovations they'd been saving for. The front half of the house was gutted to make room for shiny new wooden floors, a sparkling state of the art kitchen and a plush sunken-in living area. A little nineteen-seventies if you asked me, but Mom had always wanted one and for this particular project she got everything she desired, including her "suite." After years of having kids in their faces all day, my parents finally earned themselves a private wing that we were basically banned from entering.

I did love the alterations. I loved the open expanse, the way it lead to a huge sunny deck area. They did good, and out of all the siblings, I've reaped the majority of the benefits. At least there was one cool thing about being the youngest by miles.

I pulled out my regular chair and took a seat, still not wanting to look my mother in the eye. Her super quiet mode was slightly unnerving. It didn't help that Dad was away on some golfing weekend. I mean I liked that he was, because I so didn't want to face a disapproving frown from him too. I'm his "little peanut." Seth and I look just like him with our dark blonde hair and blue eyes; the other three all took after Mom. In spite of Dad's effort, he couldn't help a touch of favoritism when it came to his eldest and youngest children.

Much to my siblings' angst, my dad has laxed out big time on discipline. I think Toby used up all his will power and now I basically get away with everything. Luckily for him, I'm a good kid. I think he'd be gutted about my behavior with Chase though, even if I knew a smile or two would win him over, earning me some back up.

"She's eighteen, Suzy," he'd say to my mom. "Let her be."

In saying all that, the idea of his peanut getting it on with her boyfriend...may not fly so well. No, it was definitely better that he was not here!

A fresh chicken salad with a side of homemade bread was plopped in front of me. I eyed the brown bread, stuffed full of seeds and various nuts...I had no idea what they were. I know Mom's heard of plain white bread before, because I've mentioned it several times, but she just gives me that look and asks me why I'd want to put pillow stuffing into my system. The curse of being a nutritionist's daughter, I guess.

I picked at my salad while Mom sat across from me with her freshly squeezed guava juice. The awkwardness was somewhat painful, but I decided not to let it bother me. At least I decided that until I'd stuffed over half the meal into my mouth and couldn't handle one second more of her dark glare and repeated tutting.

"What?" My fork clattered to the table.

"I didn't say anything." She shrugged.

"You didn't have to. It's written all over your face." I threw my arms in the air. "Would you just spit it out, please!"

"Alright fine." She gently placed her empty glass on the table and crossed her arms. "I don't think teenagers understand what an emotional responsibility sex is."

"Mom, it's just—"

"Don't say, 'It's just sex.'" Her eyes were on fire.

I swallowed back my words and slumped into my chair, knowing I'd have to hear this one out.

"There's no such thing as *just sex*. I hate the way people cheapen it like that. When you're with someone in that way it should be amazing and magical and mind-blowing."

Please don't say like you and Dad. Please! I don't want that mental image!

Thankfully she let out a sigh and continued in a quiet voice. "I don't see how you can do that unless you're with someone you love. I mean do you love Chase?"

The question stumped me. I should have been able to answer in a heartbeat, but I couldn't. The truth was, I didn't really know if I loved him or not. I definitely cared about him. I liked spending time with him, but our relationship so far had been more of a heady-rush. One I'd never expected. Chase Mitchell didn't look at girls like me, but for some reason I'd caught his eye and I wasn't about to cold shoulder the unexplained phenomenon.

"We've only been dating a couple of months," I mumbled.

"Then you shouldn't be having sex with him." Her eyebrows rose so high I thought they might glide off the top of her forehead. I crossed my arms and slouched while Mom let out another big sigh.

"Caitlyn, I respect that you are now an eighteen-year-old woman and in less than six months you will be flitting off to college to live the life you choose." She blinked and I couldn't tell if that news relieved or saddened her. I tried not to think about it as she realigned her wedding and engagement ring, a habit she'd had forever. "I'm not telling you when you can lose your virginity and who you can lose it to. I just want you to think about it." Her deep brown eyes were filled with parental concern. "I know you probably think I'm an old stuff. Your father's the only man I've ever been with and I know views on sex are very different to what they were when I was a teenager. I just..." She sighed. "I don't ever want you to have regrets when it comes to your first time...or anytime for that matter." She swallowed and looked awkward again. "I mean unless you've already had your first time and this is a wasted conversation. Well, it's not totally wasted, but..."

Her hands started fluffing the back of her grey-speckled curls like they always did when she was flustered. I cleared my throat and interrupted her.

"Mom. Still a virgin." I wanted to die. Who talked about sex with their sixty-three-year-old mother?

She leaned her elbows on the table, looking all relieved. "Oh, so you haven't...yet?"

"No." I frowned, and have no idea what compelled me to continue, but I did. "And we probably wouldn't have this afternoon either."

"Really?"

I shrugged, realizing I'd just told a big fat one. If Mom hadn't interrupted us, we totally would have.

14

And Mom knew it too. She dipped her head and muttered, "I'm so glad your father's not home right now."

I couldn't help my eye roll.

"Caity, I just want you to be thoughtful about it, that's all. I don't want to dictate who you hang out with, but you've got to admit you're changing. I sometimes worry where your friends are going to take you next. I miss the sweet, funny girl you used to be. The one who played sports all the time and had fun. The one who had principles and would never in a million years just let some random guy touch her."

"Chase isn't random. He's my boyfriend."

She made a face. I tried not to let it bug me. I liked Chase. He was hot and exciting. Mom just didn't get it.

"Look, I'm not that different. I'm just growing up. And I told you why I didn't try out for volleyball again this year. I wanted to focus on my studies, which is what I'm doing." That wasn't entirely true. I probably would have gone out for the team this year if my best friend, Stella, hadn't bitched and moaned about how it took up too much of my time. Sometimes I think she's just jealous, because she's such an unco, but I conceded, like I always did when it came to Stella. It was easier that way.

Reaching across the table, Mom pulled me from my thoughts by gathering up the fingers of my right hand and running her thumb over my knuckles. "I know you're growing up." She grinned. "And I love to see it."

Her smile wavered. "Just as long as you never lose that compassionate spirit of yours, the one that always looks out for others. All I want you to do is be who you are. People should love you without you having to change anything."

I scowled. This conversation was getting under my skin and I really didn't like it. "Mom, what are you talking about? I'm still me."

"You have to admit that the likes of Stella...and Chase have brought out a different side to you." I could feel my hackles rising the way they always did when she talked about my best friend. Stella and I had been tight since first grade and sure, she had changed a lot over the years, but I wasn't just going to ditch her. I liked some of the stuff she'd gotten me into. Sure, it scared me a touch sometimes, but I'd never admit that to my mom.

It was my turn for my bright blue eyes to grow dark with disapproval. My mom grinned, no doubt trying to ensure the conversation didn't get explosive. "I'm not saying you're a bad person or anything, I just don't want you to forget who you are at the core."

I swallowed back my anger. I hated conflict, no matter who it was with. Taking a little breath, I forced a smile. "Mom, you raised me right. I know who I am, okay?"

"Yeah." She sighed again, looking totally unconvinced.

Much to my relief, my phone dinged with a text

message. I fished it out of my back pocket and unlocked the screen.

Just heard from Chase. Need a rescue? Tell your mom shopping with the girls. I have a plan.

I cleared my throat. "So Stella and the girls are going shopping tonight. Can I go?"

I'm sure twenty years ago, when she'd been dealing with Seth, Layla, Holly and Toby—my older siblings—she would have made them stay home, but she either no longer had the energy or she knew it was easier to keep in her kids' good books. I didn't care what the reason was, I loved seeing that little shrug and nod. "Be home by ten."

"Mom, it's Friday night."

"Okay, eleven."

"Thirty?" I tipped my head, giving her that look I'd been perfecting over the years. Holly taught it to me. We called it the mother-softener.

She rolled her eyes. "Not one minute more."

I jumped up with a smile, the rest of my dinner forgotten.

"Caitlyn." Mom's voice stopped me. "Just remember what we talked about, okay? I want you to really think about it."

The serious look on her face made my reply sincere. "I will, Mom."

And finally her brown eyes lit with a soft smile. "Have fun, sweetie."

two

I knew I probably should have considered what Mom said. Did I really want Chase to be my first? I knew for a fact I wasn't going to be his first. If I was entirely honest, I would probably end up being another notch on his belt. Technically I should have been running for the hills. But I really wanted to have sex. I wanted to know what it felt like...and I wanted to do it with someone I liked. And I really did like Chase...and he liked me. We'd been having fun together. He made me feel alive and adventurous. I liked that feeling.

I ran my hands through my long curls and ruffled the ends. Flicking them over my shoulder, I adjusted the ring on my forefinger and scuffed my high black sandals on the path outside our house.

Stella was always late. Ugh. But I wanted to wait outside, rather than loiter in my room. I was scared Mom would come up, having thought of something else to add to her little speech. I knew I shouldn't mind it. I guess it was nice to be cared for...but it really bugged me when that care rang with a truth I didn't want to hear.

I patted the back pocket of my pale denim, skinny jeans, checking that my phone and money were still there. I should have gone back in to find a handbag. Every girl in the world seemed to wear them...except me. I really hated them. They were just another thing for me to leave somewhere and I couldn't be bothered with the way they always slipped off my shoulder. Holly gave me a bag for my birthday last year that kind of went across my middle and sat against my butt. I needed to drag that out and actually start using it.

I was toying with the idea of running back inside to find it when I heard a car coming down the road. I craned my neck to see if it was Stella's VW Beetle, but no, it was the car that always took my breath away. Not because I'm a car chick or anything, but because the guy who drove it...my next door neighbor, Eric...was like the most beautiful human being ever created.

I'm not making that up. I mean he was hot and then some. Like movie star hot. When he moved in six months earlier, I swear I couldn't speak for like a day. I'd never seen anyone like him.

Eric swerved into his driveway and quickly cut the engine. I tried not to look, but couldn't help stealing a few furtive glimpses as he got out of his black Jeep shirtless and reached for the surfboard attached to the roll bars. His straight hair was wet, droplets hanging from the long ends before dripping onto his shoulders. I watched one droplet glide over his hard chest and perfect abs and couldn't help scraping my teeth over my bottom lip.

Ugh. Caitlyn, you little perv. Hello! You have a boyfriend!

But Eric.

Le sigh.

He would be my secret crush forever.

His hazel green eyes caught my stare and I quickly turned away before I could see his disapproving frown. That was the only problem about my sexy next-door neighbor. Friendliness was not his strong suit. I mean he was polite and everything. We'd said a few hellos, but the one time I'd had enough courage to give him one of my flirty smiles, he responded with a closed mouth grin, you know the 'so obviously forced' kind? Like he pitied my effort or something. It was so humiliating and I still hadn't forgiven Stella for forcing me into it. She'd been standing there nudging me until I'd twirled my hair and used a cutesy voice that was so not my style. "Hi Eric." Ugh! I could still hear the way I sounded. Cringeville! Stella had laughed her ass off over that one, but she'd insisted she wasn't being mean (although, she liked Eric too, so I had to question her motives), she was just trying to teach me the art of flirting. She'd done me a favor I guess. I'd scored Chase, so I couldn't complain.

My eyes crept back to Eric. I didn't know why he didn't like me and I probably shouldn't have cared. But there was something so compelling about the guy.

"Eric!" His little half-sister Lacey squealed out of the house and ran for him. He leaned the surfboard against his jeep and picked her up, throwing her in the air as if she were a football and not a ten-year-old child.

She wrapped her arms and legs around him with a giggle. I could hear him laughing as well.

See! Eric was nice!

"Hey, Caitlyn!" Lacey waved over Eric's shoulder. I lifted my hand with a grin as Eric swivelled to face me. I thought he was about to smile, his expression softened with what looked like friendliness, but then the sound of Stella's Beetle approaching stole his grin. We all knew it was Stella because pop music was blasting from her stereo.

Eric placed Lacey onto the ground and herded her towards the house. Knowing it would be my last chance for the day, I kept my eyes on him as he tucked his surfboard under one arm and grabbed his weekend bag from the passenger seat. I loved the shape his muscles made when they were bearing weight.

Man, I was pathetic.

Stella's car horn forced me to turn away. I ran up the

path and jumped into the passenger side, turning down the music. Stella didn't even notice. Her eyes were fixated on Eric as he walked up his front steps.

"I'm so coming over tomorrow."

"Why?" I knew why, but asked anyway.

"Look how long their grass is. Eric's home for the weekend. There's going to be some bare-chested lawn mowing going on tomorrow and I'm not missing it."

I chuckled. Eric was a freshman at UCLA and didn't live at home anymore. Luckily for us, he was around a lot on the weekends and Stella always kept an eye on the lawn. I will never forget the day we first noticed him mowing. I swear we both swooned like groupies. It was ridiculous.

"Here's your fake ID."

I looked at the plastic card in Stella's hand and swallowed. "I don't remember ordering one."

"Well, I knew you'd chicken out, so I went ahead and got one for you." Her perfectly plucked eyebrows wiggled and two dimples appeared on her flawless cheeks.

I smiled at her expectant green gaze, trying to look enthusiastic as I took the card from her. I had to remind myself that this was why I loved Stella—she made me do things I'd never have the courage to do on my own.

"Martha Woodgrove. Really?"

She giggled, her cheeky expression lighting with glee. "Take what you can get, sweetness." She pulled on the wheel, spinning the car back around. "You owe me a hundred bucks by the way."

"Thanks." *I think.*

I tapped the card against my thumbnail, trying to look grateful. "So where are we really going?"

Stella smoothed down her shiny, blonde hair with a deft hand. "Well, Chase and I thought we should take you somewhere where you can forget about your parental woes...so we're going dancing at SkyBar."

"Dancing." I tried not to grimace.

"Yeah. It'll be fun."

I pushed a smile over my lips, not my genuine one, but the wide toothy smile I used when I was trying to make other people happy. I hated dancing. I mean I didn't mind if it was all choreographed and we were all doing the same thing, but that awkward shuffling on a crowded dance floor to thumping loud music, was so not my style. There was no way I was going to say anything though. Stella and Chase were looking out for me. I nodded and turned up the music so conversation would cease. I didn't want Stella asking details about my mother's lecture. She already thought my mom was an old fuddy-duddy. Besides I was too stressed about the dancing to waffle my way through a conversation where Stella came out feeling on top and my mother wasn't dragged through the mud completely.

It took twenty minutes to reach SkyBar at the Mondrian Hotel on Sunset Boulevard. Stella gave the car to the valet and we joined the throngs of others waiting to get the approval of the bouncer before gaining entry into the exclusive club.

"Come on, let's see if the others are ahead of us." Stella yanked my arm before we could even join the line properly, pulling me past the hyped up crowd.

I was grateful I had chosen to wear my tight tank top and leather jacket. It was smart casual, which suited me fine. I hated dressing up, but if I didn't put in some effort, I looked like a total slob next to Stella. She always looked stunning, and the hot pink number she'd squeezed her curves into screamed sexy. She was turning heads and loving it. She even got a wolf whistle, which made her smirk.

I, of course, went unnoticed beside her until we reached the corner where Chase, Sean, Audi and Kurt were, in fact, waiting. Audi and Kurt were wrapped around each other as they always were. Chase looked relieved to be away from them as he approached us, pulling me aside for a private word. Stella continued her confident strut, enjoying the way Sean's eyes travelled over her body. He was so into her. Poor guy, Stella was never going to let him have her, but it didn't stop her from flirting up a storm whenever there were no other guys to choose from.

Chase ran his fingers over the exposed skin where my top and jeans didn't quite meet, setting my skin on fire. "So how was the third degree?"

"Not too bad." I shrugged, not wanting to get into it.

His smile went all soft and mushy as he slid his arm

around me and pulled me close. "So, I was wondering after this if you wanted to find somewhere quiet where we could finish what we started." He nibbled my ear, his warm breathing tickling the nape of my neck as he kissed my skin.

I grinned, trying to ignore my mother's warning as I let his hands slide over my butt. He pulled me toward him, pressing his hips against mine, showing me exactly what he meant. I had to nod. What else could I say? His expression lit with pleasure. Grabbing my face in his hands, he planted his lips on mine and we forgot we were on a public street.

"Come on you two love birds," Sean hollered, but Chase ignored him, continuing to kiss me until my senses were reeling.

Finally I couldn't take the catcalls anymore and pulled away. I pushed at Chase's chest, put on a sexy smile and whispered, "Later."

That seemed to appease him. He kissed me one last time, thrusting his tongue into my mouth, before grabbing my hand and pulling us back into the line in time to enter the club. My nerves were going off like fireworks as I walked through the door. I was so uncomfortable with using a fake ID. I'd already been in trouble once that afternoon and yes, it wasn't too bad, but if Mom knew what I was up to that evening, I'd probably get stuck on house arrest for the foreseeable future.

My insides twitched and buzzed as we made our way

through the club. The music was pulsing out a steady beat that seemed like a hammer to my skull. Stella was going on about knowing half the gorgeous guys in the place. Whether that was true or not, I wasn't sure, but I didn't try to correct her in front of the others. I'd done that once before and nearly lost her friendship. Pressing my lips together, I tried to tune her out, instead focusing on getting my legs to move. My brain was being fully attacked by my mother. Her words kept spinning around in my head...the fact I was changing, my decision with Chase.

Suddenly his hand felt sweaty against mine and I wanted to yank it free, but I didn't want to upset him, so I pressed my lips even tighter together.

It didn't work. With a smile, I eased my hand free and touched my lips to his ear. "I just have to duck out for a sec."

"You okay?"

"Oh yeah, I'm great, just um...give me a minute."

I left his confused side and yanked on Stella's wrist, pulling her toward the nearest exit sign on the edge of the room.

"What the hell is your problem?" She shook me off her once we made it out to the empty side street.

"Sorry." I rubbed my forehead. "I just needed a sec."

"Why?"

"Because..." I flicked my hands in the air. "Chase and I are going to...you know...after and I'm suddenly freaking out."

"Caity, weren't you going to this afternoon anyway?"

"Yeah, but that was spontaneous. This is all planned and pressure central! I don't know, what if I chicken out last minute? Do you think he'll hate me?"

Stella's irritation eased, her look softening to one of pity. She squeezed my shoulder with her jewelled fingers. "He'd be a jerk to hate you...and Chase isn't a jerk. I never would have set you up with him if he were like that. It'll be fine. You don't have to freak out. Yes, the first time hurts a little, but he'll be gentle."

Why that sounded gross, I wasn't sure, but I grimaced anyway.

Stella rolled her eyes. "Don't be so pathetic. You can't stay a virgin forever, just—"

"Can you help me?" We barely heard the feeble voice that came from the alley behind the club. I glanced down and spotted an old man huddled against the edge of the building. His torn, dirty clothing looked more like rags than actual attire. They hung off his skinny muscles, making him look weak and pathetic. His matted beard was unkempt and infested with who knew what. I tried not to make a face as I caught a whiff of his unwashed body.

"Ewww, you smell." Stella looked disgusted, covering her mouth with her hand. "Let's go, Caity."

"Please!" His feeble voice was desperate. "Just a little money for food. Please."

My heart spasmed. The poor man looked tired and

ready to give up. Without thinking, I reached into my back pocket, ready to pull out a twenty. Would that be enough?

"Don't you dare." Stella snatched my hand. "He'll probably just use it to buy alcohol or drugs."

"Come on, Stella," I whispered. "He looks hungry."

"He's not our problem, Caitlyn. Now, let's go back in." She yanked on my arm, pulling me away from the old man's pleas. He sounded so wretched, I couldn't help looking back and watching him rise from the pavement. His legs wobbled as he shuffled after us, still begging for something to eat.

Stella let out a huff and spun around to face him. "Look old man, we've got nothing for you, so just leave us the hell alone." Stepping forward, she gave him a shove. With no energy to spare, he tumbled backwards, landing with a soft cry.

My eyes rounded and I covered my mouth. "Stella."

"Come on." She straightened her shoulders as if she'd been completely justified in her actions and grabbed my elbow. It took me a moment to respond. I couldn't take my eyes off the man as he slowly rose from the pavement. A graze, red with fresh blood, ran from his elbow down to his wrist. He nursed his arm against his stomach, giving me one last look before shuffling back to his spot in the darkness.

three

I couldn't get the man, or his plight, out of my head. I wanted to have fun with my friends, but I couldn't, not after what I'd just witnessed. Plus, I'd done nothing to help. What kind of person did that make me?

Stella pulled me to the dance floor and we found the others shuffling in a circle.

Chase's arm wrapped around me the second I stood beside him.

"Where'd you go?" he yelled above the music.

"Caity just needed some air." Stella shot me a droll glare then rolled her eyes. "We bumped into this homeless jerk who tried to steal money off us."

"That wasn't—" I wished I was more assertive. I wanted to trample all over Stella's lame ass story, but she'd never forgive me, especially when Sean was dishing out sympathy cards.

"No way! Are you alright?" He ran his hand down Stella's back. Any opportunity.

I rolled my eyes and turned into Chase's shoulder.

"I'm glad you're okay," he spoke into my ear.

"It wasn't—"

But Chase was already trailing kisses down my jawline and attacking my neck. He wasn't interested in the truth. None of my friends were.

Chase's hips ground against me as he turned me in his arms and moved to the blaring music. I put my arms around his neck, trying to get into it, but I couldn't. My mind was being assaulted by that man's face. I wouldn't be able to enjoy this until I'd wiped my conscience clean.

"I have to go to the bathroom," I yelled in Chase's ear. He reluctantly let me go and after a quick apology, I worked my way through the crowd toward the bathrooms. It felt weird not having Stella beside me. I usually never took off to the bathroom on my own, but this time was different. She would not appreciate what I was about to do.

I glanced over my shoulder when I reached the bathroom door, making sure my friends were all distracted on the dance floor, before ducking down and sneaking out the closest exit where I could work my way back to the alley. It was a mission getting through the pressing crowd, but I finally made it, bursting into the fresh night air and feeling a sweet moment of release. It was actually good not having Stella beside me, making me feel bad for needing her.

Clubbing really wasn't my scene. I knew that before, but this was just confirming it. All my friends had beers in their hands and were gyrating on the dance floor before I'd even had a chance to find my equilibrium. I knew they all expected me to order one when I got back, but after this afternoon, there was no way I was going home smelling of alcohol. I'd deal with that when I returned. For now, I had a conscience to clean.

My heels clicked on the pavement as I made my way back around the building and into the alley, hoping I would find the man again. The guilt swirling through my system was so overpowering, my night would be totally ruined if I didn't help him. I reached into my back pocket, pulling out all the cash I had. Sixty bucks, it was hardly much, but hopefully it would feed the guy for a few days. I nervously clutched it in my hand as I approached the dark patch where he'd first called out to us.

I smelt him before I saw him. He was laying on his side on the hard concrete, facing away from the passing traffic, his head resting on his arm.

"Excuse me." I cleared my throat.

Nothing.

"Um..." I crouched down, not really wanting to touch

33

him, and used a louder voice. "Hello, sir?"

Still nothing.

Biting my lower lip, I held my breath and poked my finger into his shoulder. "Hello?"

He jerked and spun to face me. At first I thought he was going to yell at me, his eyes were so wild, but then he paused. His nose wrinkled, his forehead creased and his expression relaxed. The eyes that had been so full of desperation earlier that evening watched me with a deep fascination. Although it was dim and I couldn't really see the details of his face, I sensed the depth of his gaze.

Goosebumps rippled over my flesh, an uneasy feeling creeping up my spine.

I swallowed and held out the money. "I thought you might need this."

He looked at it as if trying to figure out what it was before turning his silent stare back to me.

"Take it." I jiggled my hand, encouraging him to take my meager offering.

Moving in slow motion, he adjusted his body, perching on his hip and reaching out for the cash. He didn't take it straight away—just kept staring at me as if trying to figure out if I were tricking him or something.

"I'm not...my friend doesn't know I'm out here, okay? You're safe."

The corner of his mouth twitched with what could have been a grin. He pulled the money from my grasp and unrolled it, counting the three twenties.

I wanted to get up and bolt from the spot, but I didn't want to appear callous. So I stayed squatting down until he scrunched the money into his pocket.

"I know it's not much." I cleared my throat when he pierced me with his pale gaze again. "Is your arm okay?"

He nodded.

I nodded back and went to stand, but he grabbed me before I could, wrapping both his warm palms around my left hand. I should have been grossed out by his greasy touch, but I wasn't. There was something about the gratitude in his eyes that made me feel safe.

"You are a good soul," he said.

"Oh no, it's really no big deal. I should probably do more for you, but my friends..." I pointed back to the club with my free hand, feeling ashamed for even associating with my heartless companions.

His smile was tender as he squeezed my hand. "Your kindness will not go unnoticed."

"Uh, thanks." I tried to pull my hand free, but he held it tightly. It was only then that I noticed how warm his hands really were. It wasn't a sweaty warmth, more like a dry heat that soaked into my skin. And then came a spark. I jerked my hand away and rubbed my thumb and forefinger together.

He looked completely unfazed as if he hadn't even felt it. I gazed at my fingers. They didn't hurt or anything. All I could guess was static electricity. I frowned and stood before he could touch me again.

"Well, take care of yourself." I shoved my hands into my back pockets and took another step away from him.

He nodded, a serene smile stretching his mouth wide. "You are a good soul. Your kindness will not go unnoticed."

"Okay." I stepped away, hoping I wasn't being rude.

He said the words again, sounding like a raving lunatic and making it that much easier to leave his side. It was getting weird. I raised my hand in farewell and double-timed it back to the club. The bouncer didn't even check my ID, just waved me through as he recognized me from last time. I gave him a grateful smile and immersed myself into the thumping fray.

The music felt a million times louder than when I'd left. I rubbed my temples, feeling the onset of a monster headache. It was coming on super-fast, too. Trying to ignore the pain, I wiggled and pushed my way through the crowd. Stella saw me coming and waved. I finally busted my way through to them. Chase caught me against him and placed a sloppy kiss on my lips. He tasted like more than beer and the lax way his limbs were moving made me wonder how much he'd downed while I was gone.

His hungry tongue worked over my neck, something I'd usually enjoy, but my headache was growing worse by the second. My eyes were killing me, my temples were pounding, and nausea was setting in fast. I had to pull away.

"I'm sorry," I yelled, stumbling away from him. "I

gotta go."

I grabbed my head and nearly fell over as I made my way out for the third time that night. The headache was near blinding by the time I reached the door.

"Caitlyn!" I ignored Stella's pissed off call and threw myself at the exit.

The bouncer had to catch me as I tripped out onto the curb.

"You alright, Miss?"

"She's fine." Stella snatched my arm and dragged me away from the burly guy. "What is up with you tonight?" She swung me around to face her.

"I can't." I swallowed back the bile. "I feel sick."

"You haven't even been drinking. What the hell did you do in the bathroom?"

"Nothing," I mumbled. "It's just a migraine."

Stella's frown softened a little and she rubbed my back as I braced my hands on my knees. "Are you still nervous about doing it with Chase? Because I asked him, and he said he's taking you to a motel, so you're not just doing it in the back of his car or anything. It'll be fine."

"It's not about Chase." Who I was very aware had not followed me out to check whether I was okay. "I just want to go home."

"But Caity," Stella whined. "I'm not ready to go yet."

I knew I should have been pissed at my friend's attitude. I was seriously in pain here, but I didn't have the energy to feel anything more than a desperate need to get home. "Just call me a cab. Please, Stella."

With a reluctant huff she yanked out her phone and dialed a taxi for me. I had no idea how I was supposed to ask her for money, but thankfully my best friend redeemed herself by staying with me until the taxi showed up and giving the guy my address and a fifty-dollar note.

I leaned against the doorframe muttering a thank you and asking her to say sorry to Chase. She promised to do it. I noticed her disappointment at being abandoned by me and made a mental note to apologize again in the morning. Squeezing my eyes shut, I willed the morning to come, anything to stop the excruciating headache.

four

The morning brought minimal relief. I woke after a night of weird dreams. My top sheet was tangled around my limbs, a total giveaway to my restlessness. Kicking it off, I flicked it out and let the cotton float back over me. I squeezed my eyes shut with a groan.

Mom had already been in bed when I stumbled through the door earlier than my curfew. I downed two Tylenol and headed straight for bed, stripping off my clothes as I went. I scrambled beneath my covers in my panties and tank top, begging sleep to take me.

I so didn't want to get up. I'd never been hung over before, but I was guessing this is what it felt like. I didn't get it. I hadn't had a drop. Maybe Chase's alcohol infused kisses got me drunk by osmosis or something.

I placed my hand on my forehead, expecting a temperature, but I was fine. Just aching temples and burning eyes. I'd had migraines in the past—only a couple, but none that had set in so quickly. I couldn't believe how fast it took me down the night before either. It was weird.

Rolling to my side, I pulled the covers over my shoulders, more than grateful that I could spend the day in bed. I didn't want to face anyone or anything.

My door burst open.

"You're still in bed? It's eleven o'clock already. I got home five hours after you and I'm up!"

I squeezed my eyes shut, cringing at Stella's staccato voice. Her words felt like bullets raining into my ears.

"Stella," I mumbled. "I told you, I'm sick."

"Oh come on." She nudged my shoulder. "It's just a headache. Take some painkillers. Don't waste the day in bed. The sun is shining and lawns are about to be mown."

I heard her move to the window and shuffle stuff around on my desk. She was no doubt perching her perfect behind on it so she could get the optimum view.

"Eeeeppp! There he is. Come on, Eric, take off your shirt, baby."

I swallowed, fighting the urge to get up and join her. But I couldn't. My limbs felt like Jello and there was no way my chicken neck could support my concrete head.

The lawn mower started up, another punishing blow to my ears. I grabbed my pillow and shoved it over my head. Stella's swooning was mercifully muffled. I waited it out, trying not to get pissed. I just wanted Stella to leave me alone! I wanted peace. I wanted quiet.

Finally the lawn mower cut off. With a disappointed tut, Stella got off my desk and plonked herself beside me. Her hand rubbed my shoulder.

"Sorry you're feeling sick. You missed out on a good night. I didn't get home from the club until one."

I grunted.

"Chase was pretty disappointed you had to leave early. He was really looking forward to...you know."

I wanted to mumble something about him not even trying to see me home, so "you know" probably wouldn't be happening for a while now anyway. But I couldn't be bothered.

"You guys can talk about it later today. I'll tell him to call and take you out for ice cream or something."

The word NO was on the tip of my tongue, but Stella patted my shoulder before I could talk. "Get some rest, okay?"

I was rising to my elbows in protest, but she was out the door before the pillow had even fallen off my head. I snatched it back and plonked my head down with a sigh.

"Ow."

****

Chase called at two. By then I'd managed to get some more sleep, eat a little fruit salad and yogurt, and get some more pain killers into me. My head was slowly starting to clear and my eyes only hurt a little. At first I wasn't sure if I wanted to talk to him. I was still kind of miffed that he hadn't even bothered to check on me. My thumb hovered over the screen, but then I sighed and unlocked it.

"Hey."

"Hey," Chase's voice was soft, quelling my annoyance. "How you feeling?"

"Better."

"Is it okay if I pick you up soon? I thought we could go for a drive, have a chat."

How could I say no? His voice was so soft and sweet and I suddenly wanted to see him.

I smiled. "Sure."

"See you in an hour, okay?"

"Okay."

Throwing back the covers, I shuffled out of bed and headed for the shower. I was more than grateful to find Mom's note downstairs saying she was out for the day with my eldest sister, Layla, and the grandkids. My mom was such a sucker for kids, and Layla knew it. She was always calling on Mom to help her out. They were often here on the weekends, overtaking the house. Thankfully they were never allowed in my room. That was my Dad's ruling and I loved him for it.

The shower revived me, my scented soap making me

feel crispy clean. I let my hair dry naturally, something that would take ages to do and probably give me a little frizz, but I didn't care. It felt so nice wet and cool against my back that I walked around in nothing but my jeans and bra until I heard Chase honk the horn.

I pulled on my shirt and buttoned it as I descended the stairs. Grabbing my phone and a little cash, I shoved them in my back pocket, yanked on my flat slip-on shoes and scurried out to the car.

"Hey you." Chase greeted me with a kiss.

I closed the passenger door behind me and blushed. "Hey."

Putting the car in gear, he pulled away from the curb and headed for the beach. "So, you feeling better?"

I glanced at him to answer and my breath hitched. He looked different. I couldn't figure out what it was, but there was something weird. His cool charm had vanished and now he looked plain pissed.

My stomach clenched. Adjusting the ring on my finger, I looked at my lap. "Sorry about bailing last night."

"No big deal." He shrugged, looking casual enough. Maybe I had just imagined the dark look I saw. I stayed quiet for a minute, studying him out of the corner of my eye. The longer I looked at him, the more the calm facade slipped away and I could see his anger. The smooth lines of his face were hard and unrelenting as he scowled ahead.

"Why are you so mad?"

"I'm not." Stopping at the intersection, he glanced at me and smiled, but it wasn't a kind smile at all, it was rigid and forced. I didn't get it. His voice was so calm and casual, like he actually meant what he was saying, but I could see it all over his face. He was not impressed with me, at all.

I blinked slowly and looked at him again. The anger was gone and I could see the sweet smile he was giving me. The light turned green. As Chase accelerated through it, I kept watching him, waiting for the angry change up.

It was freaking me out. Why nice one minute and pissed the next?

He didn't say anything, which wasn't helping. I wanted to hear his calm voice and assure myself that all his dirty looks were a figment of my warped imagination.

I bit the corner of my lip and stayed quiet for the rest of the trip. We were soon pulling up to one of our favorite beach lookouts. Chase parked.

"Come on," he grinned. "Let's go for a walk."

I took the picnic rug he handed me and tucked it under my arm. That black look was back in his eyes again. I almost didn't want to let him take my hand, but he grabbed it before I could pull away.

It was mega awkward, there no way I could enjoy our afternoon together if we didn't clear the air.

I swallowed as we made our way over the grass verge. "I really am sorry about last night. I wouldn't have bailed if I hadn't felt so bad."

"I said it was fine." There was that shrug again and the smile slipped into a frown. I blinked and looked at him. The frown was gone and he was smiling sweetly at me. I grinned back, but then his sweet smile disappeared and became that hard-edged grimace I saw before.

What the hell was going on?

I jerked to a stop.

"Chase, you look really pissed off...like you don't believe I was sick or something."

He let go of my hand with a huff and stepped away from me. "Come on, Caitlyn, a headache, really?"

"Yes, really."

Why would he not believe me?

The rejection he felt last night flashed across his face as he ran a hand through his hair. It was followed by a look of disappointment and then anger again. I couldn't believe he was letting me see all of this. Chase Mitchell was not the kind of guy to talk about feelings, let alone let them all show. He obviously really wanted me to know how much I'd let him down.

I so did not want to have this conversation and I wanted to die instead of ask, but I knew I had no choice. Not with him looking at me with such open anger. "You're mad because we didn't have sex."

His smile was tight, forced. "Well, excuse me for being disappointed. I thought I was going to get some and it fell through."

"You did not just say *get some*." I closed my eyes and looked away from him.

His voice went soft as he took my shoulders and gently squeezed them. "I thought you wanted this too."

"I do, but not when I have a screaming headache. It's my first time. It's a big deal." I finally looked back at him.

His smile was sweet as he tucked a lock of hair behind my ear. "It's just sex, babe."

Mom's words rang through my head, "*There's no such thing as just sex. I hate the way people cheapen it like that.*" And I couldn't help asking. "Do you love me?"

"What?" He looked incredulous and about ready to gag.

"Do you love me?" I repeated the words slowly.

His chuckle was filled with nervous energy as he rubbed my arm and gently lowered his hands, shoving them into his jean pockets. "We've only been together a couple months, it's a little early to start pulling out the L word, isn't it?"

"But it's not too early to be screwing each other?" I retorted.

"What is your problem today?" Once again his voice and face didn't match. He looked so much more annoyed than he sounded. I squeezed my eyes shut and rubbed my temples, feeling the onset of another throbbing headache.

"We're teenagers, Caitlyn. Of course we want sex." I

couldn't help noticing the way his eyes trailed down my body, hunger obvious in his dark expression.

Hugging the blanket to my chest, I looked at the grass. "You know what? Maybe I'm not ready. I thought I was but...I'm sorry, okay?" I shook my head.

"Yeah." Chase nodded, looking away. "Whatever. Cool. We can wait." I saw straight through his shrug. He was super pissed and totally lying to me.

For some reason his inability to hide his true feelings really irked me. I snapped and retaliated with my standard sarcasm. "Well if you want it so bad, maybe you should go hook up with someone else."

His face lit with pleasant surprise. "You'd be okay with me doing that? Sleeping with other girls while we were still together?"

My eyes bulged before I could stop them. I stepped away from him, not knowing whether to cry or punch him in the face.

"Babe." He grinned. "That was a joke."

"No it wasn't."

He looked confused, surprised that I was able to see that. Guilt flashed over his features and then scuttled away to be replaced by confusion again. I could see his disbelieving smile. He was opening his mouth to no doubt convince me I was seeing things.

And maybe he was right. I was seeing things.

Real things.

Things I had never noticed before.

All of Chase's sweet comments...the tone of his

voice...were all a farce. He wanted me for sex...and that was it. He had been willing to put in a few months of his time to get it, but if I wasn't going to put out then he wasn't going to wait around.

"You know what..." I passed the picnic blanket back to him. "You go sleep with whoever you want, because we're not together anymore."

He didn't really look that disappointed as he took the blanket off me and let me walk away on my own.

five

I crossed my arms tightly around my body and stumbled over the grass. As soon as I hit the pavement, I ran. I reached Stella's house ten minutes later. I wasn't usually out of breath after running for ten minutes, but I had been crying most of the way, so when Stella opened the door I was a huffing, puffing mess.

"What happened?" Her green eyes were wide as she grabbed my arm and pulled me inside.

"I just dumped Chase." I finally hiccupped when she sat me down on her bed.

Flicking the door shut, she spun around to face me. "Why?"

"Because he only wanted me for sex." I sniffed and wiped at my tears. The crying fit was so not helping my headache.

Stella perched on the bed next to me with a Kleenex in her hand. I snatched it off her and blew my nose, dabbing my puffy eyes. My best friend stayed silent as I pulled myself together. Finally I drew in a long, slow breath.

"I mean I know he's been around a little. I know it was unrealistic for him to actually like me, but I really thought he did. We got on great, you know? I thought sex would have been an added bonus for us, not the be and end all." I looked up, forcing a watery smile.

Stella sighed, her hand running slow circles over my back. I looked into her eyes and felt my stomach sink.

Was she smiling?

I blinked and looked at her again.

No, she was sad for me, but...but the longer I looked, the more I saw the sadness slip away. It was like a layer of falsehood fell off her expression and I could see the quiet glee. I gasped and sat back from her.

"Caity, are you okay?" Her voice sounded concerned, but her irritated frown told me something completely different. She didn't want to have to deal with her upset friend. She didn't even care that Chase was being a jerk...she was happy about it.

"Stella..." I didn't know what to say to her. I shook my head, bile surging in my stomach.

"Caitlyn?" Stella patted my back. "You look kind of

pale. Please don't puke on my carpet, okay?" She said it with a giggle, but her expression told me otherwise.

What the hell is wrong with people today? Why is everyone so mad at me?

"I gotta go." I jerked off the bed and nearly crashed into the door. Wrestling with the handle, I finally yanked it open and made a beeline for the front door.

"Caity?" Stella rushed after me. I didn't want to, but couldn't help myself; I paused at the door and turned to look at her. Her brow was creased with worry, her lips slightly parted. There she was. The Stella I knew and loved, but once again, the longer I looked, the more I could see. As her worry slipped away, I saw it all—her irritation with my pathetic, crying self, and her complete lack of concern for me.

Bereft of words, I flung the door shut and raced down the path. The day was only getting weirder. Why were the people closest to me acting like selfish jerks?

Finding a steady rhythm, I made it back to the beach quickly. Nature and exercise usually calmed me. It sort of worked, but by the time I hit the sand, my head was killing me. I slowed to a walk, stopping to whip off my shoes, so I could feel the grains between my toes. I scanned the beach, hoping not to see Chase. Thankfully I didn't spot him amongst the scattered faces.

Not wanting to catch anyone's eye, I kept my head down and focused instead on the lumpy sand and the sound of the ocean.

I made it to the section of beach that was parallel to

my house. We were about eight blocks inland and I was more than happy to walk that. I didn't want to go home yet. I needed the fresh air kissing my skin and I certainly didn't want to talk to anybody.

I headed up to the road, not taking notice of those around me. I did spot one surfer hustling up the beach out of the corner of my eye, but I ignored him, hunching my shoulders and keeping my eyes on the ground.

"Hey, Caitlyn."

I jolted at his friendly greeting and couldn't help looking up.

Eric? Why was he talking to me? I stared at his friendly smile and waited...waited for it to slide away and be replaced with something else...like anger or frustration.

But nothing.

His smile stayed in place only transitioning slightly to a look of genuine concern.

"Hey, are you okay?" He pushed his surfboard into the sand and held it to his side.

"No." I have no idea what compelled me to be honest. I think it was utter confusion at the friendly expression on his face.

"What's up?" He tipped his head, his expression and voice matching perfectly.

I squinted up at him, my sore eyes and head making me unaware of his luscious form. Maybe I had imagined Chase and Stella's reactions to me. Maybe I had just projected what I thought they might feel.

No, wait a sec. That didn't work. If the day had been normal then Eric Shore would not be looking at me as if he were interested in what I had to say.

"You're not an asshole." I shook my head, rubbing at my aching temples.

"Um..." He frowned, but not a mean one, more like a confused, comical one. "Okay, uh thank you? I think." His brows dipped together and he grinned. "How am I supposed to respond to that?"

"You're not." I waved my hand, feeling out of it. "It's just...why are you being nice to me?"

His hazel eyes softened. "Because I've never seen you look so pale. Plus I'm a nice guy." He shrugged, putting on a nonchalant air, but I saw straight through it. Was he blushing?

"No, you're not a nice guy." I murmured.

Wait. What did I just say? Where is this honesty coming from?

I cringed and shook my head. "You're always ignoring me."

He pursed his lips and looked out to the ocean, wrinkling his nose. "That's only because you're always with your friends...and all they seem to want to do is drool over me. I'm not a huge fan of being mentally undressed every time I step out my front door."

I loved his answer and if I hadn't been feeling so sick I would have smiled and no doubt giggled like his little sister always did. Instead I went for sarcasm and rolled my eyes. "It must suck being so good looking."

"Well, you should know." He grinned.

I don't know how I remained standing. He was flirting with me. My eyes must have totally bugged out, because he kind of snickered and looked to the ground, trying to hide the fact he'd just blown his cover, but I saw it. He thought I was cute.

Eric Shore thought I was cute.

"This day could not get any weirder," I mumbled.

His steady gazed pierced me, his concern obvious. I didn't think he'd be that interested in me explaining it all and to be honest, I didn't even know if I could. I had no idea what was going on. I was freaked out, tired, aching and confused. All I wanted to do was crawl into bed and forget the day had even started.

I turned to leave, not even bothering with a goodbye, which was so unlike me. My parents were all about the manners.

"Hey, Caitlyn." Eric's soft voice was consistent with his tender touch on my arm. "Seriously, if you do ever need someone to talk to, I'm here, okay?"

I could barely comprehend what he was saying, so I just nodded like an idiot. His smile was sweet and true as he tucked his surfboard under his arm. With a short wave, he headed back toward the ocean. Normally I would have stayed and watched his divine body hit the water, and admire the way his arms moved as he paddled out past the break. But it was not a normal day, so instead, I crossed my arms and headed home.

six

I crawled into bed and stayed there, refusing dinner. I kept my head under the covers when Mom came in to talk to me. She didn't seem overly fazed. I'd had migraines before and she knew the best cure was sleep and lots of water. She brought me a big glass of ice and a pitcher of water then left me alone.

It was a relief. I didn't want to see her. I didn't want to look at her face and see her soft expression slip away to reveal something I didn't want to know.

I didn't want to see people differently. I wanted things to go back to normal. Why was this happening to me?

My plan was to spend the rest of eternity locked in my room, but unfortunately a new day dawned and brought with it a fresh wave of Stella.

She called and texted me relentlessly until I finally answered my phone. I should have just switched the damn thing off and was annoyed I only thought of that when I answered.

"Caitlyn." Her voice was crisp. "I don't know what the hell was up with you yesterday, but you need to get out and come with me to the beach. We can sit in the sand, watch the guys try to impress us with their sporting skills and you and Chase can sort it out."

"I don't want—"

"We're all meeting at Will Rogers Beach. See you in thirty minutes."

And she was gone.

I checked my watch. Eleven-thirty a.m. Stella time meant I had until at least twelve-fifteen. I could probably pull that off. I sat up slowly, expecting my headache to kick in the second I moved, but it didn't. Rubbing my forehead, I blinked a few times and had the fleeting thought that yesterday must have been a nightmare, one I had finally woken from.

That made me feel better and helped me get my body moving. After a shower and a big glass of water, I bounced down the stairs. I was still a little nervous about bumping into Mom. What if she looked different?

Pausing at the landing, I drew in a slow breath, trailing my hand along the wall as I walked towards the kitchen. She was out on the deck, her feet perched on the table, a magazine in her hands. The wind was ruffling her hair as she sipped her steaming cup of herbal tea.

"Morning," I mumbled, taking a seat beside her and pulling her leftover fruit towards me.

"Hey, sweetie. How are you feeling this morning?"

Popping a grape into my mouth, I squinted in the sunlight and nodded. "Okay."

She ran her hand over my head, smoothing down my drying frizz. I tried to read her expression, but with shades on it was hard to tell what she was thinking. I liked that. I didn't want to look into her eyes just then.

"You weren't drinking on Friday, were you?" Her tone was light, but I could see the tightness of her smile.

"Mom, really? You have to ask me that?"

"Well, I don't want to, but I feel like it's my parental duty to check."

I sighed and reached for some apple. "No, Mother. I was not drinking. I don't know what brought the headache on, but it's gone now. I'm heading to the beach with Stella soon."

"The fresh air will do you good." She smiled, lifting her glasses. At first I was afraid to look, but I had to check. Gazing into her eyes, I searched for any trace of falsehood, but what I saw was real. Mom's expression didn't waver as she grinned at me. I smiled back, relief flooding through me. The headache must have been messing with me. Everything that happened yesterday was just a warped reality...although the Chase thing still seemed pretty real.

I stood from the table and muttered something about getting my stuff. I was nervous about seeing Chase again...and Stella, even though Mom had just proved to me that yesterday might not have been real. Grabbing my keys and a towel, I stuffed everything inside my bag and headed for my car. Well, it wasn't my car. It was Holly's hand me down. She threw me the keys the day she moved to Hawaii. I had only been fourteen at the time. My father had snatched them off me and told me he'd keep it in good knick until I was old enough. It would never be the nicest car in the lot, but I liked it. My 1999 Mini Cooper. I tried to imagine that I was in the Italian Job when I was driving it. It didn't make my car any shinier, but it definitely made me feel cooler.

I made it to the beach at twelve-ten and to my surprise, Stella had beaten me there. She was waiting for me on the brown grass. I smiled at her and she waved back with a grin. My static nerves began to settle as I hitched my bag up on my shoulder and walked toward her.

She was wearing shades, like me, but that was okay. I didn't need to see her eyes to know things were back to normal. Her whole demeanor was friendly.

I was about to give her a warm hello when she lifted her shades. Her eyes were alight with lust. That was the only way to describe it. Glancing over my shoulder, I followed her line of sight and saw Eric jumping out of his jeep with his two little sisters in tow. Poppy and Lacey were squabbling over a frisbee, which Eric quickly snatched off them. They jumped and tried to reach it, giggling and pushing each other while yanking on his shirt. He grinned and ran ahead of them.

I turned back to spot Stella watching the exchange. Her hungry eyes were on fire and I couldn't see a scrap of her usual subtle flirting. Eric took the trail that led straight toward us. His eyes were down, obviously trying to avoid coming in contact with Stella's leering gaze. Were we that obvious? No wonder he hated it. Stella was repulsing me too.

"Hey, Eric," she said in a husky voice, running her tongue over her top lip.

Oh she didn't.

I grimaced.

He nodded politely, lifting his hand with a short wave. He wouldn't look at either of us and I didn't blame him.

"Hi, Caitlyn." Lacey grinned as she bounced past me. I waved, unable to form any words. I was still too grossed out by Stella's mental undressing of Eric.

"Come on, Stella, let's go." I tugged on her arm.

"Just one more minute." She spun to watch Eric's sleek frame make it all the way to the sand. I mean I got it, I enjoyed watching him too, but Stella looked ready to eat him alive.

"Do you have to leer at him like that? I don't think he likes it very much." I kept my voice light, hoping not to offend her.

"What do you mean?" She whipped around to face me, looking guilty and surprised. "I wasn't leering."

An innocent veneer swept across her face, but it didn't take a second for it to fall away. She was totally exposed to me...and she had no idea. She shrugged; smiling with what she obviously thought was her adorable grin. To me it just looked forced and weird.

Yesterday was clearly not going to be a one off.

I tried not to let it bug me as I made my way to the sand. I noticed Eric had taken his sisters as far away from my crowd as possible. Part of me wanted to go and join him and his sisters. Playing frisbee with them seemed so much more appealing than what I was about to do. But my friends would never get it and Stella would kill me, assuming I was flirting with a guy she had her eye on.

Dragging my feet a little, I forced myself to catch up with Stella, dumping my bag on the ground next to Audi and Indie. I greeted both of them, but didn't really want to get into a conversation. Instead I kept my eyes on the ocean.

Audi was going on about Kurt and their night of clubbing. I so didn't want to hear about it. Friday night was the beginning of the end for me. Stella started giggling as Audi went on about Sean and Chase getting drunk off their faces and dancing like fools.

My mood grew blacker by the second. I wanted to get out of there. I wanted to go back to bed. It didn't help that I had spotted Chase. He was playing volleyball with the guys. They were all shirtless and looking mighty proud of themselves as they spiked the ball and jumped around heroically. They made it look so dramatic. I rolled my eyes before taking in different facial expressions, frowning as every emotion was laid bare before me.

Chase was feeling smug because a group of tweens was checking him out. They were all openly drooling over the high school seniors. The guys loved it, except a few who were serious about the game and became majorly pissed with the show offs trying to impress the girls. Their emotions were all so raw and apparent. I was surprised no one else noticed.

Cheers went up as a point was scored. Chase ran his hand through his hair, looking annoyed that his team hadn't gotten to the ball in time. He caught my eyes on him and I saw a flash of guilt, but it was quickly replaced by disdain. He looked away from me as if I were a stranger and focused back on the game. I couldn't believe how quickly our relationship was over. I also couldn't believe how much I didn't care.

And I had been planning on sleeping with him. Ugh!

I looked away from the boys with a frown.

Running my fingers through the sand, I zoned in on the feel of the grains on my skin. My head was starting to hurt again and my insides were buzzing.

"Hello! Caitlyn?" Stella's sharp tone made my head snap up.

"Huh?"

The girls all giggled at me. It was hard to tell what they were thinking. All of them were wearing big shades that covered most of their faces and hid their expressions.

"So do you want to come?"

I had no idea what Stella was talking about and I didn't have a chance to ask, because Libby Phelps bounced up to us with a cheerful greeting.

Man she looked nervous. I watched her chubby arm wave frenetically before she stopped at our feet.

"Hey, girls." She beamed. "How's it going?"

Poor Libby. I'd never really noticed her desperation before. Behind that bright smile of hers was a nervous wreck. Her eyes darted to each of us as we smiled back. I didn't know why people had a problem with her. I mean, sure, she used to hang out with the brainiacs, which made her a slight know-it-all, but she was really sweet. Stella thought she was fat and repulsive, which was way harsh. She wasn't that big and she had a gorgeous smile. But Stella just seemed embarrassed at having her nearby.

I didn't really know how Libby suddenly made it into our group. It had been a mystery that perplexed a few of us. One day we weren't talking to her and then all of a sudden she was in. But from the expression on the faces beside me, I could tell that no one really wanted her included. I thought she was really nice. I liked her, although being the sheep that I was I behaved as though I couldn't care less.

I was so weak sometimes.

I glanced at my best friend. Stella's legs were squirming and I could tell by the tense set of her shoulders that she didn't want the guys to see us conversing with the chubby brainiac.

I smiled at Libby, hoping to ease her nerves a little. I could practically hear her begging us to like her as she chatted about the sun and how nice it was that the weather was warming up. Indie kept the conversation going a little, but it was so forced. It was like she was doing it under duress.

"I love that summer is coming. Sand, surf, and bikinis. Yay." She giggled.

Stella's nose wrinkled and I could tell she was picturing Libby in a bikini.

I winced. Did she have to be so openly repulsed by it?

I felt guilty just being near her radiating animosity.

"You okay, Caitlyn? You look kind of pale." Libby's gentle, brown eyes were filled with concern as they landed on me. Genuine concern.

It threw me a little.

Shaking my head, I mumbled. "Just a headache."

"Still?" Stella looked at me. "You've had it all weekend. What's wrong with you?"

"Wow, all weekend?" Libby's brow creased with

compassion. "Maybe you should go to the doctor. When did the headache start?"

"She's fine, Nurse Libby. Thank you." Stella flicked her hand, raising her shades to get a better look at me. I could see that she didn't like someone else fussing over her best friend. Was that insecurity I glimpsed? That didn't seem right. Stella was the most confident person I knew.

Glancing back at Libby, I saw her face crest with disappointment over Stella's sharp words. She looked about ready to cry, but there was a smile on her face. It took me a second, but I told my brain to see past the smile and I spotted it again. The watery grin, the wobbling lips—the effort to remain in control so we didn't know how desperately she needed us to accept her.

"Well, see you around then." She waved, looking dejected as she slumped away.

"Stella," I whispered. "That was a bit harsh, don't you think?"

"What?" Stella looked confused.

"Libby. Look how rejected she feels." I pointed after her.

"What are you talking about? She's smiling."

Glancing back, I noticed Libby was, in fact, smiling and waving at people as she passed. She looked like a happy, carefree girl who was friends with everyone. I frowned and rubbed my temples, feeling stupid for even saying anything.

"Seriously, Caitlyn, you have been acting so weird this weekend. What is wrong with you?"

"I don't know." I squeezed my eyes shut.

"Ever since Friday night at the club." Stella shook her. "Did aliens snatch you and mess with your brain or something?"

I froze. "What did you say?"

Stella frowned. "It was only a joke, Caity. Chill out."

Chill out? I couldn't! My heart was racing too fast. My mind was ready to explode.

Friday night.

That man...on the street...the electric shock.

No freaking way. Did he do something to me? Was that more than just a shock?

I had to know.

Grabbing my bag, I flicked it onto my shoulder.

"Caitlyn, what the hell are you doing?" Stella snapped.

"I gotta go." I pulled on my shoes and dug the keys out of my pocket.

"Where?" She looked seriously pissed.

"I'm sorry. I just...I have to go. I'll call you later, okay?"

"Caitlyn! Caity!"

I ignored her calls and kept my head down as I walked up the sandy path. I was on a mission and for once I wasn't going to let Stella's anger stop me.

seven

I put my foot to the floor and cruised along Pacific Coast Highway, up the California incline to Ocean Avenue, and steadily made my way back to Sunset Boulevard and Skybar at the Mondrian Hotel. Coming from the beach wasn't the most convenient drive, but I needed to get back to the club. Although I found my way easily, I still had to park down the block. Clutching my bag to my shoulder, I walked back down the street, keeping my eyes to the ground. My emotions were zinging like bullets inside of me. I couldn't pinpoint which one to focus on. Everything from fear to outright rage was turning my brain to spaghetti.

The homeless man wasn't in the spot from Friday night. Stamping my foot, I swore loudly, scaring off a woman walking past me. I ignored her. Part of me wanted to head back to my car and forget the whole thing. It was ridiculous. I was out on the street looking for some beggar, because I thought he cursed me with the ability to see everyone's true emotions.

I jerked to a stop.

Yes, that was what it was.

I was seeing who people truly were. How they really felt. The facades everyone normally hid behind weren't there for me anymore. It was like they were laid bare, for my eyes alone.

It felt good to define it.

But it didn't change the fact that I didn't want it. I didn't want to see what people were feeling. It was fully messing with my head and there was no way I could continue life that way.

Shoving my hands into my pockets, I looked up the street and then down, trying to decide which way to go. How long did I look for the guy? What if he'd moved on?

I wasn't overly keen on searching through alley after alley of homeless people. Not to sound judgemental, but it scared me a little. What if something bad happened to me?

Something worse than what you're already dealing with?

I rolled my eyes.

The mental argument raged within me as I kept walking. The least I could do was check the full length of the street. If I didn't find him after that, I'd head back home and I don't know...start seeking out a psychiatrist or something.

My feet were aching by the time I reached the Standard Hollywood Hotel, further down Sunset Boulevard, and still I hadn't seen the man yet. I was fully fighting tears as I turned to head back to my car, but then the thought that the street had two sides hit me. I crossed the busy road and started my search again.

Ten minutes later I found him.

It was pure chance really. I spotted a black boot sticking out from behind a dumpster. I didn't recognize it as his or anything, but I was pretty desperate by that stage, so I headed into the fetid alleyway.

"Hello?"

The boot twitched.

"Hello, sir?"

I gingerly stepped past the green dumpster and poked my head around the corner. And there he was. Those pale eyes took me in and then a smile of recognition eased across his face.

"You're welcome," he said.

"I'm welcome?" I couldn't help my sharp tone. Was he admitting to somehow cursing me and then expecting me to be grateful?

He nodded and grinned, struggling up from his spot. He looked weak and tired, but once he was standing, something about his demeanour changed. He was no longer a desperate lowly man, but now stood with a confidence that was almost charming. In spite of the grey pallor of his skin, his face was the picture of serenity, his eyes dancing with a smile.

"You were kind to me. I wanted to repay you."

I scoffed. "By ruining my life?"

His forehead crinkled. "Ruining your— No. I gave you a gift."

"No, no you didn't. You cursed me." My finger was shaking as I pointed at him.

"No." He went to reach for my hand, but I yanked it away. "Sweet child, the ability to see behind people's masks is a gift. It will protect you."

"Protect me! I've never felt more vulnerable." I hadn't actually known that, but as I said it, I realized just how susceptible I felt. I blinked away tears. "All you've done is exposed me to everyone's true feelings...and you know what, I don't like them very much!"

"I understand." Regret flooded his expression. A big tidal wave of it crested over his face as if he knew exactly what I meant. Squinting his eyes he looked to the ground and took a deep breath.

His expression turned from sad to pensive as he gazed back at me.

"What?" I barked.

"Rather than throwing anger at me, maybe you should ask yourself why these people's feelings bother you."

"They're bothering me because my boyfriend, who I just dumped thank you very much, obviously only wanted me for sex and my best friend doesn't even care. In fact my pain seemed to bring her joy."

The man studied me for a long beat before softly saying, "Well, don't you think it's better to know this than live with a lie?"

"I—" Throwing my hands in the air, I stepped away from him, my ankle nearly rolling on the cracked surface. I winced and shook my head. "I...I don't know. Lies make life easier sometimes."

"Ah." The man nodded. "So, you'd rather play the ignorant fool."

I threw him a black glare, which made him chuckle. "It is the safer option, I guess." Once again with the regret. His eyes brimmed with it until he blinked rapidly and shook his head. "What is your name?"

"Caitlyn," I murmured, crossing my arms and wrinkling my nose as a fresh whiff of garbage stench wafted up my nostrils.

"Well, Caitlyn." He smiled. "The first time I saw you, I knew you were a good soul, and when you came back to prove it, I knew I had to pass this gift to you. I have never shared it with anyone before."

His warm voice made me feel privileged somehow, but I still couldn't stop my head from shaking. "Look mister, I appreciate that you were trying to be nice and all, but I don't want it. So can you please just, you know, take it back?"

He looked hurt by my suggestion, but not offended.

It didn't really matter what he felt, because he still shook his head. "I can't do that. It's yours now. I passed it onto you. I can't take it back."

"So, you, you don't have it anymore?"

He shook his head, looking at peace about the whole thing.

I frowned. "Well, if you liked it so much, why'd you give it away?"

"I'm dying." He shrugged, leaning back against the dirty, brick wall.

My breath evaporated along with a little of my anger. I swallowed as he kept talking.

"I don't know how much longer I have. The day the doctors told me, I had a bit of a breakdown." He rubbed the back of his neck. "When you can see what people are really feeling, it's easy to tell when they think you have no chance. I knew I was terminal before they even told me."

"I'm—I'm sorry."

He flicked his hand as if it didn't matter. "I was a busy businessman...driven. Being able to read people gave me power and I abused it." Shame flooded his expression. "I never gave myself time to fall in love or have...a family." His voice wavered and I could see the lie. He'd had a family all right. One he'd probably abandoned, which was why he didn't want to say anything. What was the bet he couldn't handle seeing what they really thought of him and so he left. My eyes narrowed as he continued talking. "And then when I had no time left, I realized I needed to pass this gift on. But I knew no one worthy of it."

"How did you end up on the street?"

"When you know your life is coming to an end, things don't matter anymore." He tipped back on his heels. "I gave away everything I had. There were others who needed it more than me. But this gift of sight...I knew that was for someone special. I wanted someone compassionate to have it. Someone who could use it to help others."

"I'm not that person," I whispered, shaking my head frantically. "Look, I'm really sorry, but I think you've made a mistake."

"On Friday night, you came back to give me money and make sure I was okay." His eyes glimmered with an assured smile. "I've made no mistake. Seeing the way people react to the homeless is fascinating. I knew I'd find someone this way."

"So you planted yourself here? Just looking for someone?"

He nodded. "I wanted it to be someone with means. Someone who could use their position in society to help people."

"I don't have any position. I'm not famous or anything." I spread my arms wide; incredulous that he'd chosen me, thinking I was something special.

"But you don't want for anything. You have money. I could see that you're loved and cared for. You have no emotional baggage to speak of." He tipped his head, his piercing gaze making me feel exposed and vulnberable. "You seem restless, but not unhappy. You have space in your life to help others."

"How do you know I have money?"

He raised his eyebrows as if to say, "Are you kidding me?"

I blushed and looked to the ground. "Besides, I'm a teenager, of course I have emotional baggage. You've read me all wrong."

He snickered, seeing through my lie. "Caitlyn, I want you to use this power to help people. Don't do what I did."

"But...but Good Samaritan isn't one of my career choices," I practically whined.

He smiled. "This is your path now, you must accept it."

"I don't—I don't want to! How am I supposed to help people? Everyone has something to hide! Everyone has problems!"

"Focus on the ones who touch your heart. It may be one. It may be five. Spend time with them—peel back the layers. As you learn to control your vision, you'll know what to do." He pointed at my heart. "Ignoring this will only make you miserable. Trust me, I know."

The deep shame and failure on his face made me want to cry.

"Help those around you, one person at a time, and you will have a full and happy life. You can do what I never did."

Man, he wanted me to do this so badly, and I didn't want to let him down, but this was a life-changer. Like massive. Huge. And damn it, I didn't want it.

"I liked my life the way it was." I frowned. "I never asked for this. Please, don't do this to me."

"I can't change it, Caitlyn. I've already told you that."

"But..." I sighed, probably looking as desperate as I felt.

His eyes were warm with a compassionate smile as he squeezed my shoulder. "You can do this and you will be richer for it."

Tears lined my lashes as he turned and shuffled down the alley. He looked weak, and the idea that his regret over being a selfish businessman may have been a lie flittered through my head, but I had seen his face. He had told me the truth.

I walked out of the alley and leaned my head against the wall, feeling desperate, afraid, annoyed...everything I probably shouldn't have.

The urge to chase after the man and demand more was pretty strong, but I knew it was pointless. I was stuck with this gift and there was nothing I could do about it. With a reluctant sigh, I realized that if I was going to take this on then I should probably understand how it all worked. Like how did he get his power in the first place and how did he learn to control it?

I stepped back into the alley.

"Wait! I have a few more questions." I looked in the

direction he'd shuffled off, but he was gone. "Hello?"

Running further into the alley, I looked into doorways and searched for any other exits, but there were none. Had he seriously just vanished into thin air?

I was basically at the dead end when I found him. He was lying on the ground, a serene smile perched on his lips. I knew it before I touched him, frantically hunting for a pulse. There was none. He had obviously waited around long enough for me to find him again. One last explanation before he left.

The tears I'd been blinking back hit me full force then. They dribbled down my cheeks, dripping off my chin and landing on his dirty face. My insides shook as I drew in a quivering breath.

What was I supposed to do now?

I staggered to my feet and backed away from the body. I needed to report his death, but the idea of talking to the police freaked me out. My limbs were trembling as I headed out of the alley, hoping no one spotted me when I ducked back onto the sidewalk. I found the first pay phone I could and dialed 9-1-1. I gave the details swiftly then hung up before leaving my name and address. I didn't want to use my cellphone in case they somehow traced the number. I felt bad, but I was in survival mode.

Scrambling for my keys, I walked as quickly as I could to my car. I was wrong about yesterday. It hadn't been the worst day of my life.

Today had.

eight

I didn't remember the drive home. My brain was too full to really focus, so it was probably a miracle that I made it in one piece. As I slammed the door shut, I noticed Dad's car. I'd forgotten he was coming back from golf that afternoon. I didn't want to see him. Not because I didn't love him, I just knew that if he gave me one of his tight squeezes and asked how his little Caity was doing, I'd lose the plot completely.

Opening the side gate, I decided to sneak around to the back of the house and get to my room via the laundry room. I was just ascending the stairs of the back deck when I spotted my neighbor. He was sitting on the back steps of his own deck, sipping on a Coke and looking content.

Damn, he was hot.

And damn, why did I think that every time I saw him?

He glanced my way. "Hey, Caitlyn."

"Hey." I pushed a smile over my lips. It probably looked so weak and pathetic. I still wasn't used to him being nice to me. Maybe I looked pale again.

I bit my bottom lip.

His eyes narrowed slightly. There was that concern again.

"You want a Coke?" Digging into the cooler beside him, he pulled out an ice-cold bottle and held it out. I skipped down the stairs, a little euphoric that Eric Shore was offering me a drink. It was both unnerving and thrilling. My woes still sat heavy and present on my shoulders as I reached over the fence for the bottle, but his enigmatic smile was certainly dulling the impact. Maybe I could forget about my day for just a second.

Eric leaned against the fence, his long body looking comfortable as he took a swig of black gold.

"So, I saw you hustling away from the beach today. Everything okay?"

I definitely didn't want to get into it. I could feel the tears brewing and highly doubted he'd appreciated me falling apart in front of him.

Nodding with another plastic smile, I downed a few large mouthfuls so I didn't have to talk. I nearly choked, but managed to gulp down the fizz before spraying it all over him. I wiped the drops from my bottom lip, feeling like an idiot.

He snickered.

Wanting to remove all heat from my blushing face, I perched my arms on the fence and cleared my throat. "You heading back to your dorm tonight?"

"Yeah, I'll probably leave in an hour or so." He looked at his thick leather watch. It was one of those massive, chunky ones and looked so good on his wrist. He had thin leather bands sitting above it. He wore those on both wrists. Some of them had beads woven in, others were just strips of leather. I always wondered if they were a collection or if they symbolised something more.

He was looking at me, probably trying to figure out why I was staring at his styley wrists.

I scratched the corner of my mouth. "So, um, why is it that your house is only twenty minutes from campus, yet you don't live at home? Because that tells me you don't want to be here, but then you're home almost every weekend. I don't get it."

His eyebrows dipped together, his hair covering his face as he looked to the ground. After a moment's pause he snickered and looked at me, slightly abashed. "Well, I live on campus because I can only handle so much of my mother's steady stream of boyfriends. I come home every weekend because my half-sisters' father got a one-year contract in Colorado and they're missing him big time."

Swoon! He was looking out for his sisters.

I fought to control my quivering lips. "Wow. That's pretty cool."

He shrugged, taking another swig of Coke. "It's only for a year and I feel like I owe them."

"How so?"

"I took the year off after high school to go traveling. I spent some time with my grandpa in San Diego and then spent the rest of the time checking out national parks and just exploring."

"Where'd you go?" I leaned forward, totally fascinated. I loved exploring.

"I went rock climbing in Utah, hiking in the Grand Canyon, checked out Mesa Verde. Spent time in Fire Valley. Then I started missing the ocean, so I came out to the coast and worked my way up to Washington State."

My face was beaming. I could feel it.

It was my dream to do that kind of thing. Holly, Layla and I did a girls weekend in Yosemite National Park once and I adored every second of it.

"I'd love to do that one day. Just travel off with no agenda or schedule. That must have been awesome."

He grinned, tucking a lock of hair behind his ear. "It was. One of the best years of my life actually."

"I bet." I smiled. "I can't wait to get college out of the way and just be able to go, you know?"

"Why wait for college?"

I shrugged. "I don't know. I guess I want to get it

done."

"Yeah, I get that. Although I don't mind being a year older than all the other freshmen. It's not too bad."

So he was twenty. For some reason that just made him even more attractive.

"What do you want to do at college?" he asked.

"I don't know yet. I thought I'd take a bunch of different classes and see what inspires me."

"You going to UCLA?"

"Most likely, all my brothers and sisters went there."

"It's a good school." He shrugged. "I like it anyway."

"Have you figured out your major yet?"

"Nah." He shook his head. "I like a psychology class I'm taking. That could be cool."

I raised my eyebrows. Psychology. Maybe he could become my therapist. I certainly needed one! Rubbing my forehead with a wince, my day suddenly slammed back into me, stealing my smile and all the niceness of the heavenly moment.

"Hey." Eric nudged my arm with his bottle. "You sure you're okay?"

"Just a bad weekend, I guess."

"You want to talk about it?"

"No." I licked my lips and spun the bottle in my hands. I was too afraid to look at him. I didn't know what I'd see. Annoyance at not opening up to him, maybe? Or sweetness. That would just make me cry. I kept my eyes on the bottle, just waiting for him to say something.

"Okay, well, can I give you some advice then?"

"Do I have a choice?" I couldn't help stealing a glance at him. Thankfully a small smile played on his lips.

"Of course you do. If you don't want to hear it, I won't tell ya."

"Okay, well now I want to know."

His smile grew to full beam. Man he was gorgeous. I smiled back and felt instantly better, but then I saw how serious his gaze was. His hazel eyes were rich with concern...for me.

My top teeth caught my bottom lip.

"Caitlyn, whatever it is that's eating you up, you either can't do anything about it and you have to let it go, or there *is* something you can do about it and you have to do that thing."

I swallowed and willed my eyes not to start leaking. Finally, once I'd cleared the boulder from my throat, I whispered. "That's good advice."

"I thought so." His mock smugness made me chuckle. We both grinned at each other and then it got awkward. He was thinking I was cute again and I just had no idea what to do with that. Stella was like a power cat when it came to guys. She knew exactly how to play them.

Me? I was the swooning klutz who stumbled over my words and ended up looking like a moron.

I guzzled down the last of my drink and handed over the bottle, praying I didn't burp in his face. I willed my tummy to behave itself.

"Thanks, Eric. For the drink...and the advice."

"Anytime, Caity."

Caity on his lips was like melted chocolate on a marshmallow. It took every ounce of self-control not to blush up a storm and beg him to marry me right then.

I turned away before he could even get a whiff of my thoughts and scurried up my back steps. I paused at the door and waved one last time, nearly flying when I realized he was still at the fence watching me. The look of open admiration on his face made my insides turn to mush.

I wasn't sure if he wanted me to see it, but at that moment I didn't care. I may have not wanted the freaking power I'd been given, but in that second I was almost grateful for it.

nine

I wasn't grateful for it.

What the hell was I thinking?

Grateful?

I felt like my brain was going to explode and I'd only been in school for ten minutes. I avoided my parents before school, not wanting to know if they had any secrets to hide. I didn't know if they actually had any, but I sure as heck didn't want to find out. I knew school was going to be bad enough, but I never expected this.

I went to Palisades Charter High School. It catered to the wealthy, Westside families and was considered one of the better schools in L.A. The grounds were pretty wicked. I loved all the outdoor walkways and how the orange brick buildings were connected. If schools could be good-looking, Pali High definitely was. A few movies had even been shot on site. That was testament enough.

Basically the school was filled with privileged kids from privileged homes. I had grown up with most of them and, for some reason, I had been living under the naive assumption that my perfect school was filled with together kids who had no issues.

Man, was I wrong.

No matter where I looked I spotted hidden emotions. It sucked. Was no one in this place genuine? I thought all my friends were nice and amazing, but it turned out half the people I hung out with were self-centered jerks. Chase wasn't the only guy with a dick for a brain. The amount of leering looks I spotted walking down the corridor with Stella was revolting. She seemed to love it though. Her smug smile and arched eyebrow said it all, but the longer I stared at her, the more layers seemed to strip away and her smug smile dropped to a wide-eyed insecurity that I didn't want to know about.

Not Stella. She was the strong one. The confident one. The one who showed me what to do. I didn't want to know about her inferiority complex.

I stopped looking at her after that, making sure I kept myself busy whenever she was talking. Candy Crush on my iPhone became a lifesaver. It would eventually tick her off, but it was all I could handle that morning.

Libby bounced past our blue lockers with a friendly hello. I tried to make my smile genuine to counter Stella's aversion to Libby's presence, forgetting that both girls were unaware I was seeing it all. Libby flounced away, feeling rejected, but looking like the chirpiest person at school. Stella strutted off with her boobs sticking out, feeling I don't know what because I couldn't go there, and looking like the belle of the ball.

So much for a gift.

I told the guy he'd picked the wrong person.

I couldn't even look my best friend in the eye and I didn't want to delve any deeper than that one layer. How was I supposed to help people if I could barely handle a walk down the hall?

The bell rang, saving my life. I shuffled off to class avoiding eye contact at all costs. I nearly smashed straight into an open locker at one point, but Micah pulled me out of the way in time. His bemused grin made me blush.

"See you in Biology," I mumbled to my lab partner and shuffled into class.

Algebra brought with it a new type of anguish, partly because it was Algebra and secondly because the girl sitting next to me was a tightly wound mess. She answered all the questions perfectly when asked, but the look of sheer panic raking her features as she spoke was enough to give me heart palpitations. The guy behind her spent the whole period rolling his eyes at the girl and loathing her...probably for being right all the time. His dark vibes unsettled me, so I kept my eyes on my book, only looking up when I absolutely had to.

The day continued in that fashion. Me spotting things I didn't want to see. I even noticed Chase looking at me a couple of times. For some weird reason he still wanted me. I couldn't help wondering if I had sort of become a conquest to him. It made me want to avoid him like the plague and I spent a good portion of my day walking the long route to every class in an attempt to not see him.

I couldn't believe how quickly my feelings for him had faded. I'd gone from major crush mode and thinking I was going to sleep with him, to pure repulsion. Would I ever be able to like anyone again? Knowing everyone's secrets just made me want to stay away from them and if they ever found out what I was capable of, they'd treat me like a flu virus. Who wanted to hang out with someone you could never hide anything from? It'd be isolation city if I didn't figure out how to handle it.

When it came to fight or flight, I had always erred on the side of running, but with nowhere to go, I had to settle for head-in-the-sand syndrome, staying quiet and keeping my eyes down for almost every interaction I had.

By the end of the day, Stella was furious with me. I glimpsed the hurt she was feeling over my quiet behavior, but I couldn't explain it to her. How could I tell her? She'd never look at me the same if she knew. And there was no way she'd be able to keep it a secret.

I was alone, and struggling to face that reality. I'd never been a 'blab my feelings to everybody' type of person, but Stella and I usually talked about everything. It was good to have one person to offload to. The idea of calling one of my sisters nudged at me, but I immediately rejected it. Holly would have a hard time quelling her laughter...even if I was in tears. Layla would go into mother mode and that always irked me.

No, this time, there was absolutely no one I could confide in.

Or was there?

I rejected the idea instantly. Was I insane? I'd only just figured out Eric thought I was cute, I wasn't about to ruin it all by telling him I was a teenage mentalist.

No, my options were few...actually they were one.

Escape.

By the end of the next day I was done. Before Dad got home from work and Mom returned from babysitting Layla's kids, I stuffed my car full of everything I thought I'd need. My plan was to drive to the most isolated place I knew and finish high school online. I was sure there was a way I could do it. I hadn't really researched it yet, but I had my phone and every town had some kind of Internet access, didn't it? My cash card was in my back pocket and I had enough savings to get me through to June at least. I didn't leave a note for my parents; I figured I'd just email them when

I got there.

It was illogical thinking, but two days of intense high school stress was more than enough. I couldn't seem to control what I saw. Everyone was an open book and it wasn't like I could keep walking the halls with my eyes on my shoes. I either had to face it head-on or run for the hills.

I was weak. I was pathetic...and I didn't even care.

I knew L.A. pretty well, having lived there my entire life, so I had no idea what my stupid brain was thinking when I decided to skip town by driving past UCLA as if it were the only route I could take. My subconscious must have been working overtime and then, thanks to the traffic lights outside the college, my foolproof, or epically foolish, plan was foiled. I never intended to turn into campus, but I'd gotten into the wrong lane. As I drove through the massive university I was consumed with the thought that Eric was there somewhere.

Probably in class. Probably learning something about how to help psychos like me.

A desperate need to see him surged through me and before I could stop myself, I pulled over and asked for directions to Hedrick Summit. That was where Eric's dorm room was. I had overheard his mom chatting with mine and stored the information away. I assumed I'd never need it, but it had to do with Eric, so of course I remembered it.

I parked my overloaded Mini and headed for the entrance. My nerves were going mental as I clutched the keys in my hand and walked into the lobby. I had to ask several different people until I found out that Eric lived on the fifth floor in room 503. I made sure to keep every conversation quick, avoiding eye contact as much as possible. I received a few curious frowns, but most people pointed me in the right direction without even looking at me.

The hallways weren't that crowded. Most people were probably still dribbling in from classes. It was only four o'clock in the afternoon. I got bumped from behind as I came to a stop outside Eric's room. I ignored the mumbled apology and just stared at the door, unsure whether to knock or walk away.

The decision was stolen from me when the door flew open.

"Oh! Hi." The guy in front of me looked surprised to see a strange girl ready to knock on his door, but he also looked intrigued. His gaze was open, his pale brown eyes sparkling. His spiky hair was the brightest orange I'd ever seen, but it was obviously not from a bottle. Poor kid probably got hassled mercilessly growing up. The freckles dotting his pale skin wouldn't have helped either. I must have been cringing in pity, because his head tipped to the side, his expression going from friendly to droll.

I averted my gaze, my cheeks flaring with color.

"Sorry, um. I'm looking for Eric." I tucked a lock of hair behind my ear and glanced at him, making sure to look him straight in the eye.

A smile grew on his lips and he extended his hand. "I'm Scott and you must be..."

"Caitlyn."

"Right." He nodded. I could tell he'd never heard of me before.

"I don't go here. I just...I'm a friend. Well, maybe. I mean, I don't..." I took a breath. "He's my next door neighbor."

Scott's smile was in full beam by the time I was done. I waited for him to start laughing at me, but he swallowed it back, his lips trembling with the effort.

It didn't bother me. Talking to him was easy for some reason. Maybe it was because no matter how long I stared at him, he looked the same. No slipping of facial expressions or hidden emotions.

He just...was.

"Well, I haven't seen him this afternoon, but you're welcome to wait here. I'd wait with you, but I've gotta go, sorry." He felt bad. How sweet.

"No, that's okay." I waved my hand. "I might...I can come back another day." I swallowed, half-relieved that I had an excuse to lose my nerve.

"Caitlyn?" Eric's voice reached me from a few feet away. He was behind me, so I couldn't see what he was feeling, but he sounded happy. My lips twitched as I turned to face him and that was all it took. He was standing there looking gorgeous in his ripped jeans and checkered shirt with the rolled-up sleeves. I loved that one. It showed off his impressive forearms and those wristbands I loved. But it was the look on his face that did me in. His hazel eyes with green flecks were gazing at me with such open admiration that I lost it. My eyes began to shimmer with tears and my chin started quivering.

Eric's face washed with concern as he stepped toward me, shooting Scott a quick look of inquiry. Scott shrugged and mumbled a quick goodbye before taking off.

I felt like such an idiot. Swiping at my tears, I sniffed and said, "I'm sorry. I just came by to...um...to um..."

"Talk?"

"Yeah." I swallowed and sniffed again.

In spite of his obvious concern, the edge of his mouth lifted with a smile. "Come on. I know the perfect place." He took my hand and pulled me down the hallway. He didn't say a word as he wove me through the human traffic and out of the building. We walked across campus in silence and I was glad for it. I kept my head down, letting my hair work as the ideal curtain. I didn't look up until Eric pulled me into a quiet grove of trees. We stopped at a lone park bench situated under a huge willow tree. The long branches created a quiet haven, the dappled lighting giving it a magical feel.

"Wow," I breathed. "How'd you find this place?"

"I was exploring." His right shoulder popped up with a shrug as he let go of my hand.

I wrapped my arms around myself and scanned the ancient-looking tree. I was just buying time really, trying to work out how I was supposed to get any of this stuff off my chest. Eric watched me in silence; maybe he was trying to work out where to start as well.

Eventually I gave in with a sigh. Running my fingers through my hair, I brushed it off my face and looked at him.

"I don't even know how to start this conversation."

"Why don't you start with what's bugging you." He pointed at the bench seat.

My chuckle was dry and lifeless as I walked towards the seat and sat down. "That's too huge. Start with something smaller."

"Okay." Eric stretched his arm along the back of the seat. It touched my back, feeling strong and warm...both a comfort and a thrill. "Let's start with you telling me what compelled you to come here."

I nodded, tears building in my eyes again. "Well, I was on my way to Wyoming and I took a wrong turn."

"Wyoming?" He scratched the light stubble on his chin.

"Yeah." I nodded. "I Googled it this afternoon and it's the least populated state in America."

"Right." Now he was looking at me like I was mentally deranged. "And you want to go there because...?"

"There are hardly any people there." My laugh was pitchy and near hysterical. "I could maybe even go a whole day without looking at someone. Without seeing all they had to show me." My face crumpled as the tears took me again. I covered my mouth, trying to rein them in, but a few still slipped out.

Eric was working on figuring me out. I watched the confusion and concern flit across his face. His lips pursed to the side and he was worried about what to say next.

"Caity." When he finally did speak, his voice was low and soft. "Why are you running away? What's spooked you? Are you in trouble or something?"

"No." I sniffed. "I'm not in trouble, well I mean I'm not in physical danger, I just, I'm not coping with my new eyesight and the stuff I can see... This *stupid* gift!"

He grimaced, searching for the right words. Unsure what to say, he ran his finger down my hairline and gently over my ear. "You know you sound like a crazy person." He smiled. "And I really want to help you, so you need to figure out how to tell me exactly what's going on."

He could see my torment and this made him hurt for me. I knew I liked him for good reason. His hazel eyes were near anguished because he wanted to help me and wasn't sure how. I took in a deep breath and slowly expelled it, focusing on the dappled light dancing over my hand.

"Okay. Okay. I don't know how this works, but I can..." I licked my bottom lip. "I can read people."

Eric's eyebrows rose. "Like...?"

"Like I know what they're feeling. I can see it on their faces. Everything is just laid bare and I know all their secrets. I mean I don't know what they're thinking, but feelings can tell you a lot, you know. And I can't...it's too much. I mean I don't want to know this stuff, Eric. I can't handle it. I can't...I can't..."

"Okay." Eric cupped my face with his hands, putting an end to my stuttering drivel. "Just take a breath."

I did as I was told.

"And another one."

As I was expelling the second breath, he gave me a gentle smile. "I need you to start at the beginning. Did this change happen last weekend?"

I nodded.

"Tell me about it."

And I did. I spilled it all out, starting with Friday night. I even humiliated myself by mentioning Chase's sex obsession and how he was supposed to be my first and it would have been the biggest mistake ever. And then I finished with how I left a dead guy in an alleyway. It was such a relief to say it, to finally come clean as if I was confessing to a crime or something. I couldn't look at Eric while I was talking. I ended up pacing from the tree trunk and back to the bench, rabbiting on about everything I'd seen over the last few days.

I had no idea what he was feeling as I spoke, but the fact that he remained in his seat was a good sign.

"And now I'm here and I want to run away and not face this, but then I thought of you..." I finally looked at him.

He was stoked I'd said that and it made me blush. I

rubbed my cheek and began playing with the ring on my finger as his pleasure morphed to a frown. He licked the corner of his mouth, obviously trying to decide what to do with my freak of nature revelation. It unnerved him, and so it should. I mean I got an electric shock from a homeless guy and could now read people's emotions.

I wanted to turn away, tell Eric to forget I'd said anything, but I couldn't. And the main reason I couldn't was because he believed what I was saying. There was no scoffing, no scuttling away from me in terror, just a quiet, calm acceptance.

What was up with that?

Maybe I wasn't the only non-normal person around here.

"You believe me."

He glanced up from his fidgeting hands. "Why do you sound so surprised?"

"Because, it's weird. Stuff like this doesn't happen in real life."

"Sorry to break it to you, Caity, but this is real life."

"No it's not." I shook my head.

His smile was tender. "You hear about supernatural stuff happening all the time. It's not like you've grown a second head or can suddenly fly or shoot webs from your hands. You're just seeing things differently."

I gave in with a sigh.

"Explain to me how it works. You look at people and you see everything they're feeling?" He shifted in his seat. It was obviously starting to dawn on Eric that I could do that with him as well. I looked to the grass at my feet, not wanting to make him feel uncomfortable.

After a short sigh, I tried to explain. "It's like layers fall from their faces. The homeless guy described it as masks. People hide behind a mask and I can pull it away without them realizing it. If I can look into their eyes it happens much faster. I glimpse them normally and then everything changes, all their real emotions start to show."

"And that's what's freaking you out? You can't handle the onslaught of what you're seeing."

I nodded. That was exactly it, and the fact that people I thought I knew were not at all who they appeared to be. My heart did a painful hiccup and I pressed my hand to my chest.

Eric placed his elbows on his knees and loosely threaded his fingers together. He tapped his thumb against his knuckle as he thought, no doubt trying to figure out a way to help me.

"Well." He pursed his lips. "I don't want you to go to Wyoming and I don't think your parents would be overly excited about that either. So that plan is now off the table."

I chuckled. "So what do I do?"

Sitting back, he stretched his arms across the seat and thought for a minute. "I know you're having a hard time and rightfully so. But you've got to come back to what that guy said. He chose you for a reason."

I groaned and dipped my head.

He brushed his fingers down my arm. "Hey, I'm not saying you have to embrace it. You're obviously not ready and that's cool, but running's not going to help you either. You're going to have to learn how to process everything you can see."

"You mean like, control my..."

"Power. Yes."

I gave him a sideways look. "It's so not a power."

"Are you kidding me? It's like a super power."

"How can you say that? This is like the world's worst hex."

He grinned. "Just wait 'til you can control it. You'll be like Mind Girl."

"That's..." I wrinkled my nose. "That's a really lame superhero name."

"Yeah, yeah I know. I'll keep working on it." He winked.

I blushed. "You just told me it wasn't that weird. Turning me into a superhero is *not* helping."

"You're right. I'm sorry. No more superhero names."

I crossed my arms and sighed, "Thank you."

His grin was adorably boyish as he slapped his knees and stood tall then turned and held out his hand. "All right little lady, come with me. Let's go work on your mind control."

I took his hand, trying to quell the nervous bubbles that burst through me as his fingers curled around mine. I could get use to how awesome it felt to hold his hand.

As we walked out of the quiet grove, the human population came back into view. Reality returned like a hard slap and my immediate response was to grimace and look down at the grass.

"Caity, you've got to face this." Eric tugged my hand. "Now, look at that couple over there. Tell me what you see."

I followed his pointing finger and took in the guy about ten yards away. He was good-looking and knew it. His smile was near blinding as he chatted to a perky blonde who didn't know how to stand still. She kept bouncing on her toes as she talked.

Taking a breath, I studied their faces. "He's into her."

"Obviously."

"But he doesn't want to be. I mean he does, but he feels guilty, like he shouldn't be flirting. They're not a couple. He's hitting on her, because she talked to him first. She's totally into him. Like stalker into him. She's..." I paused.

"What?"

"She's scared he's going to reject her and she doesn't know if she can handle it. She's doing everything she can to impress him. I don't know why, it's almost warped, like maybe he reminds her of someone or she's trying to make up for something."

I looked back at the guy and anger surged through me as I watched him touch her cheek. His eyes were filled with that hungry lust Stella studied Eric with. I squeezed Eric's hand and made a move to turn away.

"Wait." He pulled me back around. "Keep looking at them."

"I don't want to." I frowned. "Why's he feeling guilty? He's probably got a girlfriend already, one he cares about...sort of. With this girl, he's after one thing and she's after everything. She's gonna end up hurt. It just makes me sad...and annoyed."

"I know." His sincere look was so sweet I didn't want to pull my eyes away from it. "But keep looking at them. I want you to try something."

I turned back with a huff. "What?"

"Put the layers back on."

"What do you mean?"

"Well, the longer you looked at them, the more you saw, so just put back what you saw."

I'd never thought about it that way. I'd probably done it accidentally a few times when the power first hit me. One big blink had seemed to reset my vision. I closed my eyes and tried to picture them the way I originally saw them and opened my eyes, but no luck. The masks slipped away in a nano-second and I was back seeing open emotions that hurt to look at.

"I can't do it. I can't hold onto the image. Tell me what you see right now."

"I see a guy flirting with a girl who obviously likes him."

I closed my eyes again and tried to empty my brain of anything I'd already seen. Taking a deep breath, I opened my eyes and gazed at the couple, willing the snapshot to hold.

"I see it." I grinned, but it didn't last long. The layers started falling away and I was once again back to guilt and desperation. "I'm losing it."

"Don't." Eric squeezed my hand. "Hold on to it. Put the layers back on, but don't close your eyes this time. Try to do it while you're looking at them."

Squinting my eyes, I ordered my brain to see what I'd first captured. Painfully slowly the guilty expression morphed to one of carefree flirting and the girl's desperation eventually ebbed back to pleasure.

"How's it going? Is it working?"

"Yeah, yeah I guess so. I'm trying to work backward. It's really hard, but I think I can see what you're seeing now."

"Excellent." Eric spun to face me. "So if you can do that, then you just need to focus on what you see first...before that mask slips off. I know you only get a second to take it in, but if you can practice holding on to what you see in that second, then you can put that back on and not be swamped by all these emotions and secrets. Do you think you can do that?"

I nodded, feeling calm for the first time in days. A smile crept over my lips and I nodded again.

Eric's solemn gaze made my smile slip a fraction.

"Caity, I'm not helping you so that you can ignore this amazing talent." He squeezed my shoulder. "I just want to give you a strategy that will stop you from bolting to Wyoming. You're gonna have to face this at some point."

"I know." I nodded, not wanting to hear it but knowing that he was right, and he would want me to agree.

His gorgeous eyes studied me for a beat too long before he was finally satisfied. My steady gaze must have put him at ease, because he eventually grinned. "Okay, cool, let's go practice on someone else."

ten

Eric pulled me around campus for the next hour, working my brain and eyes until they were aching. By six o'clock, I'd managed to read and unread eight more people. I saw nothing sinister, just little secrets, and it was refreshing to find that at least one of those eight had nothing to hide. It gave me hope in humanity, if only for a moment.

As a thank you, I took Eric out to dinner. He wasn't happy at all about me paying, but I could be stubborn when I wanted to be. He then told me the only place he wanted to eat was In-N-Out Burger. I thought that was a lie and he was just trying to save me spending too much on him, but he was telling the truth. So we sat at In-N-Out Burger dining on fries animal style and juicy, beef burgers.

I slurped up the last of my vanilla shake, making a ridiculous noise. Biting my lips together, I pushed the cup away from me, willing my cheeks not to turn red yet again.

Eric grinned. "So, you feeling better?" He wiped his hands on a napkin and balled it up.

"Definitely. Thank you."

He shook his head. "You can really stop saying that now. I think you're up to about forty thank yous. It's getting kind of old."

My nose wrinkled and I rubbed a hand over my face. He just laughed at me, but when I looked up, his smile was missing. His serious expression made me swallow.

Dropping the balled up napkin, he reached for me, drawing soft patterns over the back of my hand with his forefinger. "Caity, can you promise me something?"

"Sure." With that voice, I'd promise him anything.

"Now that you know how to control it, don't read me."

My insides clenched. This was why I didn't want to tell people. They wouldn't be themselves around me if they knew. I went to pull my hand away, but he grabbed it before I could.

"I'll always tell you the truth, I promise. So don't read me, okay? I want us to be ourselves around each other and if I think you might be reading me then I know I'm gonna act weird. I feel privileged that you've told me this stuff and I don't want you to ever worry that I'll hide anything from you, so you don't have to worry about reading me. Does that make sense?" His warm, hazel eyes flickered with bashful concern and I had to nod.

"It might still happen without me meaning to, but I'll trust you, Eric. I promise."

He met my shaky smile with a beaming one of his own. I didn't even have to read him. What he was showing me was pure honesty and my insides buzzed with that euphoric giddiness I always felt when I was around him. Except in that second, it was running on overdrive.

****

I practically floated to school the next morning. Eric and I had parted ways shortly after dinner. He hadn't kissed me goodbye or anything (like he even would!), but he'd hugged me tight and told me to keep him posted. He even took my phone and programmed his number in. It would remain to be seen if I'd ever have the guts to call him. I'd respond in a heartbeat, but to actually initiate? Scary!

I took my time walking to my locker. This time I kept my head up and took in those around me. It was an effort and I failed at least three times, but I did manage to hold onto those first glimpses for some people. I resisted the layers falling away and scrambled to put them back in place before I saw it all. It helped that most of the people I chatted to were friends so I remembered what they looked like normally. The skill was going to take time to master and I'd still slip-up and spot stuff I didn't want to see, but the more I practiced, the more I could do it.

It was a triumphant feeling and I would be eternally grateful to Eric.

Eric.

Le sigh.

"What are you smiling about?" Stella's voice was sharp. I could see that what sounded like annoyance was actually hurt, and I had to quickly work to put her normal face back together. "Caitlyn? What is your problem?"

Okay, so I obviously needed to work on my concentrating face. I shook my head and smiled. "Nothing. I'm good." I squeezed her arm and looked her in the eye. "I'm really good. Sorry for being so weird the last couple of days, I've just been struggling with this headache."

"Still? Have you seen a doctor?"

I hesitated, then grinned. "I saw one after school yesterday...and I'm already starting to feel better."

"Good." Stella looked exasperated. "Because I was getting really over you."

"Thanks." My droll look elicited a cheeky giggle from Stella and she threaded her arm through mine and hauled me to U.S. History. That was our favorite subject together. Mr. Winright was such a boring and unobservant teacher, we ended up passing notes and fooling around most of the time. It was fun.

The day progressed easily. I kept practicing and it did get easier. I couldn't block out everything, but I would be able to eventually. I was determined. The cafeteria at lunch got a bit too much for me, so I left early, making up an excuse about needing to finish some homework. I got a bunch of weird and disbelieving looks, but I didn't care. I needed a breather. And in all honesty, I could use a little extra study time. Work was piling up. With SATs less than three months away, the pressure was on. I still had some big assignments ahead of me too. I couldn't afford to slack off.

No one else in my group seemed overly fazed. I was either a dumbass or a super slow worker.

Probably a combination of both, dumbass.

I snickered at my self-deprecating joke, knowing it wasn't true. I wasn't the smartest kid at school, but I'd do okay, especially if I didn't slack off. I cringed when I thought of how little Stella was doing. Surely she'd start to freak about her grades soon. I'd no doubt get sucked into a last minute study-fest, cramming for SATs until the early hours of the morning.

The corridor was pretty empty as I walked to my locker. It was a pleasant relief. I nearly made it all the way there without a single interaction, but then I heard Libby's sweet titter and I couldn't help looking. I peered down the adjacent corridor and spotted her leaning against her locker. Her face was practically shining and it wasn't hard to figure out why.

Carter Hanson was leaning over her with a charming smile.

Really?

What the hell was Carter doing chatting up Libby? Not to be mean about Libby, but she was hardly in his league.

I couldn't help myself, I ducked around the corner and played spy.

"So I was thinking, maybe you could join me." Carter ran his finger down Libby's cheek. Her body was quivering as she gazed at him with a nervous smile.

The layers fell away before I could stop them. I was too intrigued to fight it...and the intrigue quickly morphed to concern.

Carter's gaze wasn't leering; if anything, he actually looked a little reluctant to be doing what he was doing. It wasn't until the reluctance fell away that I noticed the malicious gaze beneath it. What was he up to?

"Liam's parties are always the best and he's having it at Indie's place, which is, you know, a mansion. We'll have a great time."

"I'd love to come."

My insides hitched as I studied Libby's face. She was ecstatic that Carter was even talking to her, let alone inviting her to a party. Part of her couldn't believe it was true, but it was being overridden by her desperate need for acceptance. Her slight fear was shunted aside by a dreamlike euphoria.

I got it. I mean Carter was hot. Liam's parties were amazing, if not a little overwhelming, and Libby had never been invited to anything like it before. She always tried to tag along, but I'd never seen her at a Liam Donovan party. Whether she chickened out at the last minute or was turned away at the door, I didn't know. Judging from the current look on her face, she'd be chickening out over her dead body. With Carter taking her rather than showing up on her own, it would be a given.

The question was, why was Carter taking her? What did he really want?

The black gleam in his eyes scared me. He was up to something, and although Libby and I weren't super-close, there was no way I wanted to see her get hurt. She was a sweetie and didn't deserve whatever Carter and his friends had planned. I knew him well enough to know he wasn't working alone.

I had to do something about it.

Swallowing back my nerves, I approached Libby's locker just as Carter was walking away. I figured Libby would be the easier one to talk to. If I tried to call Carter on anything, he'd probably tell me to go screw myself. He was on the basketball team with Chase and Sean. A bunch of good-looking guys who thought they ruled the school. Most girls swooned...just like I had. Spotting Chase's true feelings had helped stunt my deluded admiration.

"Hey Libby." I kept my voice light and casual, not wanting to scare her.

"Oh, hey Caitlyn."

Her smile was nearly blinding.

"Did I just see Carter Hanson ask you out?" It was really unlike me to get straight to the point. I had 'dancing around the bush' down to an art form, but the bell was about to ring and if I went for small talk I'd lose my nerve altogether.

"Yeah," Libby breathed. "He's taking me to Liam's party on Friday. Everyone's going there after the game."

It was pretty standard. Friday night basketball was often followed up with some sort of event—normally to celebrate the win, sometimes to blow off steam. Stella would no doubt drag me along this Friday. She never missed Liam's parties. He was a bit of a legend at this school. He and his girlfriend Indie were the couple everyone wanted to be like.

"That's cool." I nodded. "But um..." How did I say this?

I glanced at Libby's expression. She was nervous about what I was going to say, in spite of her smile.

"I don't want to sound rude or anything, I just wanted to make sure you're comfortable going with Carter."

"What do you mean?" Her nerves were picking up big time. I had to get this out quickly.

"Well, he's not really...I mean you guys don't really hang out much. Don't you think it's weird that he's suddenly asking you out?"

"What are you saying?" Nerves were being replaced with anger. It was a jittery anger fueled by her underlying insecurity and I really didn't like it, but how could I not say something?

"Libby, I don't know if you were aware of this, but when he was talking to you, he looked kind of...untrustworthy. I can't help wondering if he's up to something. I'm worried you might get hurt."

"Worried? You're worried about me? Really?"

Shame crept over me. She was right. I'd never given a rat's ass before. I'd always just stayed quiet as my friends made her feel like pond scum. She'd have to be blind not to see through their plastic smiles. You didn't need any kind of super power to pick up the get lost vibes that radiated off them whenever Libby was around.

Lifting her chin, she gazed up at me with a steely glare. "You know what, Caitlyn, I think you're jealous."

My head jolted back in surprise. "Of what?"

"Carter liking me. I know you and Chase broke up and now you're probably on the prowl for someone new."

On the prowl? Was she serious? That was so not my style.

I closed my eyes, forcing a calm softness to my voice. "Libby, I'm not trying to take Carter off you. I don't even like Carter...like that. I'm just not sure if he's being honest with you."

I was sure. I was one hundred percent freaking sure, but I couldn't say that to her.

Libby's face bunched up tight, her obvious and hidden emotions blending together. I tried to put back the layers, not wanting to see how much I'd hurt her. I finally managed to settle on an indignant anger, which wasn't exactly fun to look at either.

"You know what, Caitlyn. You can have any guy you want. You hang with Stella and Indie and all the cool girls, so it's not hard for you. Why would you want to take this from me?"

"I'm not trying to—"

"Guys like Carter never acknowledge my existence so when one finally does, I'm not going to reject it. Why can't you just be happy for me?"

"I'm sorry. I just—"

"Stay out of my business." Libby shouldered past me before I could say anything else. I didn't bother chasing her. I'd probably end up doing more harm than good.

Dammit. Blocking people out was so much easier. I didn't want to get involved with this drama.

With my mood fully blackened, I headed to my locker. The hallways were crowded again and I worked overtime making sure to put layers back on every single person's face. I didn't want to see another damn thing.

eleven

By the end of the week I could block out most things. I was surprised by how quickly I'd managed to get a handle on my power. I guess I'd been practicing...a lot. It felt good though. I was in control, mostly, and I was determined to keep it that way.

The basketball game went well with an easy victory against Santa Monica High. Micah, the star player, who also happened to be my biology lab partner, had been on fire as usual, pretty much winning Pali High the game. Stella and I followed the revellers to Indie's house in my car. She was planning on getting plastered and asked me to be the designated driver. I was more than happy to do it. I still hadn't really acquired a taste for alcohol and only drank it when I absolutely had to. That night, I had the best excuse in the world not to swallow a drop.

We bustled into the party, knocking shoulders with the crowd. Indie Swanson was the daughter of Dominic Swanson, big time movie producer. They lived in a palatial mansion and now that her older brother, Maverick, was at a college in Texas, Indie basically had the house to herself. Her father was away shooting yet another film and the live-in housekeeper was so passive, she basically let Indie do whatever she liked. I had heard that Liam, Indie's boyfriend, slept over most nights. They were like living together. Some girls thought it was so romantic. I still hadn't decided what I thought.

The humongous house was crowded. Liam had obviously invited everyone he knew. I hated being around so many people at one time and made a beeline for the quietest area I could find. It was the movie room, just off the main living area. It was dark and filled with couples mauling each other on various couches and beanbags. Stella was not impressed with my choice and pulled me back into the main area. The doors leading out to the pool were all open making the partying space a massive expanse, chocked full of people. Knowing I'd lost the battle, I pressed myself against a free space of wall and studied the crowd. Stella was flirting overtime with the guy beside us. I didn't recognize him. He looked older than us, just Stella's style.

Not being able to help myself, I practiced putting people's masks on and off. I didn't study what lay beneath their expressions, I just let the layers start to slip then quickly put them back in place. I loved that I was getting better and could do it in under ten seconds. I spent the next half hour happily controlling myself, feeling proud for doing it.

But then I spotted something I couldn't ignore.

It wasn't Libby, who I had secretly been keeping an eye out for. I hadn't seen her since we arrived and part of me hoped she'd chickened out and gone home after the game.

No, what I saw was something totally unexpected. It kind of threw me and I ended up having to look again. It was Indie, the quiet auburn-haired beauty that everyone wanted to be like. She was an enigma almost. Her soft smile and kind blue eyes made people like her, but she was so cool that no one had the courage to really go near her. She was like a celebrity at her own school. I had to admit that I was proud to call her my friend. I mean I didn't know her that well, but we hung out together all the time.

But I'd never seen this about her before.

Fear. It was stark white all over her face.

I blinked, quickly replacing the mask. Her calm veneer was back in place. She was smiling at Liam as he said some joke to the people in front of him. His arm was around her waist, keeping her close. They looked so in love.

I frowned and tentatively let the smile slip from her face. There it was again. She was scared. Not like timid scared, but like hell scared. Her eyes were wide with fear, her lips quivering. The hand perched on Liam's shoulder was practically shaking.

I put her mask back on to compare what I was seeing. Her fingers were fidgeting with Liam's collar as he spoke. He gazed down at her tenderly and whispered something in her ear. She giggled and gave him a coy smile.

I whipped her mask away and saw her neck muscles strain tight. The smile was hiding a grimace and when she looked up at her boyfriend I saw a mixture of terror and loathing.

My lips parted as I reverted my gaze to Liam. Stripping away his affectionate smile I snatched a glimpse of something that gave me goosebumps, a dark possession that had my stomach clenching. The arm around her waist wasn't loving at all, it was holding her in place, keeping her in line. Another layer began to slip from his features and I flinched, quickly putting it back in place.

I didn't want to see that. No. Indie and Liam were the perfect couple. Everyone at school aspired to be like them. They were cool, but really nice. They were accepted by every social set in the school. No one despised them. They were like the golden couple.

My breathing was punchy as I looked away. What had I just seen? What was I supposed to do with that?

Poor Indie. I hadn't seen fear that stark before, not ever. She was petrified and I didn't want to know why.

"I'm getting a drink." I nudged Stella and took off before she could follow me. I made it to the kitchen, keeping my eyes down. I didn't want to look at anyone. I didn't want to practice with masks or layers. I just wanted to be normal again!

The kitchen was devoid of ordinary drinks. I opened one of the fridges, looking for anything non-alcoholic and finally spotted a small can of Sprite in the back. I felt a bit bad for taking it. It obviously wasn't designated for the party, but I needed something to quell my pulsing nerves.

Popping it open, I was about to take a sip when someone practically bowled me over.

Sprite splashed up my nose, dribbled down my chin and soaked into my shirt collar.

"Sorry," the person mumbled tearfully as she bustled past.

I glanced up to see Libby frantically pushing her way through the crowd and my drink was forgotten. I forged after her, squeezing past people and trying to keep track of her.

She made it to the main entrance and started running for the door.

"Libby! Libby, wait!"

Her short legs slipped on the shiny marble. She obviously wasn't used to heels. Her ankle twisted and she hit the floor with a thud.

A couple of people around her snickered, some of them pointed. No one bothered to help her up. I wasn't bold enough to glare them down like I wanted to. It took all my courage to openly approach her and offer my hand.

Libby looked up at me, tears spilling from her eyes, making her mascara run.

"Come on," I murmured.

She reluctantly took my hand and I hauled her up. After a few hobbling steps from Libby, I wrapped my arm around her and supported her out of the house, toward a dark patch of grass off the main driveway.

"Are you okay?" I rubbed her back as she hiccuped and cried. It was hard to see her in the dim light and I was glad. I didn't want to read her. I just wanted to talk and find out the truth the conventional way.

Libby popped open her purse and pulled out a Kleenex. Her shoulders shook as she dabbed at her eyes. I kept rubbing her back, not exactly sure how to make her feel better.

"I didn't think you were here," I eventually said. "I was looking for you and thought maybe you'd changed your mind."

She rubbed her eye and shook her head with a sniff. "I wish I had."

"What happened?"

"You were right about Carter." She sniffed again.

"Did he—" I frowned. "Libby what did he do?" My insides were curdling. I didn't want to hear what she was about to say as my mind raced to the worst scenario I could think of.

Libby was quiet for too long, making it worse. My imagination was working overtime.

"He took me upstairs. We'd only been here like ten minutes." Her voice wobbled.

"Lib—"

"Don't worry, he didn't try to..." She flicked her hand. "He didn't force me to do anything."

The way she said it made me squeeze her shoulder. "What *did* you do?"

"Nothing." I could just make out her eyes shining in the dim light. Tears were busting to break free once more. "He wanted me to give him a blow job and I was really uncomfortable. I've never even kissed a guy before and Carter just expects me to blow him?" Her voice pitched high and she took in a shaky breath. "He started undoing his pants and I said I didn't want to. He got all annoyed and told me I owed him because he'd brought me here. If I wanted to be cool then I had to earn it and that if I didn't do what he said, he'd make my school life hell." Her face bunched with stress lines. "I thought about it, Caitlyn. I even got down on me knees, but I just couldn't go through with it. I freaked out and ran...and now the rest of this year is going to be so much worse than what it already is."

She leaned her head against my shoulder and broke down with unrestrained sobs. I could feel my shirt getting wet and no doubt stained with mascara. It would simply add to the Sprite. I wrapped my arms around her.

Black rage was an understatement for what I felt. I wanted to find Carter Hanson and squeeze his balls until they popped. I knew about his asshole tendencies, but why go after Libby? There were plenty of other girls far more experienced and willing. It was almost like he was trying to scare her. I didn't understand it.

Libby's sobs slowly ebbed. I had no idea how long it took. I felt like I'd been standing there forever. Her fingers dug into my back as she clung to me. I knew she wasn't ready to step away and I didn't have the heart to push her. So I stayed where I was, giving her the silent comfort she so obviously needed while trying to hide her from prying eyes as party-goers wandered up the driveway and into the house. It became increasingly challenging as whispers spread, and when two giggling girls actually came down the driveway to investigate, I couldn't take it anymore.

I squeezed Libby's shoulder. "Come on, let's get out of here. Go for a walk on the beach or something."

"Are you sure?" Libby's eyes rounded with surprise. "What about Stella?"

"She'll understand." Not really, but I wasn't about to tell Libby that. Pulling out my phone, I texted Stella and told her to call me when she was ready for a ride.

There'd be backlash, but Libby needed me and I wanted to be there for her.

twelve

The night air was cool and refreshing. Libby and I walked for only a few minutes before finding a nice little spot on a sandy dune. We sank into it, not caring that our butts would get covered. I whipped off my shoes and dug my toes in, loving the feel of the cool grains against my skin.

There was no doubt about it. Nature was good for the soul.

The pale moonlight was glistening against the gently surging water and I felt safe in the dark, magical haven.

I hoped Libby felt the same way. I peeked a glance at her. She hadn't said much as we drove down the hill and parked at a nearby beach. It was pretty much deserted, perfect for what Libby needed—a private place to cry.

She wasn't sobbing anymore, but I noticed her lips pucker every now and then, and a few more tears would descend.

I rubbed her back, not knowing what else to do or say.

Swiping at her tears, she finally drew in a shaky breath and muttered, "It was so insane to think that Carter would even be into me."

"Don't say that."

"Why not? It's the truth, isn't it? You told me so."

I bit my lip, suddenly wishing I hadn't.

"It's so unfair." Libby scowled. "I have two gorgeous sisters who sailed through high school, a mother who could pass for a model and I take after my fat father." She winced and grabbed my arm. "I love him. Really I do. But why? Why did I have to inherit his genes?"

I licked my bottom lip, wanting to sound sincere. I didn't have to try hard; I meant was I was about to say. "You're gorgeous, Libby. You have great genes."

"That's easy for a skinny person to say." She shot me a sardonic frown.

"Hey, at least you have boobs. My brother spent most of my teenage years comparing me to a surfboard."

Libby tittered. "You're not that flat."

"Yeah, I think I graduated to a B cup last

year...maybe." I rolled my eyes. "Come on, look at you, you've got a great set." I pointed at her breasts, which made her giggle.

She thrust them forward and jiggled them. We both laughed, bumping our shoulders together like comrades. But the laughter soon died away, the crappy events of the evening not far from reach.

"I wish I could just disappear sometimes," Libby whispered then scoffed. "Like a girl this size could vanish, right?"

"Hey," I softly reprimanded, squeezing her arm.

"Maybe I should just go back and do what he wants. Five minutes of torture could save me from three months of agony."

"Don't say that." My tone was much firmer than I meant it to be, but I was annoyed that she'd even consider it. "You'd hate yourself."

"What if it's the only chance I'll ever get?"

"What are you talking about?"

"For physical contact. I mean what guy is ever going to be into me?"

"Libby, stop it. There's a guy out there for you and he'll be kind and sweet and not some jerk who demands blow jobs. You don't want to be with someone like Carter. No matter how caring they might seem at the time, you'll come away feeling shallow and tainted."

She nodded, knowing I was referring to Chase.

Libby sighed. "When Carter first started taking me upstairs tonight, I thought about what you said at school. You know about him being untrustworthy?" Her nose wrinkled. "I was so annoyed with you and I didn't want your voice in my head." Her eyes landed on me, sparkling with a gratitude I wasn't expecting. "But if you hadn't warned me, maybe I wouldn't have seen through his gentle persuasion. He was being so nice to me and even when he started unzipping his fly he was making it sound like we were going to do this intimate thing that was special." She shook her head with a cynical snicker. "He made it seem like we were already a couple. I would have fallen for it, but I couldn't get past what you said."

I gave her a soft smile as my insides flooded with intense relief. Thank God I'd said something. What if I'd just walked away?

"I'm sorry for going off at you the other day," she whispered. "Out of all of Liam's group, you're one of the nice ones—you and Indie. I should have listened to you in the first place. I guess I so badly wanted to fit in."

"I know. I wish high school was easier for you and I'm sorry guys like Carter even exist, but like I said, the right guy is out there."

Her lips puckered and she shrugged. "I've dreamed about having a boyfriend for forever. I keep fooling myself into thinking he's waiting for me somewhere. Any guy who ever talks to me, I practically fall all over them. I'm pathetic. The only thing people want me for are my smarts. Whoopdeedoo."

"What do you mean?"

She shrugged, her features overrun with a guilt I didn't understand. "Just people always want help with their homework and stuff. That's the only time they ever talk to me."

I frowned, trying to decipher her expression. Maybe I was reading it wrong, the light was dim, but did she feel guilty for helping people with their homework? I didn't get that.

"Libby—"

"It'll all be over soon anyway. I've applied to a bunch of schools on the east coast. Soon I can fly away from this place and start anew. No sisters to compete with, no mother to feel fat beside. Just me." She drew in a shaky breath, but then turned to me with a smile. That thought calmed her and I didn't want to disrupt it by bringing up the homework thing.

"That's cool, Libby. You're gonna be great." I grinned at her, my insides tripping as I suddenly wondered what my future held. No matter where I went, I now had this power. I felt like there was no starting anew anymore. I was cursed...or maybe blessed...until I died.

It felt good to know that Libby hadn't crossed her own line because of something I'd said. It was with a sinking realization that I knew I wouldn't have said anything if I hadn't been able to see. I mean, yes, Carter talking to Libby was weird, but I probably would have brushed it off as none of my business. My newfound power was making me curious and that curiosity just helped someone.

Maybe blocking everyone out wasn't the answer.

"Help those around you, one person at a time, and you will have a full and happy life."

The stranger's voice was clear in my head. As Libby and I sat quietly on that beach, I couldn't help admitting that maybe the homeless guy was right.

thirteen

Stella was pretty steamed that I left her at the party. I dropped Libby home before going back to collect her. I toyed with the idea of reading my best friend on the way home, but I didn't have to, she was so drunk she told me everything. She didn't like that I was changing and so ready to ditch her all the time. She felt abandoned by me and wanted her friend back.

I felt bad and decided to make up for it the next day, but she was either too annoyed to talk to me, or sleeping it off. When the afternoon rolled around and I still hadn't heard from her, I was forced to put it to rest and deal with it the next day. My house was being overrun with little people and lucky me had been ordered to babysit. I didn't mind too much. My nephews, Jake and Brody, were gorgeous. They were so full of fun and we always had a blast together.

Isla, my two-year-old niece, was staying with her dad's parents so it was just me and the boys for the night. My parents were being taken out by their two eldest children for the evening. Seth and Layla did it every year...and I was never invited.

Why would I be? I was the babysitter!

Thankfully, Seth's girls were somewhere else. I loved them as much as the boys, but put all four together and it was an explosive concoction. I had done it once and my exhausted self had kicked up such a big fuss when everyone got home that I was never asked to do it again.

I checked my watch as I headed down the back steps. Everyone was leaving in half an hour. It would soon be game on and I wanted a second to collect myself.

"Hey, Caity." Eric's sweet voice made my insides flutter.

He was standing on his lawn, leaning his surfboard against the fence. He finished drying off his hair and spread the towel out to dry.

I tried not to stumble as I descended the stairs toward him. He propped his arms on the fence as he waited for me. His bare skin smelt fresh and salty. I wondered if he knew how much his shirtless form undid a girl. I was sure he'd wear more clothes if he knew how much it undid me anyway.

Trying not to gaze longingly at his chiseled frame was hard work. I licked my bottom lip and forced myself to look into his eyes. They were glimmering with a small smile.

"So you never called me."

I ran my hand down my ponytail, wondering how to respond. Was he annoyed or sad that I hadn't? I was tempted to read him, but forced his mask back in place when it started to fall away.

"I guess the rest of your week was okay." He touched my elbow as I leaned against the fence.

"Pretty much." I nodded. "I've been practicing a lot."

"Is it working?"

"Yeah." I grinned. "I can block out most emotions now. It's good."

"But..."

I glanced away with a snicker. "I thought *I* was the people reader, not you."

"I don't need a super power to know there's something more." He leaned his chin on his hands and looked up at me. The green flecks in his eyes seemed to shimmer. "You don't have to hide anything from me, Caity. I like that you're letting me in."

My lips twitched with a smile as I looked at him. I could have stayed that way for the rest of the night, locked in the silent connection, but then the back door swung open.

"Caitlyn and Eric sitting in a tree, K-I-S-S-I-N-G."

Jake.

I closed my eyes and wanted to die. I could feel my cheeks flaming.

Throwing a molten glare at my seven-year-old nephew, I was happy to see him yelp before running off with a giggle.

"Sorry about that." I winced, rubbing my forehead to hide my eyes. "I'm gonna go strangle him in a minute."

"Have fun with that." Eric laughed, a bright smile taking over his face.

I took a second to admire it.

"Caity is in lo-ve. Caity is in lo-ve."

Brody. No doubt spurred on by Jake.

Their giggles filtered down from the top window. I glanced up and saw it slam.

"Okay, now I'm gonna go kill both of them."

"Are you sure your sister won't mind?" Eric fought a smile.

"She's leaving in like ten minutes, it'll just be me and the boys. I'll hide their bodies before she gets home. No one will ever know."

"You'll have to come up with a good cover story."

"Or drive to Wyoming." I chuckled.

He laughed with me. "I'm sure you'll come up with something believable."

"Well, I've got all evening to do it." I winked, probably way too suggestively, and walked up the stairs before he could spot my fierce blush.

Ugh!

Could I have made it any more obvious that I would welcome him coming over to keep me company after the boys were in bed? Was that the only thing on my mind?

I slammed the back door shut and closed my eyes. The quiet patter of feet creeping down the hallway made me grin. I stayed still and kept my eyes shut until the door creaked open, then...

"BOO!!"

They both squealed and took off. I chased them with a growl, happy to run from my humiliation. I caught Brody halfway down the hallway and swung him into the air. He was laughing so hard his giggles were silent. His red face and wide-open mouth were too funny. I lowered his quaking body to the floor and tickled his tummy. A squeal burst free, giving him a chance to breathe properly.

"Don't hype them up too much before dinner. They'll never eat."

I kept my eyes down, so Layla couldn't see my eye roll.

Poking out my tongue at Brody, I let him scramble free and rush down the hallway. His father caught him as he tried to dash past and do a swan dive onto the couch. From the boys' perspective, the best part about Grandma's sunken in lounge was the opportunity to sky dive from the wooden floors to the couches below.

"Jake, don't you dare!" Layla raised her finger. He paused, his eyes dancing with the thrill of breaking the rules and the dread of getting in trouble. He stayed where he was, trying to weigh up if it was worth it.

I winked behind Layla's back, letting him know he could do it later, once the adults had gone. He grinned at me and stepped back.

Layla spun back to look at me as Brody wriggled free of his father's grasp and barreled into my dad, who hoisted him up with a laugh.

Layla gave me a stern frown. "Don't let them do anything naughty."

I snickered. "Layla, they'll be little angels."

"Yeah right." She rolled her eyes, crossing her arms to launch into a lengthy list of instructions. I'd heard them all before, and I knew what I was doing, but I let her run through them. It made her feel better. As she raised a finger for each new instruction, I pulled her mask away, more out of curiosity than anything. I wasn't overly surprised by what I saw, although found it intriguing that the idea of leaving her boys made her feel a mixture of guilt and worry. I never realized she felt so obligated by her role as a mother.

"And don't feed them any candy." She was up to ten fingers now. Surely it was the last instruction. "I've left out the dinner I want them to have. It's in the fridge. There's enough for you too."

"Thanks." I forced a grin, knowing it would be some gross, overly healthy crap.

Inspired by my mother, Layla followed the nutritionist path as well.

"Okay, I think that's everything." She tucked a lock of her straight brown hair behind her ear. Man, she looked like Mom when she did that. Her mask was still off and I decided to try something.

"You're such a great mom." I squeezed her upper arm. "You work so hard for your kids and take such good care of them. You deserve a night off. Go relax, have some fun. Don't even think about your kids tonight. I promise I'll call if there's a problem, okay?"

Her reaction nearly made me laugh. First it was utter confusion that her kid sister was saying something so sweet and mature, but next came the look of relief I'd been hoping for. Her guilt and worry eased a little as she gathered me into her arms with a warm embrace.

"Thanks, sis." She kissed my curls and held me at arms length to give me one more smile. I popped her mask back on and saw it was the same expression she was wearing. I was glad I'd made her feel better.

With that she turned to gather up her babies for goodnight kisses while I was dragged into my daddy's arms.

"Have a good night, honey."

"Thanks, Dad." I could barely talk past his bear hug.

"Be a good peanut." He flicked my nose, something I hated, but didn't have the heart to tell him. "The restaurant is on the other side of town so we'll be home late. Don't wait up. The boys are sleeping over anyway."

"I won't."

Brody and Jake came to stand beside me as we waved our goodbyes and blew kisses. The door clicked shut and I squeezed the boys' shoulders, waiting until we heard the sound of a car pulling out of the drive. As soon as we got the all clear, I pulled the boys in front of me.

"Okay, Jake, you start pulling all the squabs off the couch and Brody you start gathering up any pillow in the house you can find. Don't go into Grandma's room though, okay? But any other pillow in the house is ours." I winked, making him giggle as he dashed away.

Jake stood there with a beaming smile, just nodding at me. Yeah, at that moment in time, I was the coolest aunt ever.

fourteen

It was eight o'clock and I was attempting to put the living room back exactly how it had been before the grown ups left. Thankfully I'd made the boys help me return some of the pillows earlier. What a mission!

By some miracle, both the boys were asleep already. It probably helped that after half an hour of launching from the top step onto the mountain of pillows, blankets and couch cushions, I had taken them to the beach and run them ragged. After that, they devoured their tofu, stir-fry, brown rice noodle concoction and were too tired to do anything else but play in the bath and fall into bed.

I had missed a call from Stella while I was entertaining the boys and had tried calling her back, but she wasn't answering. It bugged me a little, but I decided to let it rest. I couldn't be bothered grovelling. Yes, I did ditch her on Friday night, but for a really good reason and I went back to get her afterwards. She'd never understand what I did for Libby, but I knew I'd done the right thing and that felt good.

As I shoved the last couch cushion into place my thoughts returned to Eric...again. I'd been thinking about him all afternoon, wondering what he was doing. The idea that he got my hint and would come over skimmed through me, but I knew I was dreaming. As if he would. I laughed at myself as I turned to look at the pile of blankets. Once those were folded and put away, I was free to do as I pleased. I could tell my obsessional thoughts of Eric weren't going anywhere so I needed a heavy-duty distraction once I was done or I'd go insane. I shouldn't have been thinking about him at all. If Stella knew how bad my crush was getting, she'd flip a switch. It wasn't like he belonged to her or anything; we'd both liked him for the same amount of time, but that was under the understanding that neither of us would ever actually get him.

I cringed. I seriously had to stop thinking about him.

I was trying to decide whether to go for my kindle or the TV remote when the doorbell rang. I rolled my eyes. It was no doubt Stella. Not exactly the diversion I was hoping for, but probably exactly what I needed. With a deep breath I tried to summon the energy for the encounter. But when I opened the door I was flooded with a mixture of relief, astonishment and giddy joy.

"Hi." I leaned against the frame.

"Hey." Eric was now in ripped jeans and his pale-green Quicksilver shirt. I loved that one on him. It was just tight enough to see the curves of his chest and shoulders.

"You want to borrow a cup of sugar or something?"

He grinned. "Actually I was wondering if you needed help burying your nephews."

I swung the door open and stepped aside to let him in. "Actually they redeemed themselves by being adorably cute this afternoon, so I let them live."

"That was good of you."

"I'm a nice person." I shrugged.

Eric walked into our open living space, looking at the artwork as he went. He seemed impressed by my parents' collection of photography and scenic oil paintings, giving me a nod of approval. I pointed to the sunken lounge area and followed him into it. His eyebrows rose as he pointed at the pile of blankets.

I shrugged. "Little boys doing sky diving practice." I pointed from the top step then onto the pile. "That's the last of the aftermath."

He chuckled as he reached for a blanket and threw it toward me, keeping the other end for himself.

And so began the folding session.

"I hope you don't mind me just popping over."

Uh - that would be a NOT AT ALL, I can't believe you're actually here and trying to hide my ecstatic joy is taking major effort right now.

I could feel my hips wanting to break into a happy dance, but I quelled the urge and managed a demure smile as he stepped toward me, touching the corners of the blanket to mine, before stepping back so we could make another fold.

"Poppy and Lacey have gone for a sleepover and Mom's boyfriend just arrived." He rolled his eyes.

"You're welcome here anytime." I took the blanket off him and placed it on the bottom step as he reached for another one.

"Thanks." He cleared his throat, looking slightly nervous, and I wasn't even reading him.

"Are you okay?"

As if suddenly aware that his edgy behavior was showing, he gave me a sheepish grin and reached for another blanket. "You said your week was better, but you were hiding something. I wanted to come over and see what that was."

I caught the edge of the blanket and found the corners, holding them wide until he nodded at me and we folded together. I stepped toward him, touching our corners together and felt him looking at me. As his fingertips brushed mine, I stole a glance up at his face, his intense gaze and those perfect lips. I wanted to stretch up on my toes and "accidentally" knock our mouths together. But how would I ever explain that one?

Instead, I cleared my throat and took a quick step back, getting my foot caught on the edge of the blanket. He grabbed my arm before I fell, pulling me up against him.

Damn his lips were close.

What if I just—?

No. No. I would die if he didn't reciprocate and it didn't even occur to me to try reading him at that point. I was in such a fluster, my pulse thrumming in my head like a bass drum.

"So, the party."

"What party?" He let me go so we could finish folding the blanket and the moment was gone.

I was such an idiot. I suppressed my self-deprecating eye roll and as we worked our way through the next blanket, the two thick quilts, and lastly the sleeping bag, I told him about the party and Libby and what Carter tried to do to her.

"What a jerk."

"I know." I hugged the sleeping bag to my chest before placing it on top of the neat linen pile. I'd put it away later. Pointing to the couch, I invited Eric to sit down while I pulled a beanbag over and perched on the floor beside him. "Carter is a jerk and I'm so mad at him."

"Did it make you glad you'd read them?"

I smiled, knowing what he was getting at. "Yeah, I guess. I mean I know that I can help people. Libby is testament to that, but...I don't know, she was pretty annoyed that I tried to get involved."

Eric shuffled closer, dropping off the couch so he could sit right in front of me. "But she listened to you."

"I suppose. Man, if Carter knew what I'd said though. He hangs out with a lot of my friends, I don't want to cause any waves."

Eric's brow dipped as he ran a finger up my arm sending my brain into frizzle mode again.

"A few ripples never hurt anybody," he whispered. His voice was so soft and sexy.

Was he making a play for me right now? Oh man, I hoped so.

I tried to stop my voice from shaking. "But what if I see something really big one day...something sinister or scary?" I was thinking of Liam, but I couldn't say it aloud. Eric didn't know Liam, but he was part of my group, not to mention Indie's boyfriend. I didn't want to speak badly of him. I didn't want to hurt or betray her either. Besides, what if I'd just imagined it? Maybe she'd been worried about something else. "I don't want to meddle where I don't belong."

"You'll know what to do, just like you did with Libby." Thankfully Eric was looking at his finger trailing down my arm rather than my face. I didn't want to mention what I'd seen. I didn't want to waste my time with Eric talking about how the nicest guy in school might actually be a depraved hard ass.

I was worried about Indie and I wanted to help her,

but there was nothing I could do right then.

I focused on the feel of Eric's finger trailing up and down my arm. He was watching me now, a soft expression on his face that I forced myself not to decipher.

"You're trying not to read me right now, aren't you?" His eyes narrowed perceptively.

I pressed my lips together and dipped my head.

His fingers caught my chin and gently nudged it. I looked back up at him, drinking in his soulful gaze. His eyes filled with tenderness. "I was thinking how nice this is and how much I want to kiss you right now."

My eyes rounded with surprise. "You want to kiss me?"

"Yeah," he chuckled. "Why? Is that weird?"

"No, it's just... You're...you're Eric Shore."

The edge of his mouth curled up. "And is there something wrong with kissing Eric Shore?"

"No. Most definitely not." I raised my eyebrows. "But..." I scratched the side of my nose, slightly flustered. My cheeks were quickly heating with color as I smiled. "You're like Hercules hot, and I'm just...the girl next door." I shrugged.

He placed his hand on the side of my face, the look in his eyes enough to melt my heart into a puddle of mush. "Caity, you *are* the girl next door and I've liked you ever since I moved in."

"How is that possible? You only started talking to me a week ago."

He snickered. "I've been watching you for a while now, and not in a creepy stalker way, just in the I hope to get to know you better way."

I couldn't help raising my right eyebrow the way my dad always did. "I hope you weren't drooling over me or anything."

His thumb rubbed across my cheekbone and his nose wrinkled at my teasing. "Haha."

"Seriously though, why have you only started being nice to me now? It's hard to get to know someone when you never actually talk to them." I touched his watch, gently running my fingers down his forearm.

He looked embarrassed to say it. I could tell by his blush. "I've seen the way you interact with your family. Maybe I know you better than you realize."

"That still doesn't explain why you've never tried to strike up a conversation."

He held his breath for a second then left out a soft huff. "Every time I had the chance to talk to you, someone would show up... that blonde friend of yours who mentally undresses me every chance she gets. The one who's always forcing you into being something you're not." I tensed, hating the way he sounded like Mom. I didn't have a chance to respond, because he kept going with a small frown on his face. "Or that idiot boyfriend with his arrogant strut. I hate the way he always checks you out. Never looks at your beautiful face, always your body." He sighed, his fingers lightly gripping my face while his voice deepened to a soft carress. "Last weekend on the beach was the first time we've ever been alone together, without your friends or my nosy little sisters. You were so real and vulnerable and I couldn't help it. I had to talk to you. I had to somehow let you know that you've gotten under my skin." He drank me in as he leaned toward me, his lips cresting with a smile.

I couldn't believe it. I mean I seriously could not believe it.

Eric Shore!

My teeth brushed over my lower lip as I quelled the urge to bust out with nervous giggles. "I never thought a guy like you would be interested in me." My voice trailed off as his lips hovered before mine.

"Well, Caity Davis, you thought wrong."

His warm, breathy words were followed by two tender lips. They pressed against mine, soft, sweet and magical. There was nothing hungry and demanding about it, just a warm kiss that sent my brain cells spinning to Jupiter. Closing my eyes, I melted into the kiss, running my fingers around the nape of his neck and into the back of his hair.

I couldn't believe it was actually happening to me. Eric Shore was kissing me. Not my idea. His!

His tongue skimmed along my bottom lip. It felt natural to respond, to let him in, so I deepened the kiss, the pleasure of his tongue against mine sending shivers down the back of my legs. I wanted to pull him on top of me, to feel his weight pressing me into the beanbag, but I'd never be that bold. Not with him. I didn't want to come across as some hungry slut. His hands stayed on my face, his thumbs gently running up my jaw before he pulled away and leant his forehead against mine.

He didn't say anything, just looked at me with those dancing eyes. I grinned back, that giddy feeling winning the giggle battle. I let out a breathy laugh.

"Aunt Caity, what are you doing?" Brody's question made me jump. My forehead collided with Eric's and we both sat back with a groan.

"Sorry. Sorry, are you okay?" I winced, keeping my eyes squeezed shut so I didn't have to look at him. He'd never want to kiss me again.

"I'm fine." I heard him move beside me and then felt him tug on my hand. "Hey buddy, I'm Eric. Your Aunt Caity's friend."

"Hi."

My eyes opened in time to witness the cute bashfulness of my four-year-old nephew. I walked past Eric and took Brody's hand.

"We were just hanging out." I ruffled his hair. "You go back to bed and I'll come tuck you in again."

"I can't find teddy and Mommy says I'm not allowed to turn the light on after I go to bed." His voice was small and fragile.

I kissed his nose and held his chin. "I'll be up in just a sec. We'll find him together. I'll even let you turn the light on." I winked.

He grinned and waved goodbye to Eric before

padding toward the stairs.

I turned back to my gorgeous neighbor, suddenly feeling shy. Tucking a curl behind my ear, I tipped my head and walked over to him.

"Your head okay?" I tentatively reached up to rub the pale red spot on his forehead.

He bent down and kissed mine. "I'll survive."

"I guess you want to go."

"No, not really, but I think I probably should." He took my hand as we walked toward the door. "Hey, do you want to go surfing with me tomorrow or walking or I don't know...exploring? There are some great hikes up around the San Bernadino area if you could spare a day. Or we could drive up the coast."

"I love all those options." I couldn't remember if I had any plans. My brain went blank the second he invited me out.

"Okay, cool. I'll come over around nine?"

I nodded, probably way too enthusiastically.

He gently squeezed my hand and I was sure he was about to kiss me again when a little voice from upstairs stopped him. "See you tomorrow, Caity."

"Bye." I closed the door behind him and leaned my head against it.

Holy. Wow.

fifteen

"Where were you yesterday? I called like three times."

I knew I shouldn't have smiled, Stella was really annoyed, but every time I thought about Sunday, I couldn't help it. Eric had collected me right on time and driven me to the San Bernadino National Park. We had talked the whole way, not one second of silence. I found out all this cool stuff about him, like the fact his ex-serviceman grandfather took him away for an entire summer, up into the mountains and taught him all about surviving in the wild. Eric was having some anger issues to do with his non-existent father and his grandpa had basically saved his life. Teaching him how to get the anger out by running, climbing, surfing...even boxing, which I thought was weird, but Eric said it helped. His grandpa moved in with them and stayed for around six months until Eric learned to channel his energy in more positive ways.

Once we got to the hiking trail, Eric spent the next few hours asking about me, and my family. We talked like all day. I'd never talked that much in my life, and I loved every second of it. There was never an awkward pause between us. The whole day was just...easy.

And the goodbye kiss was...

I grinned.

"Hello! Earth to Caitlyn!" Stella waved her hand in my face.

"Sorry," I mumbled. "My cellphone was out of range."

"How?"

"I went hiking." I shrugged.

"Did Toby drive up from San Diego?"

It was a good assumption. Whenever my PE teacher brother came up he always forced me into surfing or hiking. I liked to complain, but secretly loved it. Stella would spaz out if she knew I'd been with Eric, so I went for casual.

"I didn't go hiking with Toby. It was just a family friend."

Not a one hundred percent lie. I could live with that.

It was enough to appease Stella who I could read

didn't give a rat's ass about my family friend. She was too annoyed and hurt that I hadn't made her the central focus of my weekend. I should have probably felt bad about that, but for some reason it just pissed me off, which totally helped stunt my guilt over the whole Eric situation. On Saturday night while I was trying, and failing, to fall asleep, I had toyed with the idea of cancelling with Eric, not wanting to cause waves with Stella. I'd started to freak out that Stella would somehow find out and go ballistic on me.

So glad I'd gotten over that brain fart!

Even so, I hated conflict, so I buried my anger and put on a smile, deciding that turning the attention back to her would put an end to our friction as well as ensure that she wouldn't probe into my weekend any further. I was just about to ask her what she got up to when Indie walked up.

"Hey guys." For the first time ever I saw her soft voice as something other than sweetness. I pulled her mask off with ease and saw a battered girl. Not physically, but there may as well have been bruises all over her face. She looked wrung out, emotionally beaten...defeated.

"Hi, Indie." I pushed as much warmth into my smile as I could. "How's it going?"

"Good." With her mask back in place, I could see the sweet smile again. She nodded and started telling us about how much fun she'd had at the party. "Did you guys enjoy it?"

"Those of us who were there did." Stella shot me a baleful glare.

I was tempted to roll my eyes, but chose to ignore her scorn.

Indie looked really awkward, glancing between us. I could tell she didn't want to get involved. I pulled back a layer and saw the idea of open conflict was too much for her.

Grabbing Stella's arm, I swiveled her in the opposite direction. "Could you excuse us?"

"Sure." The speed with which Indie took off was a testament to her relief.

"Let go of me!" Stella shook her arm free.

I met her glare with a stern look of my own.

"Would you stop, please? I said sorry about the party and it's not like I didn't come back and get you. Plus I tried calling you a bunch of times on Saturday and I know you were ignoring me."

She lifted her nose with a haughty scowl. "I'm your best friend. I shouldn't have to chase after you all weekend and I certainly shouldn't have you ditch me at a party."

"You looked pretty entertained when I left."

Her cheeks flushed scarlet. "That's not the point, Caitlyn. You should have been there for me."

This argument was getting us nowhere. I hated fighting with Stella. I always lost. From the fiery expression on her face, I knew I'd lose this round too.

With a soft sigh, I relented. "I'm sorry. I didn't realize

you needed a wingman so badly."

Appeased by my servility, she gave me a nod of forgiveness. "What were you doing with Libby anyway? Is she working for you or something?"

"No." I frowned, confused. "What does that mean?"

Stella blanched, her shoulders pinging back. "Nothing. I just meant I know she sometimes helps kids with homework and stuff. She's a tutor." Stella was lying. I didn't need to pull anything away to see that.

"Tutoring on a Friday night? Really?"

Stella couldn't respond to my sarcastic reply. Shame washed over her features like dirty dishwater.

I crossed my arms, wanting to question her, to strip away her secrets until I could figure out what the hell she was talking about. But behind that layer of shame was a fragile insecurity I didn't have the heart to mess with. I put her mask back in place and was met with a haughty, nose in the air, scowl.

I knew the only response to it was the truth, but I didn't want to get Libby in hot water or say anything that would annoy Carter. I still had three months of school to go as well.

Ruffling my curls, I flicked them off my face and went for a half-truth. "I bumped into Libby in the kitchen. She was really upset because some guys had been mean to her. I just offered her a ride home." I didn't want to go into detail about our awesome chats on the beach and how I actually felt closer to her than I did to Stella at that moment.

Stella's lips dipped. She wasn't overly friendly with Libby, but she'd never be openly cruel. I liked that her expression sunk slightly. "You should have come and got me. We could have driven her home together."

Yeah, like that would have gone over smoothly.

"I didn't want to mess up whatever you had going with that cute guy." I wiggled my eyebrows, needing to bring humor into the conversation.

Stella's grin was instant, followed by a blush.

"Who was he?"

She winced, not looking ashamed in the least. Putting her arm through mine, she turned me in the direction of class and confessed. "I have no idea what his name is. We just drank and made out until he said he had to go. I didn't even notice you were gone until then." At least she looked a little abashed by that one. She shook her head, her perfect blonde hair rustling. "Just promise me you won't ditch me at a party again."

I wanted to tell her that I hadn't, because I'd come back and got her, but I guessed that was just a technicality. In Stella's mind, I should have been there for her, standing by her side even while she made out with her mystery man.

It really stung to say it, but I mumbled, "I promise."

Squeezing my arm with a charming smile, she air kissed my cheek and strutted off. "See ya later, sweets."

As I watched her flounce past the blue lockers, I thought back to my day with Eric and how enjoyable it had been. Not because it was Eric, although that was huge, but also because I had spent the day hanging out with someone who was just as interested in me and my thoughts as I was in his. He had kept asking me what I wanted to do, not demanding that I follow him everywhere. In fact he hadn't made any demands of me at all. It was a refreshing change.

I loved my best friend. She was fun and lively. Hanging out with her was always an adventure, but I was starting to see sides of Stella I really didn't like.

The new eyesight was a trip with some really bad repercussions, but there were some good things about it too. As I walked to Algebra, I thought of Libby and what I'd done for her, which then made me think of Indie...and how badly I wanted to save her too.

****

I decided to start my "Save Indie" campaign in Biology. The cafeteria could have worked, but there were always so many people around and Liam was there. I figured Indie wouldn't let anyone in if she knew Liam was watching. I still wanted what I saw to be a figment of my imagination, but Indie's face that morning told me otherwise and made my heart sink. I didn't just feel duty bound to help her. I wanted to.

I spotted her auburn hair as I walked into the lab. Her head was down as she read over the day's experiment. Class didn't officially start for another couple of minutes so I paused by her desk.

"Hiya."

She glanced up, her blue eyes wide and gentle. I noticed how long her straight bangs were getting. They nearly touched her eyelashes now. That would drive me insane, but they looked so good on Indie. She really was gorgeous in a waif like way.

"What's up?" Her top lip perched over her bottom one and I could see how much she didn't feel like talking. I didn't want to hassle her, but I had to know.

"I was just wondering if you wanted to hang out after school today."

I pulled her mask free as I said the words, wanting to know the truth. A flash of panic scuttled across her features before settling into the ever-present fear.

"I'm busy after school. What do you need?"

"Nothing particularly. I just thought it'd be cool to hang out."

She was trying to figure out what I was up to. Her suspicion was strong and she didn't trust me at all. "Are you trying to get back at Stella or something? I don't want to come between you guys."

"Oh, no." I touched her arm. A tendon in her neck flinched as I did it. I moved my hand away. "It's not that at all. I..." Licking my lips, I willed my courage not to fail me. "I thought you looked a little worried about something on Friday night and I wanted you to know that if you need to talk to anybody about it, I'm here for you."

The flash of panic turned into full-blown terror. It was

an effort not to show her how much I could see. I put her mask back in place to compare and was astounded by her calm chuckle.

"I'm fine, Caitlyn. I'm not sure what you saw, but I'm not worried about anything." As she shook her head, I whipped the mask away and she looked ready to burst into tears. Her nostrils were flaring and her lips were quivering.

With a gentle hand I patted her back. "Okay, my mistake. Sorry."

Relief washed over her, but only briefly. I was about to pull another layer off when Libby arrived looking subdued. I gave her a friendly smile, but she just dipped her head and slumped into her chair, totally confusing me.

As I slid into my seat beside Micah, I caught Indie looking at me. As soon as our eyes connected, she spun back in her chair and I couldn't help wondering if I'd had the chance to talk to Indie for a little longer what I would have seen. The idea that maybe she desperately wanted help wouldn't leave me alone.

I turned my attention back to Libby, wondering how she was coping with her day. She was obviously nervous. Had Carter done something already? He would no doubt be lurking the halls ready to do serious damage. I'd have to keep my eye on that one. I kept my gaze on Libby until she peeked over her shoulder. I smiled again. This time her grin was jittery, but there. Friday night had been good. I'd really enjoyed our chat.

I'd helped calm Libby down, but it still felt like there was something she wasn't telling me. She was pretty scared, but she wouldn't say why. I was sure I could crack her more easily than Indie, but Indie's fear seemed so much more palpable; and therefore more important to me.

I couldn't take my eyes off the back of her long, russet curls as I sighed. This was going to be hard work.

"Hey." Micah nudged my elbow. "Don't worry about it. She's never let me in either."

Glancing at Micah's strong, dark face I watched his mask drop away and was surprised by what I saw. Micah Wilson was a tall, muscly African-American senior. He came to the school last year having already been expelled from other schools in the area. People were kind of scared of him, but he joined the basketball team and quickly became a super star. He was potentially NBA good. His adopted parents were working on getting him a really awesome scholarship and I knew he was studying his ass off. He was in head down, good behavior mode. In spite of this, people still seemed to avoid him. He was pretty quiet and didn't smile much. Sometimes he just looked plain mean. I wondered if it was a protection thing. He'd always been super nice to me. Maybe he played mean to avoid being pulled into anything that could take him off track.

Maybe I wasn't that surprised by what I saw on his exposed face. His gaze was on Indie, his dark eyes drinking in every little move she made. He was in love with her. It was so obvious. Not a lusty love, but a real, genuine, 'I want to protect that girl and cherish her' kind of love.

My heart melted to putty as I smiled at him.

"What?" He scowled, pulling the experiment sheet toward us. His mask fell back into place and I let it. I felt a little bad for reading him and discovering his secret. Man, I wished people knew what a marshmallow he was. He would be the perfect boyfriend for Indie—a strong knight for a fragile princess.

I kept everyone's mask in place throughout Biology so I could concentrate on what we were doing. The experiment went smoothly, and Micah and I agreed on all our results. Once it was done, we were supposed to write up a report and that's when my eyesight began to wander. After fifteen minutes of studying the three people around me, I had my mission set. I needed to figure out what was worrying Libby and help her enjoy the last few months of school. I didn't feel like that would be too hard. Indie was going to be a much tougher case. I had to work out what was going on between her and Liam and then if I could somehow work it, get Micah an in with the celebrity's daughter.

sixteen

"Hey Libby, wait up!" I ran down the corridor after her.

She was forced to slow down and wait for a group of ambling students so I was able to catch up to her.

"How's it going?" I nudged her shoulder with mine.

Putting on a smile, she nodded and told me all was good. She was lying and I decided to be brave and call her on it.

"You're still worried about what Carter might do, aren't you?"

"Mhmm." She looked to the ground.

Concern scampered through my system. "Libby." I

squeezed her shoulder. "It's going to be okay. You did the right thing."

"Yeah, yeah, I guess."

As soon as she looked up, I read her and she looked really nervous...and defeated.

I tipped my head and asked, "Is something else going on? Has Carter approached you today?"

"No." That was the truth, but she was hiding something. She wanted to tell me and I was sure she was about to, but her eyes suddenly rounded and her lips pinched tight. "Look I don't really have time to talk about it. I have a bunch of work to do and I don't want to waste my free period. Thanks again for Friday, but I'm cool. You don't have to worry about me or you know, be my friend or anything. Let's just accept Friday for what it was...a one-off...thing." She didn't want to say that to me. Her lips could only just form the words. "I'll catch ya later, Caity," she whispered before scuttling away like a scared bunny rabbit.

Completely thrown by the swift change up, I looked over my shoulder to see if Carter was standing there. Something had her spooked. But it wasn't Carter.

It was Liam.

He strolled toward me, his friendly blue eyes sparkling. That half-smirk that all the girls fell for was perched on his lips, but it grew into a smile as he drew near.

"Hey, Caitlyn." He grinned.

"Hi." My voice didn't come out as friendly as I'd

hoped.

His brows dipped together, but then he smiled. "You okay?"

"Yeah." I chuckled. "I'm good."

"You heading this way?" He pointed with his book filled hand.

I nodded and dropped in step beside him.

"So, you enjoy the party on Friday?" Liam's tone was sweet and casual, the familiar one I knew so well.

"Of course. Your parties are always the best."

He liked that. I pulled down his mask and saw that it was a genuine feeling. He loved being in charge—that was obvious. I studied him as we walked down the hallway. He was chatting about the game on Friday and how epic our win was. He thought the boys deserved to celebrate. His enthusiasm seemed genuine. It was easy to see that control and fame suited him. I wanted to see more. I wanted to spot that dark, sinister glare from Friday, to prove I hadn't just imagined it, but it wasn't there. Sure, he was hiding a cocky arrogance beneath his sweet smile, but whatever he was feeling at that particular moment had nothing dark about it.

A small part of me was disappointed. I mean I should have been ecstatic that the Liam I was looking at seemed pretty close to the Liam I knew, but then why was Indie so scared of him? Glancing away from my friend, I spotted Andy Chen, the school math guru. I didn't know him very well and his mask slipped away before I could stop it. His eyes went wide with fear then he looked to the floor, his shoulders tense as we walked past. I turned back to look at him and he was eyeing Liam.

Not wanting my discovery to show, I grinned at Liam and asked him another question to get him talking. He chatted easily and I then spent the next few minutes roving the halls. Almost every person who walked past Liam had some kind of reaction. They either loved, loathed or feared him.

What the hell was going on at this school?

And how had I never noticed it before?

As our walk together came to an end, I started to notice a pattern. There was a pocket of students who stood out to me. Not to categorize too much, but the slightly eccentric kids. The ones who had no athletic prowess or good looks to glide them through high school. Yeah, well them. They feared Liam. Some of them looked up to him, some of them hated him, but all of them feared him.

"Well, it's been nice chatting, Caitlyn." Liam grinned, his blue eyes gleaming. I hadn't put his mask back on and I spotted a flicker of warning run through his gaze.

I swallowed, putting the mask back in place. The scary thing was, when I did, my nerves were no more settled. In spite of his smile, that warning look was still emanating from his gaze. He licked his lower lip.

"Hey, I heard about Carter and Libby. I've had a chat with him, so you don't have to worry about her. He'll leave her alone."

"Okay," I murmured.

He was telling the truth about the Carter part, but I didn't believe him about Libby. I did need to worry about her. Carter hadn't been working alone. Liam put him up to it and the big question now, was why.

****

It didn't take long to figure out that Liam ran Pali High. I had spotted it by the end of the day. I didn't ask any questions, I just watched. Lunch was a real eye-opener. He had sway in every social grouping. I knew he was powerful before, but I had always believed it to be in a positive, cool kind of way. Now I knew better. I just wished I knew what he was up to.

I had subtly asked around at school, but seemed to get stonewalled no matter who I asked. Libby was obviously avoiding me and Indie was still nice, but even more closed off than before. Being able to read them all helped. I figured out what I was up against whenever I approached them and I saw when to back away before going too far. It didn't take much; both Libby and Indie were jittery messes.

It was driving me nearly insane trying to figure it all out. I tapped my pen against my open textbook. It was Thursday night and I knew for a fact that Stella and most of our group were heading out to the movies. I had been invited, but had said no, which so wasn't helping the Stella situation. I couldn't figure out how my friends managed to fit in so much socializing when I felt like I was working overtime to keep up with the amount of schoolwork constantly being dumped on us. It certainly wasn't making me very enthusiastic about college.

My phone buzzed and then started playing "Kiss You" by One Direction. Stella had made it my ringtone when I started dating Chase and since my phone hardly ever rang, I hadn't gotten around to changing it.

I checked the screen and grinned, unlocking it with fumbling fingers.

"Hey, Hercules."

"Hey, girl next door." I could hear the smile in his voice and my insides turned to mush. "Watchya doin'?"

I groaned. "Trying to study, but finding it hard to concentrate."

"Too busy thinking about me, huh?"

I giggled. "Yeah, yeah, that's it."

He chuckled at my sarcastic reply and then cleared his throat. "You okay? You sound a bit flat."

Did I?

My forehead crinkled. "How can you tell that over the phone?"

"I don't know. You just...there's no smile in your voice."

"I'm talking to you. Of course there's smile in my voice." I shifted the notepad on my desk and started doodling down the edge.

"Come on, Caity. What's up?"

I sighed, dotting my pen on the white paper. "I've

seen something at school that I can't figure out."

He paused before replying. "Something or someone?"

"It's just a guy that I've been friends with for a while and he's really nice and his girlfriend is like awesome, but..." I licked my bottom lip.

"But?"

"She's totally scared of him. In fact a lot of people at school are and I want to know why." My dotting grew harder, nearly puncturing a hole in the sheet of paper.

"Well, have you asked around?"

"Yes and no one wants to talk to me." I rubbed my thumb over the doodles, smearing the ink. "I don't know what to do."

"Maybe you should drop it?"

"What?" My question came out snappier than I meant it to.

"Caity, you've just told me that everyone at school's afraid of him. They must be for a reason. He sounds dangerous to me."

"But he's not, I mean, he's Liam." I resumed my drawing, switching to swirly lines that soon formed the letters L-I-A-M.

"Well, what do you know about the guy?"

"He's..." I frowned. What did I know about Liam? I darkened the L of his name. "Not much. He started at Pali High two years ago and fitted in really easily. Everyone likes him."

"You just said everyone was scared of him."

"No, just his girlfriend and a bunch of students that don't even hang out with him." I shook my head. "He's up to something, but I have no idea what. I'm friends with his girl, so I figure that's my in. But she's a closed book."

"You can't read her?" Eric seemed surprised.

"No, I can read her. That's how I know she's scared. But she won't tell me anything." I started writing her name beneath Liam's, swirling the letters beneath his so they twisted together like vines.

"Caity, I don't like this. You need to be careful. If everyone's this afraid of him and he finds out you're trying to meddle..."

"I'll be okay. I'm not worried for me or anything. I just wish I could figure this out."

Eric paused. Even though we were on the phone and I couldn't see him, I could sense his reluctance. "Before you start throwing yourself into this, why don't you take some time to try and figure out who this Liam guy is? Find out anything you can about his past. See if he's hiding any secrets you should know about. That's what I'd do."

I loved that idea. It was a forward step and hopefully a step that wouldn't have me meeting a brick wall head on. I leaned back in my chair with a grin. "You give the best advice, you know that?"

His laughter was dry. "Just promise me you'll be careful and don't do anything until you've found out more about this guy."

"Yes, sir."

"Caitlyn," he chided.

I smiled. "I promise. I won't get myself in trouble. I really want to help these girls, Eric. They're my friends."

"I know. And I really like that you're embracing your whole super power thing, but I'm allowed to worry about you. It's my right as your...next door neighbor."

I thought for a second he was going to say boyfriend, but that was ridiculous. We'd been on one official date; admittedly it lasted an entire day, but still. And yes, we had been texting every day, so the whole Eric Shore becoming my boyfriend thing felt totally natural, but I didn't think either of us actually had the courage to admit it aloud yet.

I bit the end of my pen, fighting a giddy grin. Eric Shore just might become my boyfriend one day!

It was an effort not to giggle into the phone like a fangirl. I dropped my pen on the desk and cleared my throat. "Well, I feel like a very lucky neighbor right now. I'd feel even luckier if you were just over the fence at this moment, but that's okay."

His chuckle was soft. "Yeah, well I'd be getting luckier if you were just over the fence right now."

What did he just say?

The way he cleared his throat and nervously tittered made me think he hadn't meant to say it that way.

I giggled. "You're blushing right now, aren't you?"

"I'm sorry." His voice was stretched tight. "I didn't mean to sound like some depraved jerk. I just meant I'd want to, you know, kiss you."

"Don't worry about it." I grinned. "Maybe you can show me what you meant this weekend." Ugh. My flirty voice was so lame.

Eric hissed. "Actually I'm going to see my grandpa this weekend, so I won't be around."

I did my best not to sound totally gutted and focused on the fact that I was even talking to Eric Shore, my possible future boyfriend, which certainly helped ease the sting.

"That's cool."

"I'll make it up to you, I promise."

"You don't have to. It's your grandpa. You have fun and I'll spend my weekend pretending to be a PI."

"Cait—"

"I'll be a safe private investigator. I can read people, remember? I'll know if they're going to attack."

My joke was obviously no comfort to him.

"Promise to call me if you need me, okay? San Diego's not that far away."

"You're not coming back because of me. Go see your grandpa. Have fun and don't think about me."

"Not think about you? That's not gonna happen. I'll see you next weekend, girl next door."

I hung up with a grin, gently placed my phone on the desk and threw my head back with a swoon.

seventeen

I spent the rest of the night and most of Friday researching Liam Donovan and got nowhere. The guy was an enigma. No one knew his history and none of my friends seemed bothered by the fact he was so mysterious. If anything, it made him more appealing.

In the hopes of finding out more, I decided to spend as much of the weekend with my usual crowd as possible. Surely I'd spot something new outside of the school setting.

I traveled with Stella to the Friday night away game. It was at Malibu High School. Stella was still flirting with the role of ice queen when it came to our friendship, but it was nothing I hadn't experienced before. I kept the conversation focused on her, reading her the entire time in an attempt to keep her happy.

It was probably slightly selfish of me, but I needed to stay close to Stella in order to stay close to the people I was investigating.

I grinned. Investigating. What was I? A cop?

We eased across the bench seat and found a place next to Indie. She seemed less stressed than usual.

"Where's Liam?" Stella asked as we took a seat beside her.

"He's hanging out with his brother tonight. We'll see him after the game."

She was lying.

Not about seeing him after the game, but about what he was up to.

She took a sip from her water bottle and grinned at me. I smiled back, wanting to put her at ease. It was a good chance to make her feel comfortable with me. Maybe if I kept the chatter light and easy, she'd let something slip.

"So, who do you think'll win?" I asked.

"Us, of course." We chuckled. "With Micah playing we've always got a good shot."

I liked the way she said his name. There was a gentle admiration to it. I was already reading her, but had to peel back a second layer to see a soft blush tinting her cheeks.

Did she like Micah?

As our team ran onto the court we all stood to cheer. Her mouth opened with a big whoop. She was watching Micah. His large hand held the basketball easily as he pointed at his team, directing them through a few quick warm ups.

Indie couldn't take her eyes off him as he easily danced around the court. I peeled back another layer, past the affection and spotted the caged longing. Tears glistened in her eyes, her face pinching tight as she tried to deny herself the desire she felt. Another layer later and I was once again looking at that stark, white fear.

It unnerved me, so I quickly layered her back up until I was looking at the Indie everyone admired.

"So, I didn't know Liam had a brother." Poor girl, I knew the last thing she felt like talking about was her boyfriend when she finally had a night to herself.

I spotted a flash of irritation as she cleared her throat. "He's in college, I think. I'm not sure. Liam doesn't talk about him much. I haven't met him."

Liar.

"Have you met anyone else in his family?"

Indie brushed the bangs out of her eyes, keeping her gaze on the court. Her jaw clenched. "His father lives in Burbank. He never sees him."

"So who does he live with?"

"Me, mostly." Indie's voice was soft, but her eyes were blazing blue as she turned to face me. "Don't judge, okay? He had a tough time growing up. His father's a loser. His mother's dead. His brother and me are all he has."

I nodded, taken back by her vehement defense of him. "Sorry, I didn't mean to pry."

"You're really a nice person, Caitlyn." She touched my arm. "I know you don't mean any harm, but Liam likes his privacy. I'd respect that if I were you."

Her warning was loud and clear and the expression behind her mask knocked the breath from my lungs.

The buzzer went and Indie's attention was drawn back to the game...or at least Micah. I kept my mouth shut after that, more intrigued than ever. I had rattled her big time and didn't want to push it any further. All my other research would have to be done on my own.

Without meaning to, I spent the rest of the game quietly distracted. It drove Stella nuts and I didn't even notice until we were back in her car and she started going off at me.

"Well, that sucked!" She yanked on the parking brake and slammed it down.

My forehead wrinkled as I looked at her.

"Don't play dumb. I went to the game to hang out with you and you spent the first quarter chatting to Indie and the rest of the game playing mute robot. You didn't even hear half the stuff I said to you!"

"I'm sorry," I mumbled, annoyed that I'd let her down yet again, but also annoyed that she was pressuring me with her bullshit when I had so much else to worry about.

"You know what, you're becoming a really lousy friend, Caitlyn. I used to be able to rely on you and now you're just not there for me anymore."

Irritation tickled my insides. I pressed my lips together and looked out the window.

"Do you want to be my friend or not?"

"Of course," I muttered, wondering if I actually did. I could probably tell her the truth about my quiet behavior, but something warned me against it. She'd gossip. She'd turn all my insights into big drama, which it was, but the school didn't have to know about it. Indie needed to be approached quietly. Stella would turn this information into a circus and do major damage along the way.

"Well start acting like it then." Stella spat as she braked for the red light. "Stop focusing on everyone else all the time and hang out with me."

It was taking major effort to keep my lips pressed together. I wanted to boil over at her and tell her everything I was thinking, but I couldn't. I mean, I never had before, always afraid she'd be mad at me.

We pulled through the intersection and had to slow down a short while later for another red light.

"It's so embarrassing going to a function with my best friend only to have her ignore me. How do you think it makes me look, Caitlyn?"

She did that kind of thing to me all the time!

"I mean, think about it from my point of view. I'm sitting there like a loser as you chat away to Indie and then—"

"You're not the only person in this world, Stella!" I thumped the edge of my seat, making us both jolt. I'd never raised my voice to her. It actually felt pretty good—scary, but good. I swallowed. "Other people have problems too, and I can't keep pouring all my energy into you, all the time."

She gaped at me for a second before finding her voice again.

"Oh well I'm sorry for being such a burden." The way she elongated the word sorry made it obvious how little she meant it.

In spite of the way my skin was bristling, I licked my bottom lip and kept calm. "You know I didn't mean it that way, Stella. I just meant—"

"Whatever." She flicked her hand in my face. "Go hang out with Indie then."

"We both hang out with Indie. I don't see why I can't talk to her."

"I'm not saying you can't talk to her, I'm just saying... Oh, forget it. You're not hearing me anyway."

"I'm trying."

"No, you're not. You don't care about me anymore. And I don't think I can be friends with someone like that."

I saw past her scorn to the betrayal beneath and felt awful...but also annoyed. I had been a good friend to her for years, always at her beck and call. The friendship had never been about what I wanted or needed; it was always about her. I even got together with Chase because she said I should...and if she ever found out something was brewing between me and Eric, she'd cut it off at the knees. She'd do anything she could to sabotage it out of plain jealousy and spite.

Why was I still friends with her? Our history didn't seem a good enough reason to be bossed around by her anymore.

Normally I would apologize and work it out so that Stella got her way, but I just couldn't form the words.

"Fine." I crossed my arms. "Can you drop me at home? I don't feel like going to the beach with you guys tonight."

"It'd be my pleasure." The ice queen accelerated toward my place. She ordered me out of the car at the bottom of my street and I was left to walk home alone.

The idea of losing Stella had always speared me with dread, but as I reached my front door, I realized that I wasn't as sad as I thought I'd be. Maybe I'd been losing Stella for a while and just didn't know it. Or maybe my new eyesight showed me that Stella didn't have to be my only friend, that there were nice people in this world who did need me. They may not have realized it, but I was going to be there for them anyway.

****

Between my homework load and my research quest, I spent most of Saturday in my room, on my computer. I

Googled different variations of *Liam Donovan*, *Burbank* until I went cross-eyed. I found a few pictures of Liam at Burbank High when he was a freshman. I also found the name Mason Donovan and one grainy picture that was obviously scanned from a yearbook. They looked like brothers, although Mason's face was more refined and angular, his blue eyes darker. He was a senior at Burbank High when Liam was a freshman. There was a strong chance Mason was the brother Indie was referring to.

On that assumption, I researched Liam and Mason Donovan together. Nothing really popped out, even when I scoured the online *Burbank Leader*, the newspaper for the area. The only thing of significance I could find from two years back was concern from citizens about teenage parties and car thefts in the area. I figured it was unrelated and I gave up with an annoyed sigh.

Homework was calling and I needed a break.

No matter what I researched online, I kept coming back to the same thing.

Indie was my way in.

If I could get her to trust me, then maybe I could set her free and expose whoever Liam Donovan really was.

****

Monday morning brought with it the opportunity I'd been waiting for. I walked into Biology, still grinning after reading Eric's text. I'd been getting them all weekend. He'd had the best time with his grandpa, but couldn't stop checking up on me. Not wanting to burden him, I'd kept all my frustrations to myself, making sure my texts were flirty and light, yet informative enough not to arouse any concerns.

I couldn't wait to see him in the weekend. My parents were leaving for Hawaii on Friday to visit Holly for ten days. Ten days! I was super stoked about having the house to myself and purposely hadn't told anyone. I didn't want Stella launching some surprise party on me... not that she would anymore.

It was the first time my parents hadn't waited for Spring Break to visit Holly. I was always dragged along, but this year they decided I was old enough to handle things on my own. Thankfully their tickets were already booked and paid for before the Chase incident. I'd managed to ease Mom's worries over that by telling her we'd broken up. She was aware of Eric, but seemed to "like the Shore boy very much."

When Eric came over on the weekend, there'd be no little boys interrupting our Saturday night and no mothers walking in on any make out sessions. The very thought was simply delicious.

"You keep grinning like that and it won't be hard for people to figure out you're crushing big time."

I shunted Micah's elbow, my cheeks heating quickly.

We were waiting for Mrs. Mackerly to arrive. She was always late for Biology. She left out assignment sheets usually, so we just got on with it, but not today.

"So who is he?"

I shrugged, trying to hide the way my heart hiccuped every time I thought about my sexy next-door neighbor. "Just a guy. He doesn't go to this school."

"I take it you want to keep it on the down low." Micah's eyebrows rose.

"Maybe." I blushed. Although Stella and I had now "broken up" she would still freak if she knew. She'd wanted Eric for as long as I had, and I was pretty sure she somehow felt more entitled to him.

"It's cool. I won't say anything." Micah's big lips pushed to the side, his standard lopsided grin.

"Thanks."

He nodded, reverting his attention back to Indie. I couldn't help peeling back his mask. And he thought I was crushing big time. I wondered how he'd react if he knew she liked him too. I wished I could do something to help them. I was really worried about Indie...and Libby. They had both shut me out. They weren't being rude or anything, just really distant. If I could just get some time with them, I might be able to crack their veneers, get them to tell me what the hell was going on in this school. They both knew something and I was pretty sure the thing they feared was the same—Liam Donovan.

"All right class, sorry I'm late. The school server is on the fritz and the photocopier was being mean to me." We all grinned as Mrs. Mackerly strode into the room looking flustered. "Hand these back, please." She shoved a pile of papers at the people in the front row, who took one each and passed the pile along.

Micah grabbed two sheets and handed me one before passing the rest back. I scanned the top of the page and saw it was a huge assignment.

"This is your last graded assignment for the year. It's worth twenty percent of your lab assessment, so I'm expecting a really big effort on this one. You will be working in groups of four, but there will also be individual components you are expected to complete. I was going to let you choose your own groups, but I've decided it'll be quicker if lab partners just go with the people behind them."

I quickly counted from the front of the class and saw that we would be paired with Indie and Libby. Sweet! It was the chance I'd been looking for.

The girls both turned to acknowledge Micah and me. I glanced at his face, peeled back a layer and saw him beaming. He was even more excited than I was.

I nudged his elbow without meaning to, accidentally letting him in on the fact that I knew his secret. His intense scowl made me regret my decision, but then he rolled his eyes and shook his head.

"Is it that obvious?" he whispered.

"Only to me." I winked.

Appeased, he gave me a small smile before tuning in to Mrs. Mackerly's instructions again. My stomach clenched as I glanced at my new assignment partners. It was my one chance and I didn't want to screw it up. It was going to be hard and part of me was worried by what I might uncover, but I had to try.

I was chosen for a reason. Maybe the homeless stranger sensed my quiet stubbornness; I'd never be sure. But whatever he thought about my good soul, I oddly found myself not wanting to let him down.

eighteen

The girls both looked reluctant to be in a group with Micah and me. I read them quickly and decided that Libby found Micah scary and Indie was petrified I might try to pry again. As we sat down in the library that afternoon we were all nervous. If my stomach hadn't been such a wreck of nerves, I probably would have found it comical. Micah was nervous of Indie, Indie was nervous of me, Libby was nervous of Micah and I was nervous about screwing everything up. It was slightly ridiculous.

I cleared my throat, not wanting to be the leader of the pack; that was always Stella's role, but she wasn't in my Biology class. I looked to Libby and raised my eyebrows, but she just scratched her upper lip. Indie was eyeing me out of the corner of her eye, no doubt waiting for me to pounce, demanding more info on her boyfriend.

Pressing my lips together, I decided to keep my mouth shut and looked to Micah instead.

I silently told him to get things started with a little flick of my head. He was reluctant, but I put on my pleading eyes and he huffed.

"Okay, fine. I'll start." He tapped his pen on his blank notepad. "First we need to decide what we want to look into. I don't know about you guys, but I want the aim of this investigation to be kind of unique, so we stand out a little."

"Me too." Libby perked up. "We've only got three weeks, so I don't think we have time to do a proper observation study, so we need to choose something where we can gather lots of data quickly."

"Good idea." Micah didn't smile, but the soft way he agreed with her made Libby relax instantly. She toyed with a smile as she looked at him.

"Why don't you tell us what ideas you've had so far?" He gazed back at her, his expression open and non-threatening.

She was pleasantly surprised and her round cheeks bloomed as she launched into a list of ideas she'd come up with since reading the assignment brief. Man, she was one smart cookie.

Her expression was animated as she described her two favorite ideas in detail, and I thought her chest might burst when we unanimously agreed to go with the second one—classification of native plants along the Pacific Coast Highway, which involved producing a dichotomous key. I'd never really done that before and Libby wanted to get quite complex with it by making several keys for different types of plants. It was huge, but if we could pull it off, it'd be awesome.

"Cool. Thanks guys." She accidentally met my eye as she said it. She hadn't meant to. I could tell by the way her unmasked face balked and she looked away from me. It hurt a little. We got on so well after the party on Friday. I had to remind myself that it probably had nothing to do with me and everything to do with a silent threat from Liam. But I couldn't let that show.

We spent the next fifteen minutes reading through the assignment together and allocating specific jobs to each person. Our first task was to make sure we clearly understood the difference between monocotyledonous and dicotyledonous plants. I was surprised that I understood more than I realized. Libby explained everything so clearly and I was soon jotting down notes that actually made sense.

"So we obviously can't do the entire highway, but even if we go up to Point Mugu State Park, that should give us a pretty decent sample. Indie and Caitlyn, are you happy to collect flower samples? And Micah, are you cool to focus on trees with me?"

We all nodded and Libby grinned back, catching the edge of her lip with her teeth.

We had worked really well together. Everyone so happy to be led by Libby. As the session came to an end we were all calm and smiling...if anything, we were actually enthusiastic. It was a good feeling and I wanted to cling to it.

As the bell rang, I made a decision.

"Hey Indie, can I talk to you for a sec?" I waited until Micah and Libby were away from the table before asking. Indie's face paled as she reluctantly nodded.

"I just wanted to apologize again for prying the other night. I really didn't mean to offend you or Liam."

Her tense shoulders began to sink, her posture loosening a little.

"I don't want to lose your friendship by being a Nosy Nelly."

She grinned at the term I'd coined from my mother.

"I won't ask any more questions, so you don't have to be nervous about doing this assignment with me or anything. Let's just have fun with it."

Her eyes warmed, in spite of her clammy skin. "I'd like that."

"Cool." We walked out of the library together and I purposely kept the conversation light, talking about re-run episodes of "Pretty Little Liars," a show I knew she loved.

****

I kept that up for the rest of the week, trying to act as though I didn't care one bit about Indie and Libby's fears. It was working too. The more time we spent together, the more relaxed everyone became. We even skipped lunch on Thursday to hang out and study the samples we had all collected. Libby was stressing about fitting all her schoolwork in and Indie was the first to support her, saying we could easily skip lunch if it helped her out.

I couldn't figure out why Libby was so snowed under. School seemed a breeze for her. Working with her on this assignment showed me just how smart and capable she was. Of course working hard added to natural smarts, but I thought she was pushing it a little.

"I can't believe how hard you work. You're amazing. Your GPA must be so freaking high." I was expecting her to grin at my compliment or at least blush, but she did neither.

A pained expression wafted over her face as she mumbled, "I just want to do well."

My comment had closed her off completely. It didn't take much to realize I'd hit a sore spot. To say it baffled me was an understatement. I was more confused than ever. I glanced to Indie, but she was looking just as pale and forlorn as Libby.

I didn't know how much longer I could keep up the charade that I didn't care what was troubling them. But I didn't have the guts to come out and say it. Not after we'd made such good ground during the week. I wanted them to trust me, to relax around me.

"Well," I licked my lips. "Let's help you get another A+ then." I winked, pretending that I hadn't spotted her morose mood change.

Micah arrived a second later and saved the day. Everything seemed better with him around. It hadn't taken Libby long to figure out that he was a nice guy. Indie already knew it, but it was nice to see her come out of her shell. She was so much more open when Liam wasn't around, laughing at Micah's jokes and joining in with our friendly banter. I loved that side of her and I wanted to see it bloom, something it couldn't do under Liam's reign.

Indie's boyfriend sauntered into the library and stopped at our table. His friendly smirk was in place, he looked calm and in control, but underneath he was frothing. He despised Micah...with a vehemence that nearly choked me.

I coughed and spluttered as Micah pounded me on the back. "You okay?"

Nodding, I covered my mouth to try and hide my horror.

I didn't like reading Liam. He was hell scary.

Clearing the last tickle away, I sat back with a smile, hoping nobody could tell how forced it was. Liam was chuckling at me, but I didn't see that. I was too busy reading the insidious glint in his eye as he stroked Indie's hair. His very touch brought her into line. She was internally squirming, wanting to pull away from it, but knowing she couldn't.

"So, how's it going guys?" His voice was friendly and charming, but I knew better. His congenial blue gaze landed on Libby and she quaked beneath it. Her lips quivered as she smiled back and told him what we were up to. A few weeks ago she would have been bubbling with enthusiasm. Having Liam Donovan acknowledge her would have made her day, but not anymore. In fact she was doing a super crap job of hiding it. Micah could even tell. I noticed his eyebrows dip slightly.

"Well, thanks for helping my girl, but I've got to steal her away now."

I used to swoon when he said stuff like that. Now I just wanted to be sick.

Indie collected her stuff and Liam took her bag, smiling tenderly at her as he ran his hand down her back. At least that was what everyone else saw. All I witnessed was a stern look and eyes that told Indie she was in for a punishing.

I jerked out of my seat, grabbing my stuff. "Sorry guys, I gotta split. I didn't realize the time."

Micah looked skeptical as he nodded. It was a relief to hear him ask Libby if she wanted to stick around for another ten and at least finish off their discussion. She said yes and I left them to it, hoping I'd spot which direction Liam took Indie.

I was scared for her.

It might have been an overreaction, but I saw it. It was written all over his face.

She was in trouble.

Panic sizzled through me as I walked outside and headed down the open hallway. I didn't know what I was going to do. Would I seriously have the guts to help her if he tried to do something? Who did I think I was?

But I couldn't just ignore this. I spotted a flash of dark red hair on the grass below and raced for the stairs. When I reached the grassy quad I couldn't see them and my spirits deflated as I once again cursed my ability to see all this stuff.

Ignorance was bliss. I knew that for a fact.

I kicked a stone and headed to my next class not expecting to see Indie again until the morning. But on my way, my ears snaffled a voice that would have been familiar had it not been so terse.

I frowned and sneaked towards it.

"I told you to keep away from her!"

"It wasn't my choice. We were put in a group together. Mrs Mac—"

"Mrs. Mackerly's an idiot. She can be talked into doing anything. You should have asked for a different group."

I poked my head around the edge of the building and spotted Liam. He was standing over a cowering Indie, his hands on his hips as he reprimanded her like a little kid.

"You should know better, Indie. I'm relying on you."

"I'm not doing anything to let you down." Her voice was submissive and small, her head bowed as she spoke to him. "This study group could be a really good thing. I can keep an eye on her."

Were they talking about me?

"I just know how useless you are at keeping your mouth shut. I'm trying to run a business here, Indie. I can't have people poking into my past."

She flinched and touched her stomach. She looked ready to cry and I wasn't even reading her.

"She's apologized for prying. She said she didn't mean to and she hasn't been asking any more questions. I don't think she's a threat."

"She's something." Liam's dark mutter made my skin crawl. "We need to be wary of her. I don't like the way she looks at me."

Wow, so someone finally noticed. They were definitely referring to me.

Indie clutched her turquoise cotton dress, squeezing the fabric in her hand.

Liam noticed and gently pried her fingers loose. "You know I don't like it when you do that. It makes you look nervous."

"Sorry," she whispered. I could see she hated the feel of his hand as it skimmed up her arm and cupped her face. It looked gentle, but there was a pressure to his grip as he made her look at him.

"I don't want you to get punished like you did last weekend. Don't give Caitlyn anything else, okay?"

"I won't." Her lips quivered as they rose into a smile.

He kissed her forehead and smiled at her. "That's my

girl."

With a light pat on the butt, he sent her on her way. Thankfully she headed in the opposite direction from me, so I could stay and keep watching Liam.

I felt sick. He punished her?

No wonder she was so scared of him. Ideas of the type of punishment he inflicted coursed through my brain, making me want to hurl. I never would have believed it before, but I'd seen the soft blue tone of Liam's eyes become dark with malice. Oh yeah, he was no doubt capable of inflicting a lot of pain.

Liam's phone jingled. He yanked it from his back pocket and his face fell. His mask was already off, so I saw his fear easily. Who could he possibly be afraid of?

He swallowed and answered after one more ring. "Yeah... No it's not going to be a problem." Liam rolled his eyes. "Yes, of course I've spoken to her... She's not! And you don't need to scare her like you did on Saturday. I'd already dealt with the problem." His cheeks burned with color as he listened to the other caller. "My methods are just fine and they work." He clenched his jaw. "I am not a sicko. I love her and having sex is not a crime." A sudden shame lashed his features before his chin stuck out. "At least I never punch her. I know you made sure her bruises couldn't show, but she was pretty stiff the next day. Someone might have noticed." He paused to listen. His skin paled, his blue eyes filling with fear. "Don't you dare. Indie's mine and you will not touch her again." He wanted to say those words more forcefully, but couldn't. Whoever he was talking to had him petrified. "Yeah, yeah, the business is fine. I've done damage control and no one's going to squeak." He sighed. "She seems to have backed off. I don't think she'll be a problem... Dude, you don't have to do that." His usually confident gaze wavered. He kicked the concrete wall behind him, running a hand through his straw colored hair. "All right fine, but just control yourself this time. I don't want anymore blood on your hands."

He hung up, shoved the phone back in his pocket and swore. His limbs were shaking as he ran his hands through his hair again and cursed a few more times. But it wasn't anger I was watching. Much like his girlfriend, he was scared and for the first time since seeing him properly, I almost pitied him.

I would have stayed to see more, but he turned in my direction and I had to split before he caught me. My limbs were quivering as I raced into the human traffic that was scurrying off to class after the post lunch bell.

What I had I just heard? What did Liam do to Indie?

I felt sick for her, weak for her. I wanted to cry and scream and hit Liam until his face bled, but that would only land me in trouble.

I shuddered.

Liam was a sicko, but whoever was controlling him was obviously worse.

For the remainder of the day my mind replayed the two conversations. As the impact of their sinister nature began to ease, one thought stood out amongst the filth—business. Liam was running some kind of business and I had a feeling Libby, and possibly everyone else who was scared of the guy, were involved.

nineteen

"And be sure to lock the door each night before you go to bed. Check the windows as well."

"Mom, I'm not an imbecile." I rolled my eyes in the back seat. Thankfully we were nearly at the airport so I wouldn't need to listen to this for too much longer.

"She knows that, dear. We just want you to be safe."

Reaching forward, I squeezed Dad's shoulder. "I will be. I'm not a little girl anymore. I'm eighteen and capable of looking after myself. Besides, Layla and Seth are both around if I need them." I didn't want to need them at all, but the reminder would be a comfort to my fretting parents.

To be fair, it was the first time they'd left me alone for this long. They'd done a few weekends here and there, and I'd been away from them, but I could tell Mom felt guilty for leaving me. Not because she didn't want to go to Hawaii, but because she was torn. She felt a responsibility to me, and as much as it hurt, I knew that she sometimes lamented the fact that she was way too old to have a child still at home. They had already moved past the baby stage when I came along. They loved me, but it still must have been a hard pill to swallow. I saw through her watery smile as she turned in the seat to glimpse me.

"You guys are doing the right thing. You only see Holly once a year and I know she's desperate for you to meet her new boyfriend. She needs you more than I do right now. I'll be fine. You don't have to worry."

They were silent after that, both comforted by my encouragement. Dad parked the car and unloaded the bags, nervously handing me the keys.

"Drive it straight home. You use your Mini while we're away. I'm only letting you drive it this one time because of your mother's inability to pack sensibly."

"Craig." My mother's warning tone made Dad grin. He winked at me as he walked to the trunk and helped unload the two big suitcases that never would have squished into my little car.

"Do you guys want me to stick around until you've checked in?" I slammed the trunk shut.

"No, that's okay, sweetie. We don't want you to be

lumped with a big parking fee. You just get going." Dad's eyes glistened. I could see he was proud of me. His little girl was all grown up. I stepped forward and wrapped my arms around him, trying not to let my glee at their departure show too much.

"Love you, Dad."

He squeezed me tight. "Love you too, Peanut."

I stepped into Mom's embrace and whispered yet again, "I'll be fine. Please trust me."

She pulled back and held my face in her hands. "Promise you'll call Seth or Layla if you need them."

"I promise."

And with that, they finally let me go. I leaned against the car, waving at them until they had hauled their bags onto a trolley and headed inside. You'd think they were leaving for a year the way they kept looking at me.

With a little jump of glee, I slid into the driver's seat and enjoyed the power of Dad's engine igniting.

"Sweet ride," I whispered, tempted to drive it the longest possible way home.

I didn't. I played the good girl, knowing that when Dad called from Hawaii, he'd ask. I pulled the car into the garage as instructed and noticed that Eric's Jeep wasn't in his driveway.

Why would it be? He'd already texted to tell me he'd be home on Saturday morning as he was going out with Scott tonight. For once, Scott wasn't heading to Palm Springs to spend time with his girlfriend, Piper. She was coming to him and since Scott had a free night, he asked if Eric wanted to hang out. Eric wasn't the biggest socialite and seemed to have a very small group of friends, from what I could tell. The fact Eric was willing to give him a whole evening told me what a great guy Scott was.

I hoped they had fun, in spite of my disappointment. I really wanted to spend my evening with Eric, and having to wait was a total downer. But I refused to be a needy girlfriend. Not that I was his girlfriend...yet.

I grinned.

I thought about texting Stella, but what was the point? She basically hadn't spoken to me since I told her she wasn't the only person in the world. It was getting awkward hanging out with the group. Her evil glares and scoffing tone whenever I spoke was getting old super-fast. Between Chase and her, I was getting major outcast vibes and it wouldn't take much more until I spent my lunchtimes hanging out alone. The thought was far from appealing, but I hated the subtle cold-shouldering that was in play. It made me feel like such a loser.

I decided I was cool with my own company outside of school though. It'd give me time to think. I was still trying to work out what kind of business Liam was into. I wouldn't put it past Liam to be involved in some sort of cheating ring within the school. Like maybe Libby and her intellectual counterparts were somehow helping Liam and his buddies get good test scores or something?

That made sense.

When I thought about all the people who feared Liam the most, they definitely had some common ground. They were socially awkward...and they were hells smart.

It was a pretty decent theory, but didn't really have time to flourish because another thought hit my like a bullet in the night...

Liam had said, "blood on your hands."

What had he meant by that? Was the guy he'd been talking to a murderer?

Dashing up to my computer, I pulled up the history I'd found on Liam. I decided to try searching in the Burbank local paper again, this time looking for anything involving murder about two years ago. I found four articles—one shooting, two robberies and a domestic violence case. It was horrible reading the meaty details, but I was able to rule out two that had already been solved. The shooting and one of the robberies remained a mystery. In fact the robbery wasn't even a robbery; it was attempted. The owner of the car had been bashed over the head with a blunt instrument, but the weapon and the culprit were never found. The article suggested that the person was trying to steal the car, the victim tried to stop him, and then it got messy. I couldn't help wondering if there was a link to the other car thefts happening in the area at the time. There were a couple more articles I found about the case, but it quickly went cold.

I exited the screen and sat back with a sigh. Reading about those murders had really unsettled me. I was jittery, and my house suddenly felt ginormous and cold. Not really wanting to kick around by myself all night, I decided to walk to the nearest shops.

I should have taken my car, but I loved that time of day. The sun hadn't set yet and the air was refreshing. I was hoping it would clear my head and help me sleep.

Wandering down Montana Avenue, I stopped to buy an ice cream and sauntered past the shops, watching people out of the corner of my eye. I wasn't in the mood for reading faces, so I kept people's masks in place and found the task easy. It was such a relief to know I could switch off if I wanted to. I pretended for a while that I was just an ordinary girl, licking on an ice cream and in no particular hurry to go anywhere. My nerves stopped clanging together and my mind shifted from murder mode into swoon mode. I started thinking about Eric and what we might do over the weekend. I was thinking a Saturday-morning surf followed by a little make out session on the beach. We could then go home, get cleaned up and spend the afternoon chillin' at my place...just hanging out on our own.

I blushed, wondering if Eric would show me what he meant by getting lucky.

Crunching down the last of my ice cream cone, I wiped my hands and threw the napkin away. I needed to get home before it got too late. Mom and Dad would not be impressed if they found out I'd been walking around, by myself, after dark.

I turned to head back when someone yanked my arm from behind and pulled me into the alleyway.

The shock gave me no time to respond and it wasn't until he was shoving me behind the dumpster that I even had the notion to scream. I opened my mouth to let rip when what felt like a cannonball struck my stomach. I doubled over, struggling for air as pain radiated through my abdomen. He pulled his fist back and thrust it into me again, my feet lifting off the ground with the force of the impact.

I wanted to cry, to scream, to do anything, but I couldn't breathe.

He let me go and I crumpled to the ground, my hair covering my face like a discarded blanket.

I tried to work out who it was through my tendrils, but tears were blurring my vision. He pressed my face into the concrete, his thumb digging painfully into my cheek. I thought my heart might explode; it was thrumming so loudly. The rough ground cut into my skin as he leaned over me, pushing until my skull felt ready to splinter.

I whimpered when he brought his lips to my ear.

"This is a warning." His voice was harsh and gravelly. "Keep your nose out of Liam Donovan's business or the next time I find you, you'll really understand the meaning of pain."

He pushed off my head and strode away, his black shoes not making a sound.

Tears gathered in my eyes as I strove for some kind of composure. I had to get up and go home, but I was too scared to move. My insides hurt and my limbs were shaking. Pushing myself up, I drew my knees to my chin, another whimper squeaking out of my throat. My body trembled and I leaned my head back against the grimy bricks, noticing just how dark the sky was turning. Wrapping my arms around my legs, I tried to quell the tremors and get my brain to function. I couldn't stay tucked behind a dumpster. I needed to get home. But the idea of walking was too painful...and petrifying.

I reached for my phone and ran my thumb over the screen. I could call Stella; she'd probably come and get me if I asked nicely. In spite of her cold attitude, she still had a heart. But then she'd want details, plus I'd owe her for all eternity.

My next thought was Seth, but he'd just freak out and call my parents who would freak out even more and fly home again. I didn't want that. I didn't want to have to explain any of this to anybody. No, there was only one person I could call, because he already knew everything...but I really didn't want to ruin his night with Scott.

My lips quivered as I held my shaking finger over Eric's contact details.

Would he freak out? Would he tell me off for taking things too far? Would he make me go to the police?

I didn't want to.

What could I tell them? That a guy with black shoes

attacked me? That's all I had. For someone with the power to read people, I was pretty damn useless.

Tears stung. I pressed the back of my hand against my right eye, my lips trembling as they fought against the sobs. My limbs were shaking uncontrollably and I was on the brink of losing it.

I wanted Eric. I *needed* Eric, and even though we'd only been dating for a little while, I knew he'd want to know. He'd want to be the one to come and get me...and look after me. That was just the way he was.

Pulling in a quivering breath, I dialed his number and pressed my lips together as it rang.

"Hey, gorgeous girl." Eric's voice was light and cheerful.

I couldn't talk. Tears popped out of my eyes, dribbling down my face as I tried to find a voice. All I could muster was a shaky breath.

"Caity?" Eric's tone rang with urgent concern. "What's the matter? Where are you?"

"I need your help." I managed.

"Are you hurt?"

I shook my head in spite of the pain radiating through me. "Can you come and get me?"

"Tell me where you are and I'll be there." I could tell he was already moving. I could hear shuffling in the background. "Scott, sorry man, I gotta go. Where the hell are my keys?" More shuffling, muffled conversation. "I'll let you know." A door banged shut and I flinched. "Okay, where are you?"

I gave him directions, but he already knew where I was talking about.

"I'm sorry to ruin your night."

"Caity, stop it. Just sit tight. I'll be there soon."

He hung up and I clutched the phone in my hand, peeking out past the dumpster to make sure the guy with the gravelly voice wasn't coming back for round two.

I sat in agonized silence, mustering the courage to get up and walk to the street where I told Eric I'd be waiting. But I couldn't stop shaking and I didn't want anyone to notice me. Anyone could see I was in shock and I didn't want to explain myself.

"Caity!"

Eric's voice made me jump. I peeked out past the dumpster and saw him standing on the street. He looked frustrated and scared as he pulled the phone from his pocket. The phone in my hand began to sing "Kiss You" and Eric spun around, his eyes wide and his face pale under the streetlights. He raced into the alley, following the sound of my ringing phone and found me huddled on the ground.

"What happened?" His words were breathy as he crouched in front of me.

I wiped my dribbling nose with the back of my hand and shook my head, tears bubbling over once more as I launched forward and wrapped my arms around his neck. His strength encircled me as he gently stood, bringing me with him. We didn't move for a while; he just held me against him and let me sob into his shoulder.

Gradually, as I focused on the security of his arms around me, my cries ebbed away until all that remained was a snivelling, quivering mess. When my hiccuping tears had eased, he lifted me into his arms and carried me to his car.

twenty

Eric drove me home and carried me inside. I told him I could walk, but he wouldn't listen; he just tucked his arm beneath my knees and walked me to the front door. I shakily punched in the code and then he carried me to the sunken lounge, propping cushions behind me before taking off to the kitchen and making himself at home.

Five minutes later, he gently placed a steaming mug on the coffee table in front of me. "I hope you like Orange Blossom tea. I've never seen such a huge range of herbal tea before; I just went for the first one I recognized."

"It's perfect." I gave him a weak grin as I reached for it. Wrapping my fingers around the warm mug, I felt myself slowly start to relax.

Eric studied every inch of my face as I sipped at my tea. His thumb was gentle as he caressed my grimy cheek.

I winced.

"Sorry." He cringed. "Do you have a first aid kit or something? It might be a good idea to put some antiseptic on your face."

I nodded and pointed to the kitchen. "In the top shelf of the pantry."

He walked back into the kitchen, agitation radiating from him. I was surprised he'd managed to hold out this long. If it were the other way around, I would have been badgering him for answers the second we got into the car. He'd just stayed quiet...calm and quiet. His knuckles had been white on the steering wheel, so I knew it wasn't quite that simple, but he'd known what I'd needed.

He returned with some cotton balls, a bowl of water, and a little tube of antiseptic cream.

"Face me," he murmured. I put down the mug and turned toward him, our knees brushing together. "Where are your parents?"

"They left for Hawaii this afternoon."

His eyebrows rose as he dipped the cotton into the water.

"They're gone for ten days, so I have the place to

myself. I was going to tell you tomorrow, kind of like a surprise." My chuckle died quickly.

Looking into his tender gaze made my heart melt. There was something deeper there too, but I forced myself not to read it. I winced and grabbed his thighs as he patted my cheek clean. It stung. His brow was furrowed with concentration as he cleaned me up. I didn't want to look in a mirror. I gingerly touched my cheek and figured it must be a small graze. It stung, but felt like a quick healer.

I rubbed my tender belly and eased back onto the couch.

"Do I need to take you to the hospital?"

Drawing my hand away from my torso, I shook my head. "No. I'm okay. He just punched me in the stomach a couple of times and squashed my face into the ground. It hurt, but as far as injuries go, it feels pretty minor."

Eric studied me in silence until I tried to smile at him, and then his face bunched with an anger I wasn't expecting.

"Who did this to you? What did they want?"

"I don't know." I kept my voice soft. "I didn't see his face."

"Was he trying to rob you or something?" Eric swallowed, tortured agony flashing over his features. I could only guess what his mind was conjuring. I sat forward, wanting to ease his frustration, but knowing the truth probably wouldn't.

"It was a warning."

"Against what?"

"He wants me to stay away from Liam Donovan."

Eric's face paled, his usually gentle eyes growing hard. "What the hell have you been doing with Liam Donovan?"

"Nothing. Just asking a few questions."

That answer didn't satisfy him. His fingers were gripped together so tight I thought his bones might snap and his left leg bobbed uncontrollably. "You told me you were going to be careful, Caity. You promised."

Guilt stripped my insides bare. I hadn't seen this one coming, but I probably should have. Liam's phone call had been about me. The idea made me flinch.

"I didn't think I was being unsafe." I sighed, placing my hand on his knee. He stood, moving away from my touch. "You're angry with me."

He scowled. "Are you reading me right now?"

I nearly laughed. "I don't need to read you to see you're mad. It's obvious." I blinked, hating the conflict. I didn't understand why he was so pissed. "I'm sorry."

"I just can't believe you lied to me."

His mask fell away before I could stop it and I glimpsed a hurt boy who'd been let down by almost everyone he cared about. I quickly shoved the layer back into place, unnerved by his vulnerability. "I didn't lie to you, Eric... and I promise you I never will."

His gaze jumped to mine and I made sure my expression was open and true. "I was going to tell you everything tomorrow. You're the only person I can talk to about this stuff, and I didn't want to tell you over the phone. I had no idea this was gonna happen to me. Do you honestly think I would have ambled around after dark on my own if I thought I was in any kind of danger?"

The anguish on his face was heart wrenching. "Someone hurt you, Caity...and I wasn't there to stop them." He sank back down on the couch, lightly cupping my cheek. "I've never driven so fast to find someone before." He swallowed. "And when I saw you huddled against that dumpster, I thought my heart might break."

His voice hitched making my eyes glisten. I leaned toward him and brushed my lips against his cheek.

"I'm sorry for not being more careful." My voice shook. "I didn't know I was such a threat to them. I only asked a few questions. I just wanted to help Indie. She's scared, Eric." My lips bunched together as I tried to ward off the tears. "I don't know what Liam's doing to her, but it makes me sick. She's suffering and I want to help her, but I don't know how." I was losing the tear battle, so just went with it, letting them stream down my cheeks.

The attack scared the life out of me. I had to back away, but what about Indie? What did she face every time she was alone with Liam? If the guy who attacked me was the one Liam was talking to on the phone, then he'd obviously given Indie a beating before.

211

"How can I walk away and forget what I've seen? What kind of person does that make me?" I blubbered.

Eric caressed the tears from my face with the back of his fingers. "Caity, I need you to stop and go back to the beginning. I want to know every single detail of your week."

"Okay." I nodded. "But can I ask you to do one thing first?" I grasped his free hand, threading my fingers through his. "Can you stay with me tonight?" I swallowed. "I don't want to be on my own."

His thumb was soft as it brushed over my cheekbone. "I wouldn't leave even if you wanted me to."

I breathed out a relieved sigh.

"Thank you," I whispered.

I led him up to my room without saying a word. At first he seemed reluctant, but it only took a gentle tug to get him onto my bed. Snuggling against him, I laid my head on his shoulder. His reticence vanished as he wrapped his arm around my back and rested his chin on my head.

"Now talk," he whispered.

I told him everything I could think of. He knew some of it already, but I noticed his grip around me got tighter every time I spoke about Liam. When I mentioned the murder, he squished me so hard my stomach hurt.

"Sorry. Sorry." He pulled away, trying to get off the bed.

"You didn't hurt me, I'm okay." I wrapped my arm around him, trying to hold him in place, but he was stronger. Standing up from the bed, he ran his hand through his hair and paced to the window. "I want to kill that guy for hurting you."

"It's over, Eric. I'm all right."

"No, it's not. He said it was a warning. Caity, you have to stay away from this."

"But what about Indie? I can't just ignore what I saw. Liam needs to be stopped."

Eric spun with a fierce look in his eye. "I want you to stay away from Liam. You have to promise me you will."

"I don't know if I can do that." I felt bad saying it, but I told him I'd never lie.

His face crested with anger and sorrow. "I don't want you to get hurt again."

"I won't. I'll be more careful, more aware."

He looked unconvinced. The shadows created from my bedside lamp darkened the frown on his face.

"Eric, tonight scared the shit out of me. I'm not going to do anything careless, I swear."

That calmed him, but he still wasn't satisfied. "I still think you should call the police."

"I know...and I will, eventually. I just want to figure out a little more first. They're not going to follow a lead on some teenage girl's hunch. I need some sort of evidence."

He shook his head. I could tell he was annoyed with me. I so didn't want to lose him over this, but I couldn't just walk away from what I'd seen.

I wanted to. I wanted to run for the hills...or Wyoming, but I'd seen too much and I couldn't ignore it. I'd never be able to live with myself if I turned my back on people who so desperately needed help.

Curse my good soul.

Why couldn't I just be a selfish cow?

Eric's agitated pacing was driving me nuts. I hated anger. It stressed me out. We needed to end this conversation for the night or we'd never get any sleep, something we both probably needed. I did, anyway.

Exhaustion tugged at my brain, the aftershock of my attack making me queasy. I just wanted to lie in his arms and pretend none of this had happened.

"Please don't be angry with me," I whispered. "There's nothing more either of us can do tonight. I'm safe," I said the word safe as emphatically as I could. "Please, Eric, just come back to bed."

He stopped with his hands on his hips, his expression a mixture of longing and regret. "Caity, I was expecting to sleep on the couch."

Without warning, tears filled my eyes. "Please don't," I breathed. The idea of sleeping alone left me feeling bereft. I blinked at my tears, embarrassed by my fragile state.

With a soft sigh, Eric stepped back to the bed. "Don't cry. It's okay." Carefully untying my shoes, he placed them on the floor. He then took his off and lay down on the bed beside me.

"Thank you." I kissed his cheek. Grabbing his hand, I rolled away from him, pulling his arm over me and tucking it beneath my waist. He kissed the back of my head and shuffled forward so our bodies melded against each other. I ran my fingers down his bare forearm and closed my eyes. His solid form against me eased my rattled nerves, helping me to put the trauma of my day aside.

I was in Eric's arms. I was safe.

With that knowledge, I drifted off to sleep.

twenty-one

My head was aching as my mind worked toward wakefulness the next morning. Hands gripping me and hurting me slammed into my brain and I came to with a jerk. The arm around my waist squeezed tight.

"You okay?" And the voice behind me made my insides sing.

He'd stayed. All night, he'd slept beside me.

My hero.

I internally giggled at my swooning self. In spite of yesterday's events, I felt like the luckiest girl in the world.

"My silver lining," I muttered.

"What?" Eric's head popped up. He rested his stubbly chin lightly against my ear. Rolling over, I ran my fingers down his perfectly carved face and grinned.

"You're my silver lining," I whispered again, bringing my lips to his.

Morning kissing was the best way to wake up. I'd never done it before, but it didn't take more than a microsecond to come to this conclusion. Eric's tongue wrapped around mine as his arms slid up my back. I flung my leg over his hip, pulling him closer, relishing his firm body against mine.

Finding an opening, I wriggled my fingers beneath his T-shirt, spreading my hand flat against his back and gliding over his skin. His strong, hard muscles felt divine, and I was once again struck by the unbelievable notion that Eric Shore wanted me. With a soft groan, he pushed me onto my back, his weight pressing me into the bed. Running his hand from my knee to my thigh, he cupped my butt before sliding his hand beneath my shirt. His lips worked down my chin and over my neck, sending spikes of pleasure running through my system.

I held him tightly to me, lost in the intoxicating dance. My temperature rapidly skyrocketed as our breaths mingled together, our kissing growing urgent with our mounting desire. I started to tug at his shirt, wanting easier access to his amazing skin...his entire body. But then he jerked and pulled away.

I felt naked as he leapt off me. He ran a hand through his hair as he breathed in through his nostrils.

The light brown tendrils fell around his face and he tucked them behind his ear.

"I have to um..." He pointed behind him. "Mind if I take a shower?"

My confused frown must have been interpreted as a yes, because he spun and left my room.

Thirty seconds later I could hear the water running.

What the hell?

I frowned, slowly getting off the bed. I rubbed my slightly tender stomach that I had blissfully forgotten about, feeling fragile and worse for wear. Padding down to the second bathroom, I braved a look in the mirror and was pleased to see the grazing on my face was quite minor. My skin was a little puffy and there was definitely a bruise, but it was pale and would hopefully fade quickly.

My fingers shook as I ran the tips over my wound, but it wasn't because of yesterday. It was because my hot next-door neighbor just leapt off my bed and looked as though the last thing on earth he wanted to do was have sex with me. The thought was a depressing lump in my gut.

I clutched my shirt, noticing how dirty it was. Whipping it off, I threw it into the laundry as I walked past, unzipping my fly on the way to my room. I wiggled out of my jeans and was tempted to waltz into the bathroom in my underwear just to gauge Eric's reaction, but I didn't want to see the look on his face. Would it be disgust?

Fighting tears, I reached for a comfy pair of sweatpants and my pink Roxy T-shirt. They were both a little tatty, but I didn't care. Eric obviously didn't want me, so it wasn't like I needed to dress to impress.

I was thumping my way down the stairs when the front door jiggled open. I paused at the entrance to the living area. My heart tripped and stumbled as I wondered if someone was trying to break in. I gripped the corner of the wall, ready to scream...until I saw my older brother waltz in.

"Seth? What are you doing here?" My insides skittered.

My brother, who was old enough to be my father, was a straight arrow. His perfectly cut blond hair and dark blue eyes always took in everything. He was basically a replica of my father...and he would so not be cool with a guy he didn't know sleeping over at his kid sister's place. I crossed my arms in an attempt to quell my jitters.

"Hey, sis. Just checking in."

I rolled my eyes and blocked his way before he could come any further into the house. He didn't really want to be here, but he felt obliged. I could read it on his face. He was a busy guy with kids of his own; he didn't want the responsibility for his kid sister as well, but he was a good boy and if Dad had asked him to do it, he was going to follow through.

"Did Dad send you?"

"No."

"Liar."

He grinned. "I promised him I would, okay. Give me a break." His forehead wrinkled. "What happened to your face?"

"Um..." Brushing the back of my hand over it, I went for casual. "Got hit with a ball at school. Didn't even see it coming."

"Huh." Seth nodded. "Sounds like you."

"Thanks." I scowled. "Look, I'm fine. The house is fine. Nothing's on fire. Would you just go, please?"

His eyes narrowed. I noticed how his wrinkles were starting to show. He was turning forty soon.

I lifted my chin to counter his suspicious glare.

"What's the rush? Why do you want to get me out of here?" He looked over my shoulder, down the hallway. I followed his gaze, feigning confusion. "Whose Jeep's in the driveway?"

Shit!

I cleared my throat. "It's Eric's, our next door neighbor's. His mom had a party last night and there wasn't room for his car, so he asked if he could park here." I shrugged. "I didn't see any harm in it, so I said yes."

Seth looked unconvinced.

"He didn't want to leave it on the road. Big deal." I flicked my hand.

Seth's eyebrow arched, just the way Dad's did when he didn't believe me.

I rolled my eyes. "Oh please, as if he'd be here. The

guy's like a God, he barely knows I exist." My insides thrummed as I mentally begged my big brother to believe me. I hoped Mom hadn't blabbed about Eric taking me hiking.

Crossing my arms, I decided to change tactics and gave my brother a pointed look. "Seth, I've got my period, okay?" Surely that would freak him out. He used to hate it when Layla and Holly were so open about that kind of thing. "I'm tired, I'm cranky and I just want to be home alone. Let me enjoy this. Please."

As I expected, he took an instant step away from me. His hands went into his pockets as he reluctantly sighed. "Okay, fine."

"I'll tell Dad you came to check up on me." Although he didn't want me to see it, the thought made Seth happy. It didn't matter how old he was, Seth liked being Mom and Dad's golden boy.

He walked back to the door and eased it open, turning to look at me. "Call me if you need anything."

I grinned. "I'm cool, Seth. You go worry about your own girls."

He left with a snicker.

As soon as the door clicked shut, I tipped my head back with a sigh.

"Who was that?" Eric's voice made me jump. I spun to face him and noticed his shirtless form coming down the hall.

Seriously! Was he trying to torture me?

His jeans sat low on his hips, letting me see the full

glory of his carved torso. I wanted to study every contour of his bare skin, but I pulled my eyes away. "It was just my brother checking up on me."

Eric grimaced. "Does he mind that I'm here?"

"He doesn't know that you're here." I scratched the back of my neck, suddenly feeling awkward. "I told him you parked in our driveway last night because your mom was having a party and there was no space left in yours."

He looked impressed by my quick thinking, but also really uncomfortable that I'd lied. "Look I can leave. I don't want you to get in trouble or anything."

Looking to the floor, I tried not to let his words sting. He was just looking out for me, but I really didn't want him to go...unless he didn't want to stay.

I shrugged. "You can leave if you want, but I'd prefer you to stay."

His eyes lit with a grin as he stepped toward me. "Then I'll stay." He kissed my forehead and it took every ounce of willpower not to run my finger down that dip from his chest to his navel.

I curled my fingers into a fist, commanding them to behave.

"Want some breakfast?" I needed something to distract me.

"Sure." Eric nodded and followed me into the kitchen. We worked in silence, me getting out milk and yoghurt while he chopped up the fresh fruit. I pulled out Mom's homemade granola and a couple of bowls and we were soon sitting at the kitchen table quietly munching our food. Thankfully, or regrettably, Eric had pulled on a T-shirt before we sat down to eat. The image of his half-naked body was burned into my brain though...and would probably stay there for all eternity.

We ate in comfortable silence...at least Eric looked comfortable, gazing past me at the clear blue sky and looking relaxed. I pushed the cereal around with the tip of my spoon, willing myself to take another mouthful and just forget it.

But I couldn't.

I was so used to swallowing down my emotions and going along to keep people happy. It was kind of ridiculous. I didn't care if this was about to get awkward; I needed to know where I stood.

"Do you not want me?"

Eric jolted with surprise, looking at me as though I'd sprouted two green antennae.

I closed my eyes with a huff, dropping my spoon into my cereal.

"Sorry. I'm just trying to figure out what happened in my bed this morning. I thought..." I desperately wanted to look at him, to figure out what he might be thinking, but I forced my eyes to remain on the table. I wanted to read him so bad. "I must have imagined it." My voice quivered.

There was a long, painful pause before Eric finally reached for my chin, forcing me to face him.

"Caity." His eyes were filled with longing. "I had to

go and have a cold shower. An *ice cold* shower." He looked pained. "This morning was most definitely not about me not wanting you."

I frowned. "Then what was it about?"

A half smile pushed at his lips as he tipped his head to the side, looking almost bashful. Reaching for my wrist, he gently tugged me toward him and nestled me onto his lap.

"My mother has spent her life jumping into bed with guys before she even knew them. It's gotten her divorced twice, nearly married three more times after that and I've spent years having different guys—some jerks, some really cool—traipse in and out of my life." He rested his chin on my shoulder. "I don't want to be like that. If my mom had managed to control herself, she wouldn't have ended up with such a mangled heart."

Sitting back, he pulled me around so I was facing him, tucking my legs on either side of him.

"I don't want our first time to be this lust-filled moment... a distraction from all the crap." Placing his lips against the edge of my jaw, he kissed me lightly and whispered. "I want it to be a conscious decision. A choice. I never want you to regret letting me touch you or make love to you."

My insides were melting like butter in a frying pan. I tried to rein them in and force my breathing to slow down.

Eric picked up one of my curls and rubbed it

between his fingers. "Sex complicates everything, Caity, and we've only just started. I'm not ready to jeopardise what we've got going here."

A smile danced across my lips as I buried my head into his shoulder. My zinging hormones were very disappointed, but I was pretty sure my heart just fell in love.

"Will it be your first time?" I hated asking, but I had to know.

He cleared his throat as he ran his finger up my arm. "It takes a lot for me to trust people... so yeah. I haven't gone all the way yet."

"Me too." I had always thought that I'd want my first time to be with someone experienced. I didn't know what I was doing and I wanted them to take the lead and show me, but sitting there with Eric, hearing his sweet words, I suddenly loved the idea of figuring it out together. If our morning was anything to go by, it wouldn't be that challenging. I blushed at the thought. "I think you'll be worth the wait, Mr. Shore."

"As will you, Miss Davis." He nibbled my earlobe and trailed kisses down my neck, finishing with a raspberry just below my chin. I jumped with giggles and tried to pull away from him, but he held me tight and lavished more kisses upon my throat until his mouth ended back on mine. He pulled me against him and ran his hands up my back, deepening the kiss, promising things to come.

My senses started to catch fire and it would soon be

time to pull away, but I didn't have to make that choice. Eric's phone rang and our kiss-fest was brought to an abrupt end.

twenty-two

The phone call was a reality check I wanted to ignore, but Eric was right. Kissing our way through the weekend wouldn't solve my problems. Spoil sport.

So instead, we sat in a cafe opposite Scott Ferguson and Piper Vaughan. I didn't particularly want to meet either of them, but Scott had called to check whether I was okay and Eric had launched into the story of what happened to me. Fifteen minutes later, he was asking if I'd be cool to go and meet his friend, Scott. I was too confused to do anything but nod.

Sometimes I hated how my first instinct was often compliance. I was way too easy-going for my own good.

Always trying to make others happy.

Piper sat across from me, her tiny arms folded across her chest. Her dark hair was perfectly brushed and her sharp green eyes ran down my body as she shook my hand in greeting. She looked about as enthusiastic as I felt. I pulled her mask away. Oh yeah, there was no way she'd driven all the way from Palm Springs to spend the morning with strangers. She wanted Scott all to herself and from the look in her eye, she wanted him somewhere private.

I pressed my lips together, squashing my grin.

"So." Scott leaned his elbows on the table. "Eric told me you got into some trouble last night over Liam Donovan?"

I nodded, still nervous that Eric had let some stranger know all about what I was doing.

"Look, I know it's probably really uncomfortable for you talk to me about this." His gentle eyes were filled with compassion. "But I asked to meet you because...well, I used to know Liam."

Regret was evident. I tried to pull his mask away, to see more, but there wasn't one. What I saw was exactly that.

I swallowed. "How'd you know him?"

Scott sighed and ran a hand through his ginger locks. "I didn't know him that well; but we went to high school together and I used to hang with his older brother."

"Mason."

"Yeah, he uh..." Scott glanced at Piper. "He taught me how to...um." He frowned.

Piper reached for his hand and gave him a soft smile. Scott blushed and then grimaced, his nose wrinkling. "I used to party pretty hard with that guy and we got ourselves into some trouble."

I found that a little hard to believe. Scott, the mild looking freckle-faced guy with the cutest grin I've ever seen. That Scott? Partying hard?

He ran his pale fingers over his mouth and sighed. "He—he taught me how to pick locks and...well, I finally got busted for breaking and entering. I was kicked out of school and my parents moved me to Palm Springs."

"Thank, God," Piper murmured.

I had no idea what that was about, but there was a pretty strong connection between the couple. They'd both been through their own versions of hell—that wasn't hard to see.

Scott ran his hand up Piper's back, squeezing the nape of her neck affectionately. She grinned at him.

I didn't want to kill their uber-cute love tones, but I had to ask. I looked at Eric, who still seemed pretty tense, and he nodded at me.

My lips parted and I sat forward. "So you and Mason stole stuff together?"

"It wasn't just us. He kind of had a crew going."

"Did he ever steal cars?"

Scott cringed, telling me everything without saying a word. "I didn't get into that, but..."

"When was this?"

His nose wrinkled and he looked at Piper. "A few years back now."

"Did you go to Burbank High?"

"Yeah." He looked across the table at me, his eyebrows dipping in question.

"I read an article in the Burbank paper about a murder that happened a couple of years ago. The case has gone cold now, but it was suggested that the victim was killed by someone trying to steal his car. You don't think it would be Mason, do you?"

Scott's lips pinched tight. He wanted to shake his head vehemently, but couldn't quite do it. He scratched his forehead and frowned. "Look, I haven't seen Mason since I was fifteen. When I knew him, he was the kind of guy that just wanted to party and have fun all the time. I can't imagine him being capable of murder, but he was a reckless guy."

"What was Liam like?"

Scott shrugged. "He just wanted to be like Mason. Everything Mason did was for Liam and everything Liam did was to please Mason. Their dad was a total loser; they only really had each other and it made them pretty tight."

I nibbled my lip, thinking about Liam's phone call and what he'd said to my attacker.

"What is it?" Scott's eyes searched my face.

I hesitated and glanced at Eric.

"Tell him. It's okay." He ran his hand down my arm,

threading his fingers through mine.

I licked my lips then shakily explained. "I overhead Liam talking on the phone, and in retrospect, I think they were talking about me. I'm getting too close to something and they wanted to scare me away. Liam said not to kill me; he didn't want whoever he was talking with to have any more blood on his hands."

Scott hissed and sat back in his seat. "That sounds pretty dark to me." He shook his head. "But I don't think it was Mason."

"Okay." I nodded. "Then who's controlling Liam?"

Scott pursed his lips and shrugged. "Not sure, but I'd be really careful if I were you. Liam's had a troubled past and it sounds like he's in a pretty bad place right now." Scott shook his head. "My memory of him was that he could be pulled into anything. Whoever he's working for could probably get him to do whatever they wanted."

"I just wish I knew what they were up to." I bit the inside of my cheek. "I have a few theories, but—"

"I guess you'll just have to live without knowing." Eric squeezed my hand.

I turned to him with a frown. "But what about Indie? She's in trouble. She's scared. How can I just turn my back on her?"

"You don't." Piper's voice was adamant as she placed her coffee cup down.

"Pip." Scott placed his hand on his girlfriend's leg and warned her with a gentle squeeze.

She turned a pointed look on him. "If you'd turned your back on me, I'd be..." Her face paled, pinching tight with a mixture of past terror and regret. She dipped her head, tucking a lock of long straight hair behind her ear. "You put yourself in harm's way for me and you saved my life."

His expression softened when she glanced up at him and they were briefly caught in a moment that told me everything. These two were in love, and not just the "let's see where this takes us" kinda love, but the "we've been through big shit together and survived it" kinda love.

My curiosity was piqued, but I was too shy to ask. It wasn't really any of my business what they'd been through. I could just tell it was big.

Suddenly interested, Piper turned her sharp gaze back to me. "So how do you know all this stuff? You overheard the phone call, but what else?"

"Well, I've just noticed around school that people are kind of scared of him, but the problem is, everyone loves him."

"Okay." Piper's head tipped in confusion. "So this guy is scary, but people like him?"

"They don't know he's scary. I mean all the people with the power to actually do something about it think he's charming."

Piper sat back, her eyes piercing me. "So how do you know it then? You a mind reader or something?"

I looked down with a blush, surprised by an intense

urge to tell her. "Something like that," I murmured.

"Caitlyn's powers of observation are... pretty good." My eyes shot to Eric and he winked at me.

My lips jumped into a grin.

"So you're like a mentalist then." Piper nodded with a smirk.

I blushed. "Kind of weird, I guess."

She shrugged, looking completely unfazed. "Life is full of weird crap that people struggle to understand." She winked at her boyfriend, sharing some private joke I didn't get. "Look, Caitlyn, if I were you, I wouldn't be able to walk away either." Piper's expression turned serious. "Just be careful and don't try to save the day on your own. You've got a boyfriend who obviously cares about you and people in your life who can help you. I know your type." She raised her eyebrow and flicked her head toward Scott. "You don't like to bother people with your problems. You like to figure stuff out on your own, but don't be an idiot. People want to help you, so let them."

Her speech was good. I acknowledged her words with a smile and a nod before glancing at Eric. He wasn't totally pleased by what Piper had said, but his reticent demeanor had changed. He looked slightly more at ease and I wondered if maybe I could still pursue this without pissing him off.

****

The night had set in and we lay in bed in the darkness. Eric had popped home during the day and grabbed a few things. His mom hadn't even flinched when he'd told her he was staying with me. She'd just blushed and wiggled her eyebrows. Eric rolled his eyes when he told me.

We'd spent the rest of the day hanging out. We walked away from our session with Piper and Scott, strolling down to the beach both thinking about it, but not saying anything. I knew we had to. I wanted his blessing before I hit school on Monday, but he wasn't quite ready to give it to me. The rest of the day was quiet. We watched a movie. I did some homework while Eric studied for an upcoming test. We were like an old married couple—a comfortable silence nestled between us.

We chatted over dinner, I heard all about the weekend with his grandpa in detail. I loved it. And then that night we'd gone to bed and kissed until our bodies were on fire. He'd caressed my skin and I'd slid my hands as close to the line as he'd let me.

We finally pulled away breathless and Eric faced me away from him, holding me tight until we'd both calmed down.

"You're gonna make this really challenging, aren't you?"

I grinned. "It's not my fault you're hot."

He kissed my neck, his arms squeezing me tight. I was expecting a teasing reply, but he didn't give one.

Instead he sighed, his breath tickling my exposed shoulder. He pulled my T-shirt back into place and rolled me over, his expression serious as he ran his finger behind my ear.

"I want to keep kissing you, keep distracting myself with your soft skin, but we need to go to sleep and I can't do that until we've talked."

I pressed my lips together.

"I want you to walk away from this Liam thing."

My face crumpled and I started to shake my head.

"I know you're not going to." He sighed, and I hated that I was the cause of it.

"Eric, I'm sorry, but I can't."

"I know." His smile was pained. "I just suddenly wish I went to Pali High, so I could watch your back."

I grinned. "That'd be good."

"I was thinking about what Piper said, about people helping you. I know you don't want to tell anybody, but maybe you should ask that guy, Micah, to help you. Out of everyone you've told me about, he seems the most genuine and if Indie does like him the way you think she does, then maybe he can get her talking."

I ran my hand up his bare arm, hating the idea of burdening Micah, but knowing Eric was right.

"It'd make me feel better, knowing he was there to help you."

"I just don't want to pull anyone else into this."

"If Micah feels about Indie the way I feel about you, then he'll want to be pulled in. Trust me."

It was all I could do to breathe. I slid my hand up his neck and threaded my fingers into his hair, pulling his lips down to mine. His warm body pressed against me, a secure blanket that I wanted to hide beneath. I'd do anything to take him to school with me on Monday, but I couldn't.

Eric was right. I had to let Micah in.

twenty-three

"Hey, Micah." His easy lope didn't falter as I jogged up beside him. I knew I'd find him on the track. He always got to school an hour before first bell to run and workout. I was determined to talk to him no matter what he was doing and was relieved to see him pounding the track.

"You're here early." He kept his eyes ahead, his body straight. He was such a natural athlete; his running style was a pleasure to watch. I hoped I could keep up with him. Thankfully I wasn't a shorty and was pretty fit, so keeping up with him would be manageable as long as we didn't run for too long.

"I need to talk to you." My shoulders relaxed as I eased into a steady rhythm beside him.

He gave me a sidelong glance and I read his immediate wariness. I didn't want to push him away before I even got talking, but I had to win the conversation.

"Micah, I really need your help."

He remained silent at first; the only indication that he'd heard me was an acceleration in his pace. I matched easily, but wouldn't be able to last as long at the new pace.

"Micah, please."

Shaking his head, he pursed his lips. "Look, I don't know what you're into Caitlyn, but I can't." He felt bad saying no. "I'm usually down for anything, but this is my shot at playing college ball. I've gotta keep my nose clean."

"I'm not asking you to get it dirty... I don't think." I winced.

He scoffed and picked up his pace even more, leaving me in his wake. I had no show of catching him.

"Micah, wait!" I slowed from a run to a walk. "It's about Indie. She's the one that needs our help."

I hadn't intended to shout it across the track and was grateful we were there on our own. Micah came to an abrupt stop. He turned and walked back to me with his hands on his hips, his dark eyes anxious. "She in some kind of trouble?"

"I think so." I put my hands on my knees, trying to

catch my breath. Micah had fully recovered already, standing over me, silently demanding more. I stood tall and looked him in the eye. "I'm trying to figure out exactly what she's into, but I know she's, um..." I stood up and scratched my nose, not wanting to say it. "She's really scared of Liam."

"What are you talking about?" Micah's wide mouth turned down at the corners. "Liam? He's a bunny rabbit. They're always making goo-goo eyes at each other." This hurt him, big time. He hated it with every fiber of his being, but knew he had to accept it.

"It's fake, Micah."

I watched hope flitter across his face, dark concern followed in its wake.

"Liam Donovan is *not* what he appears to be, and Indie only looks at him that way because she knows that's what he wants. She's petrified that if she lets her true feelings show he's going to hurt her."

"He hurts her?" The black pulse of rage that shot from him made me step back. I shoved his mask back on to dampen the impact of his wrath. It worked...sort of.

I swallowed. "I don't know for sure, but I think he does."

Micah's features distorted with a deep frown. "How do you know this stuff?"

I wasn't sure how much to tell him. How did I sell it without coming across as an unbelievable weirdo? I mean, Piper and Scott bought it, but I had Eric to back me up...and they seemed to be open to the supernatural for some reason.

Micah's intense gaze wouldn't let up, so I sighed and just went for it. "I can see things that other people can't."

"What?"

"I guess you could call it a gift?" That still sounded wrong to me, but anyway. "I can read people's emotions. I don't know what they're thinking, but when you see what they're feeling...it's easier to work out what's going on in their heads. So I'm not a mind reader, per se, but an emotion reader. Does that even make sense?" My nose wrinkled and I ran a hand through my hair. "That's how I knew you cared so much about Indie."

His dark skin heated as he looked to the ground and scratched the back of his head.

"When I was at Liam's big party two weeks ago, I spotted Indie's fear and I haven't been able to ignore it since. I've been spying on her and trying to figure out how to help her. The other day I overheard a conversation between her and Liam. He was really pissed and threatened to punish her if she didn't do what he said."

Micah's jaw clenched, the muscles on the side of his face bulging as he snorted like a bull ready to charge. "What did he want her to do?"

"Keep her mouth shut about his business or something. I can only guess what he was referring to, but I do know Indie doesn't want to be involved. I have a feeling that Libby is somehow caught up in this and she wants out, too." I shrugged. "I figured because we're working with them at the moment, this might be a good chance to get them to open up to us."

"Indie's a closed book, Caitlyn. You know that."

"But I don't think she wants to be." I really wanted to tell him what I saw at the game...the way Indie had looked at him. But what if I'd just been imagining it? I didn't want to get Micah's hopes up, but... "I think she'd listen to you. She respects you, Micah. She sees that you're a good guy."

Micah's laughter was hard and dry. "No, she doesn't. She's just as scared of me as everybody else is."

"I'm not scared of you."

"You're different." He lightly punched my shoulder.

"She's not afraid of you. I've seen it in her expressions. She trusts you."

The corner of his eye twitched. He was trying to figure out if he could believe me. Like my news was somehow too good to be true.

"How am I supposed to help her?" he whispered, his vulnerable fear showing through.

"She needs to feel safe right now. You can give her that."

This made him feel good. I decided to play on the shining knight tangent.

"She's trapped inside Liam's world and she's desperate to be rescued, but she doesn't think she can be. If we...if *you*...can make her feel protected, then maybe she'll tell us the truth."

"And how am I supposed to do that?"

"Stop hiding how you feel about her."

His face dropped, his eyes flashing wide for a moment. The idea terrified him, but it was also appealing.

"We need to find out the truth so that we can help set her free," I continued.

Micah bit the corner of his mouth, his large hand cupping the top of his shaved head. "At the beginning of the year, Indie came up to me with an offer to help me get good grades."

My insides stirred as another piece slid into place. "How?"

"She was really vague, saying she had resources that could guarantee I'd have a sweet ride this year." Micah shook his head. "I could tell it was this elite thing, like only a few were being approached about it and man, because it was her, I was tempted. But there was just this flicker in her eyes, like a warning. I'd only just finished my probation. There was no way in hell I was getting mixed up in something else. It felt wrong, so I told her I didn't want to know. She smiled all sweet, but something was off. I liked her before that, but man, whatever I saw that day just made me want to wrap her in my arms, you know?" He tipped his head toward where I'd first approached him on the track. "That's why I fobbed you off before; I thought you were coming at me with something like this."

"Well as you can see, I don't know anything about it." My eyes bulged wide as I remembered another conversation. "Stella," I whispered.

"What about her?" Micah didn't even bother hiding his derision.

I ignored his expression and kept on. "She asked me if Libby was working for me. She got all closed off when I tried to question her about it." I crossed my arms. "I think Liam's business is some sort of cheating scam or something. He's using the brainiacs to do all this work for the people who can't be bothered. Do you think they're paying him? Maybe that's what he means by running a business."

"Could be." Micah nodded, not happy about my theory, probably because it was true. "Pressure's pretty high to do well here. And I gotta say, Liam's crew don't seem that stressed about school work...at least the guys in the basketball team aren't." Micah pursed his lips. "Damn." He shook his head. "You'd be opening a big ass can of worms if this is real."

I bit my lip, nerves skittering through me like frenzied fireflies. "You want to help me do it?"

No. I could see it all over his face.

My insides deflated as I watched him push his lips together and then sigh. "You know I can't afford to screw up this close to the end of the year. I can't get involved in anything that'll jeopardise what I've been working so hard for." He winced and let out a soft hiss.

"But I want to get Indie out of whatever shit she's into, so I'm in."

I wanted to wrap my arms around him and kiss him. I was so relieved.

Instead I sufficed with a friendly slap on his arm and jogged with him back to the changing rooms. We agreed to broach it at the biology assignment meeting we'd set up before school that day. I was so nervous I wanted to puke, but knowing Micah would be there to back me up was a huge comfort.

Pulling out my phone, I texted Eric with an update as I'd promised I would. It was good knowing he was there for me, even if not in the physical sense.

This day will go one of two ways. I'll find out the truth and sneak Indie into freedom or I'll find out the truth and everything will blow up in my face.

I rubbed my stomach and forced my lungs to inflate as I made my way to the library, the attack on Friday night still way too raw and fresh in my mind.

twenty-four

The study area of the library was empty, which was why we'd agreed on Friday to meet there first thing Monday morning. Libby's idea was huge and brilliant, but it was taking us longer than we expected. No one seemed to mind the extra workload. We were enjoying hanging out together, but a very different feel hung in the air that particular morning.

Indie arrived looking flustered. Her hair was mussed and she was busy adjusting her white linen dress. She caught me watching her and shame turned her cheeks pink. I could tell she'd just been made to do something she hadn't wanted to. I didn't know what, but the sick feeling in my gut made me wonder. Her hands trembled as she sat down across from me, unable to look me in the eye.

"Morning," I said with a smile.

"Hey," she mumbled.

"How was your weekend?"

"Okay." She shrugged, looking small in her chair tucked under the big library table.

"Yours?"

I tried to look casual and unfazed. "It was pretty quiet, although Friday night was interesting."

She went pale, her high cheekbones sticking out as she ruffled her bangs.

So she did know about what had been done to me. Stripping back another layer I saw her guilty tears. Any simmering anger I may have been harboring against her evaporated. She looked so wretched.

Micah strolled in—edgy, but determined. He sat down next to Indie and a calm relief descended around her. She shot Micah a polite smile, but I could see how safe she felt beside him. Micah glanced my way and I gave him an encouraging smile. We hadn't really talked about how we were going to broach the subject and I kind of I wished we had.

Who would start the inquiry? Was it better if I did? Libby was still a little afraid of Micah, but she didn't seem too keen on me either.

"Morning, everybody." Libby bubbled into the room.

I gave her a warm smile, which she instinctively returned before swallowing and slumping into the chair beside me. Everyone was silent. It was mega-awkward, to the point that Indie actually initiated.

"So, what are we working on today? Where's everyone up to?" She opened up her book of notes and began scanning them. "Did you all manage to gather some more samples over the weekend? I only got a few. I haven't had a chance to identify them yet though."

She reached down to unzip her bag and I took my chance.

I willed my courage not to flake as I leaned forward and laid my hands on the table. "Before we get started, I just wanted to say..." I glanced at Micah. "How much I enjoy working with you guys. I feel like we're a really great group. We work well together." Although confused, everyone nodded. Indie sat up with a small grin, giving me the confidence to go on. "It might sound weird, but I feel safe with you guys, like I could tell you anything and it'd be okay."

Indie's smile fled. She glanced at Micah who was watching her with the softest expression I'd ever seen. Behind his mask his face was glowing with pure affection. It was so strong, it was breaking through and Indie saw it. Her eyes glistened before she had a chance to turn away and blink at tears.

Libby squirmed in her seat as my gaze hit her. "Do you feel that way?"

She shrugged, but I could see that she did.

I took her hand. "Libby, you can tell us anything and it'll be okay."

I looked to Indie. Her blue eyes were wide with fear. "You too, Indie. No one's going to hurt you here." She flinched, her gaze pressing into me with a look that was both pleading and annoyed.

The tension in the air grew thick and suffocating, and I wasn't quite sure what to say next, but then Libby drew in a deep breath and let out this hiccuping sob. "I didn't want be involved in this, but after the whole Carter thing I had no choice."

"Libby, stop." Indie's voice was steel cold, but behind her mask she was a quivering mess.

"I can't do this anymore, Indie! I don't care what Liam threatens me with." Her bravado was only just masking her palpitating terror.

"Keep going, Libby, tell me what's happening with Liam." I tentatively touched her arm, not wanting to scare her off, but feeling like human contact might help her along.

Libby sniffed, big fat tears popping onto her lower lashes. "He started up a business last year. He recruited a whole bunch of vulnerables." She pointed at herself in anguish. "And he makes them do all this extra work - assignments mostly, but he's managed to steal a few tests as well. We have to complete them and then hand in the answers and then the rich kids who are too lazy to do their own work, pay him."

"Libby, please stop." Indie's teeth were clenched.

"No, Indie." Libby threw a vehement look at the meek redhead before turning back to me. "Liam approached me a few months ago and I was hesitant at first. It felt wrong to me, but he kept telling me how much he needed me and how there'd be these great rewards." Libby swiped at her tears. "That's why I knew whenever you guys were doing anything social. He knew I wanted to be part of your crowd and he kept inviting me and finally I caved. But then I started second-guessing myself and I tried to quit. I told Liam the workload was getting too much. That's when he set up the Carter thing. He knew I liked Carter and he also knew there was no way I'd have the guts to do what Carter was demanding. It was the perfect threat to keep me in line. Carter was going to start these rumors about what we'd done in that upstairs room. He made sure everyone saw us go up there and then people saw me leaving in tears. On Monday, Liam told me he'd taken care of any rumors, but nothing could stop him from igniting some new ones. He threatened to call my parents. I had no choice but to do what he wanted."

"Libby, shut up!" Indie slammed the table. "Don't you get it? He'll destroy you. If this gets out, you're dead." Her voice hitched.

"Indie, it's okay." Micah gently touched her hand.

"It's not okay." Tears flooded her eyes, making them a brilliant blue. She yanked her hand away and stood from her chair. "You don't know what he's like. You don't know what he's capable of doing. Libby needs to shut up and toe the line. That's the only way to be safe! You're an idiot, Libby!" Her finger was trembling as she pointed at the weeping girl beside me. "You should have kept your mouth shut! Now we're both gonna pay!"

"Indie." Micah's voice was a soothing balm. He reached for her hand again and held tight when she tried to snatch it away. "It's okay." His large thumb caressed her pale skin. She looked so small and fragile beside him.

Her chin trembled as her lips fought for control. "It's never going to be okay," she whispered.

"Yes it is." I could see Micah's anguish as he gently pulled her onto his knee. I thought she'd fight him, but she didn't. She sank into his embrace and buried her face in his shoulder. His strong arms encircled her, cocooning her from the world.

Her pitiful sobs brought tears to my eyes. I looked at Libby and nearly started laughing. We were all blubbering messes. I yanked some Kleenex out of my bag and passed one to her. She gave me a watery smile as she took it, her eyes filling with an apology that didn't need to be said. I shook my head and squeezed her hand.

As Indie's tears slowly ebbed, she turned to look at me. Her head was perched on Micah's shoulder and she didn't want to move it. I passed her a Kleenex. Our fingers brushed as she took it and her face crested with pain.

"I'm sorry about what happened to you on Friday." Her voice was small. "I didn't find out until after... and I felt so bad."

"It's not your fault, Indie."

She swallowed, looking guilty.

"What happened to you?" Micah frowned.

I flicked my hand, going for casual. "Some guy tried to give me a warning, told me stay away from Liam."

"Did he hurt you?"

"I'm okay, Micah." I didn't want to go into details. Indie didn't need to hear it. She already looked bad enough and it wasn't her fault. "Indie, who attacked me?"

"I can't." She shook her head. "You don't understand. He'll hurt me."

"Who? Liam or this other guy?"

Her lips quivered. "Both." She drew in a sharp breath. "They both have their ways of keeping me in line."

Micah looked ready to murder someone. I shot him a warning look. Indie did not need to meet his angry side. I knew he had one, that was why he'd been on probation...for fighting. He worked overtime to pull his emotions into line. I could see him using some sort of calming technique he'd obviously learned. The unnerving black rage I spotted slowly swirled away.

Satisfied he wouldn't explode, I turned my attention back to the trembling waif on his knee. "Indie, you can't go on like this. We have to stop Liam. We have to end

253

this and get you somewhere safe."

"I don't have anywhere safe to go. Liam lives at my house." Her breathy laughter was sad and broken. "He manipulated his way into my life and now I'm trapped. I can't get out. He'll kill me, Caitlyn. And as miserable as my life is, I don't want to die."

She pulled in a shaky breath and pressed the tissue to her eyes. Micah rubbed her back, placing a sweet kiss on her forehead. His fond touch seemed to jolt something inside her and she popped off his shoulder. Fear struck her features. She stumbled off Micah's knee and whipped back to her chair.

"If Liam finds out what's happening right now, he's gonna..." She pointed at Micah's lap and looked ready to puke. "He's very particular about who I talk to. Please don't tell him I let you touch me." Her quavering voice tore at my heart and it was doing the same to Micah.

He leaned over her, running his hand down her back. "I'm not going to let him hurt you anymore," he whispered.

"You can't stop him." She met his deep gaze.

"I'm not going to let him hurt you," Micah repeated slowly.

But Indie just kept shaking her head. "If he finds out about this, about what Libby told you, he'll find a way to hit us all where it hurts the most. He watches everything. He'll figure out the best way to make our lives a living hell."

The threat was frightening because I knew how real it

was. Liam did know how to get to people. He preyed on their weaknesses and always knew the perfect way to strike. Everyone around the table was at risk.

But in spite of that, there was a sense of freedom and unity among us.

Everything had finally been spilled and I could tell Libby felt a deep sense of relief. Even through Indie's fear, I could sense a spark of hope. So I decided to build on it.

"Indie, he doesn't know what's happening right now. He's not here." I pointed around the study room. "We're the only people privy to this conversation and we can trust each other. Together, we can bring an end to this."

Her fleeting hope shimmered a little brighter. "How?"

"We need to out Liam. There's bound to be some kind of proof of what he's doing." I looked to Libby. "How does his business work?"

"Well." Libby sniffed. "Every morning when I get to school there's a new set of assignments, or a test to complete, in my locker. I have to finish it three days before the deadline so whoever the work belongs to can tweak anything and make it sound more like them. If I'm late with a deadline...I find other stuff in my locker."

"Like what?"

Libby looked at Indie, who grimaced and whispered, "Photos of what's been to done to people who don't toe the line or a flash drive with video footage." Indie swallowed back the details and I didn't press her for more. I didn't want to know.

"Liam's crew can be pretty...mean." Libby squeaked.

I gripped her hand, most likely in an effort to quell my own shaking. "Who do you deliver the completed work to?"

"We leave it in our lockers to be collected."

"Liam knows all his workers' locker codes," Indie said.

"I leave the work in a manila folder."

"Are you assigned to certain students?"

Libby nodded. "I have three, some have up to five."

"Woah," I whispered. "No wonder you're so exhausted. You must be working round the clock."

"I don't know what else to do." Her voice tripped. "I can't have him calling my parents. You know what he's like. He can convince anyone to believe whatever he tells them to."

"Do you get paid for any of this work?"

"No." Libby's voice was small and full of resentment.

I looked to Indie. "But Liam gets paid, right?"

She closed her eyes, looking pale and exhausted. "One hundred bucks for test results, twenty-five for every page of standard homework, one hundred and fifty for an essay and two-fifty for a full research assignment." Her voice was devoid of life as she rattled off the amounts.

My jaw went slack. "How many clients does he have?"

"About forty-five regulars and another fifty one-offs. Mostly juniors and seniors, a handful of sophomores."

"Stella's one of them, isn't she?" My voice was hard and clipped.

Libby bit the edge of her lip. "I do her work."

Breaths punched through my nose as my nostrils flared. "We have to stop this. It's not fair."

"If he finds out you even said that, you're dead. That warning on Friday was real. You don't have to get into this." Indie's emphatic voice did nothing to sway me.

"I'm already in it and I'm not backing down. I've seen how scared you are. How scared Libby and all the other students are. It's not fair to keep going on this way. All we need is a little evidence and we can expose Liam's whole operation."

"Doing that will affect so many people...all the workers and the people paying for the services...me and Libby included."

"I know." I grimaced, glancing at Libby. "That's why the decision has to be yours. If you don't want me, or Micah, to say anything, we won't. This will be the last conversation we have about this. I'll walk away." I so didn't want to do that, but I wouldn't fight Indie or Libby on it. If they wanted to keep suffering that was their choice. I'd given them an out and I just had to cross my fingers that they'd take it.

twenty-five

The silence that followed nearly killed me. If they didn't go for it, I would have failed on an epic scale and Micah felt the same way. He was still fighting his rage, and I was worried if Indie refused that he might lose it and take matters into his own hands. I could tell he wanted to beat the shit out of Liam, but if he did, his chances of playing basketball in college were over. I didn't want him to miss out on that.

I felt bad for getting him involved and was about to start a speech about how we just needed to survive the last two months of school and then we could rescue Indie over the summer, when...

"I want out." Libby's soft statement pierced the restless quiet we were sitting in. "I don't care about the consequences anymore. I hate living in fear like this. I'd rather just go back to being unpopular, fat Libby Phelps."

Turning in my seat, I read her to make sure it wasn't just bravado talking, but she was being honest. I squeezed her forearm.

I then looked to Indie, ready to plead if I had to. She was gazing at Libby's determined face, her weak one fighting with a maelstrom of emotions I couldn't keep up with. I popped her mask back into place to give my eyes a breather.

"You're brave, Libby." Indie said softly. "But you're not fat and you never deserved to be unpopular, because you're one of the nicest people I know." She glanced at me then turned to smile at Micah. "You all are." She reached for his hand. "I never thought getting out would be an option for me. I've just been trying to survive...put on a show to keep everybody happy. To keep myself safe." She licked her bottom lip. "But I'm not safe, and I really want to be."

Micah threaded his fingers through hers and ran his other hand over her head. She was so petite beside him. I smiled watching their interaction and thinking once again about how Micah was the strong tower Indie could recover in.

"Indie, can you help us put an end to this?"

Her blue eyes remained transfixed by Micah's sweet

gaze. "Liam keeps a record of all the money collected. He has the names of every person who has ever paid him and the names of all the people who work for him, locker combinations...everything."

"Where is that?"

"It's on his computer."

"At school?"

"No, it's a different computer. He keeps it in the vault in my dad's office."

"Okay, so do you think you can put those files on a memory stick and bring it to school? We could maybe..." I felt guilty saying it and shot Libby a nervous glance. "Take it to Dean Van der Belt?"

"Man, that's terrifying." Libby bit her lip, her skin almost white. "But it's less terrifying than Liam." She was surprised by her words, but then nodded. Yep, they were true and it made me realize just how powerful the guy was.

Indie looked ready to pass out, but she did nod...sort of.

"Indie." Micah's voice was deep, yet soft. "Do you want me to come with you?"

"No." She shook her head. "If he catches you in the house, he'll...I don't want him to hurt you."

"And I don't want him to hurt you." His eyes blazed. "So I'm coming."

Her smile was soft and fleeting, but I caught the relief in it.

"We don't want either of you getting caught. What's

Liam schedule for the rest of the day?"

Indie pursed her lips. "Liam keeps tabs on me, waits for me after every class. I can't skip and I won't be able to get away."

"What about staging another study session?" I asked.

"He already hates that I'm meeting with you guys and he's only letting me do it so I can keep an eye on you." She winced.

I waved my hand, hoping to put her at ease. "Don't worry about it. It's actually worked in our favor. Do you think you can swing the lie that this morning was just a normal study session?"

A sad smile spread over her lips. "I spend most of my life lying to those around me, so I'm well-practiced."

My brow wrinkled as I shot her a sympathetic look. "It still doesn't get you back to your house alone though." I nibbled my lip.

"I'm free last period so I can leave any time after two," Micah said. "We just need to think of a way to get Indie out."

"Do you think you could fake being sick after lunch?"

Indie shook her head. "He'd make me wait at the nurse's office until after school and then insist on driving me home."

"Well, what if Micah came into the nurse after Liam had dropped you, snuck you out and then took you home? Would fifty minutes be long enough to download the files and get back again?"

"It'd be tight, and how would we get past the nurse?"

I grimaced, hating the fact that I had no idea. I dropped my head into my hands, not wanting to let my frustrations show.

"You know what, as soon as Liam finds out what I've done, I'm dead anyway. What's skipping class?" Indie's voice held a note of strength to it. She squeezed Micah's hand. "Libby, you've got double Physics with Liam after lunch, right?"

She nodded, sitting forward in her seat.

"If you could somehow distract him at the end of class then that'll give me enough time to sneak away and meet Micah in the student parking lot. As long as I'm waiting for Liam outside Art History when that final bell goes, I'll be okay."

"Where will you hide the memory stick?" Libby asked.

"I'll take it." Micah nodded. "I can keep it with me until we decide to go to the dean."

"We'll need to do it quickly. If Liam figures anything out, it puts Indie in danger," I said.

"We should see him this afternoon then." Micah's eyes were alight with purpose.

"I'll go to the office and make an appointment." Libby bit her lip. "He's friends with my dad. I'm sure he'll make time for me."

"Okay good. All we need now is a memory stick."

Without a word, Libby scrambled into her bag and

pulled out a little black stick. She passed it to Indie who took it with quivering fingers before clutching it in her hand. I exhaled and looked around the table. We were all nervous, like hell scary nervous, but we had a plan and that bit felt good.

I put my hand in the middle of the table. Cheesy, I know, but I had the compelling urge to suddenly be connected to each of them. Micah placed his hand on mine, followed by Libby and finally, Indie.

"I know this is terrifying and we're all taking a massive risk, but it's gonna be okay. We're gonna end this." I made sure I was looking at Indie when I said it. She gave me a grateful smile. It was the first genuine one she'd ever given me and it was beautiful.

twenty-six

I was a jittery mess for the rest of the day. I actually started reading people during lunch just so I could distract myself and keep my gaze off Indie and Libby who were sitting with Liam for lunch. It didn't really work. My eyes kept reverting back to a very nervous Indie. Thankfully she was hiding it like a pro. Micah never came into the cafeteria, which also helped. I was pretty sure one look at him would have her mask slipping away.

My phone buzzed and I pulled it out of my bag, nearly dropping it as I unlocked the screen.

You being safe?

Eric.
I grinned.

Yeah, I'm safe.

I didn't want to give him full details in a text. But he'd made me promise to keep him informed. My thumbs wavered over the screen wondering if I should send a second text with more, but then his reply came.

That's my girl. Call me when you get home from school. Want to hear your voice.

My anxiety ebbed. I could tell him then.

Okay. Talk to you later, Hercules.

You bet, girl next door—xx

Kisses. Cute! He left me kisses in a text. Yep, my super-crush was definitely morphing into full-blown love.

I felt calmer after Eric's text. It was nice to know he was thinking of me. I was actually looking forward to giving him all the details. I just hoped they were good ones.

I looked across the table and met Indie's eyes. Her

mask slipped and I was expecting to see a sign that she'd changed her mind, but her gaze was determined. She was desperate to get on with it.

The bell was a blessed relief. I scurried off to U.S. History, now my least favorite subject thanks to Stella's hate vibes. I kept my head down and focused, then bobbed my knee through free period in the library. After that, my heart rate was uncontrollable. As I walked to Algebra I was fully aware that Libby was currently trying to distract Liam while Indie snuck to the parking lot. I thought my brain might actually short circuit as I fluffed my way through quadratic equations.

When the final bell rang, I lurched from my seat, ignoring the surprised titters around me, and basically ran to Indie's Art History class. I had to see her meeting up with Liam. I had to catch her eye and know the plan had worked. Shooting past the blue lockers, I tore down the stairs, trying not to bump into people, and raced around the corner to where her class was located. People were milling around outside, but none of them were Indie...or Liam.

My heart jumped into my throat as I looked at my watch. *Crap. Crap. Crap!*

Spinning around, I glanced up the stairs, across the grassy quad and then over my shoulder to the next block of buildings. No Liam. I didn't see him coming from any building. In fact to make matters worse, the only thing I did spot coming was a flustered Libby.

She grabbed my wrist as soon as she got to me and

yanked me to a private corner.

"What? What is it?"

It took her a moment to catch her breath. "I tried to stall Liam after Physics." She frowned, looking guilty.

"It didn't work?"

"Sort of. I mean I could tell he wanted to get away and then he gave me that look—the dark one that scares the living crap out of me. I backed away. I couldn't... I'm sorry, Caitlyn."

"No, it's fine." I rubbed her arm. "You did great."

"I don't think I did."

"Why?"

"Well, I followed Liam to see where he was going and...well, he got to Indie's class and she wasn't there, so he ran to Art History to check on her. He actually went into the class."

"Shit," I whispered. "Did you see him come out again?"

"No, I had to get to my own class. I nearly got a detention for being late, but Ms. Caldwell was in a good mood today." She blinked at tears and I squeezed her arm.

"Do you think he figured it out?"

"How? Unless Indie let something slip."

"I don't think she would have. She's not stupid."

"So what do we do?" Libby bit the corner of her mouth, her dark eyebrows dipping.

"I don't... I don't know." I looked around us, wondering if we should walk to the parking lot and scan it for Micah's car. Maybe we were overreacting. Maybe Liam had pulled Indie away before I got there. Maybe...

"We have to find out." Libby cleared her throat; striving for courage we were both far from feeling. "We have to go to Indie's place and make sure everything's okay."

I swallowed. Libby was right. But the scary thing was I knew, like in my gut knew, that if we did find Indie at her place, it wasn't going to be pretty. Libby turned for the parking lot, clutching her bag strap as she tore across the grass on her short legs. I hesitated. Eric would be so pissed if I did this. I'd promised him I'd be safe.

"You coming?" Libby called, her face anxious.

Damn it! I had to go. It was my freaking idea! I had to make sure Indie was okay. Whipping out my phone, I found Eric's number and pressed it before I lost my nerve. I rustled for my keys as I caught up with Libby, the phone pressed to my ear.

It went to voicemail. A huge part of me was relieved. "Hey, um..." I licked my lip. "I just wanted to let you know that I'm heading to Indie's house." Libby gave me a confused frown when I reached her. I ignored it. "She was going there with Micah to get some evidence and she's not back. Libby and I are worried about her so we're going to check it out. I just wanted to let you know what I was doing. I promise I'll be safe, okay?" I sounded so nervous. He was going to see right through my message. "Okay, see ya." I hung up with a grimace, suddenly wishing I hadn't felt compelled to call him. I was worried about his anger and now I'd probably just worried him unnecessarily.

"Who'd you leave a message with?" Libby walked to the passenger side of my Mini, looking suspicious.

I unlocked the car and got in with a sigh. "My boyfriend."

I didn't want to look at her while I started the car; I hadn't told anyone about Eric and I kind of wanted to keep it that way. Besides I wasn't even sure if he was my boyfriend. Just because Piper said it didn't make it true. We hadn't had that conversation yet.

"I don't suppose you have a phone charger that can plug into a car do you?"

She shook her head and I frowned. Glancing at the five percent warning, I shoved the phone in my back pocket and decided to keep it on anyway, in case Eric called back. I was annoyed that I hadn't remembered to charge it last night. Why hadn't I?

My cheeks flared as I reversed out of my spot, suddenly remembering why. With Eric in my bed, my brain cells were acting like Play-doh.

"You have a boyfriend? Who?" Libby buckled up as I accelerated out of the parking lot.

"It's...he's a college guy...my next-door neighbor."

I shrugged, trying to not make a big deal of it. I shouldn't have called him my boyfriend. Libby's lips quirked with a grin and she shook her head. "Are you talking about the hot surfer guy that Stella has wanted

270

to get her talons into for like forever?"

Gripping the wheel, I kept my eyes on the road as I pursed my lips.

Libby giggled. "Well, you deserve him more than she does." She shrugged. "I didn't think he was that friendly though."

I grinned. "He is when you get to know him." I couldn't help wiggling my eyebrows and we both burst into near hysterical laughter. It was bizarrely inappropriate considering where we were headed but also a welcome relief.

Our laughter died a short time later, replaced with an ominous silence.

Libby finally broke it when she cleared her throat. "I made an appointment with Mr. Van der Belt." She adjusted the watch on her wrist. "I'm due in his office at four this afternoon."

"Good." I nodded. "Do you want me to come?"

"Um...I don't... Maybe?"

I threw a glance at her. "I'll be there if you need me, Libby. Just say the word."

"Thanks, Caitlyn." Her closed mouth smile was sweet. "I'm sorry for suddenly going cold on you. Liam was pretty clear about me not being your friend."

"I get it." I forced a smile, hoping she realized that I did. We had bigger things to worry about, and I think it hit Libby the second we turned into Indie's street. Her gulp was audible.

The houses along Malibu Road were huge, all

situated behind looming gates. We drove past Indie's house. The gates were open and when Libby craned her neck, she thought she spotted Micah's car.

"Did you see Liam's?"

"No."

I turned at the end of the street and kept cruising past Indie's house.

"What are you doing? Aren't we going to check on them?"

"Yeah." I bit my bottom lip. "But I think we should park down the street...just in case Liam does arrive or something. Look, I don't know, I just think it'd be better if my car wasn't on the road as a warning sign or something. I think most people know my Mini."

"You're right. Good idea." Libby's head bobbed.

I drove one block down the road and parked at the beach. It was a really quiet beach that hardly anyone came to. I looked out across the rippling water and smooth sand. They were in complete contrast to my roaring emotions. I wanted them to make me calmer and fill me with a sense of peace, something nature normally did, but this time I was turning away from it. Walking from a serene sanctuary into a potential hell pit. Okay, slightly dramatic, but I had no idea what would be waiting for us at the Swanson house and no part of my brain could convince me it'd be good.

****

It took us five minutes to walk back up the hill to Indie's place. We didn't talk the entire way, but I read Libby a couple of times. She was petrified, her skin so pale it was almost gray. She clenched and unclenched her fingers as she puffed her way up the driveway and then I thought she'd actually stopped breathing for a second when we reached Micah's car. We ducked behind it, peeking into the windows. It was unlocked, but the keys weren't in the ignition. It looked as though they'd parked with the intention of only being a minute. That had been the intention, so why the hell was his car still there?

Libby nudged me and pointed to the front door then raised her hand in question.

I pinched my nose as I thought, unsure what to do. Libby's idea of walking through the front door seemed ridiculous. I couldn't shake the foreboding in my stomach.

"Let's try around the back first," I whispered.

Libby nodded and we scurried around the side of the three-car garage, looking for an entrance. We found a gate and lucky for us, it was unlocked. We snuck through and padded our way down the path until we reached the pool house. Peeking our heads out, we quickly scanned the pool area and then peered through the glass doors leading into the main living rooms.

We ducked back into hiding and leaned our heads against the wall.

"This is ridiculous. Who do we think we are, spies or

something?" Libby tittered with nervous giggles. I couldn't help a small grin.

"We need to get into the house."

"There's a laundry room around the corner." Libby pointed. "Carter took me past it last time we were here. It's a back way to the upstairs bedrooms."

"I guess that's a good place to start."

I followed Libby's lead and soon found myself outside the laundry room door. To our surprise it was also unlocked. Had these people not heard of security before?

We crept in and closed the door softly, just as my cell phone started singing "Kiss You." I scrambled for it, turning it off before I could even check who was calling me. I turned to Libby with an apologetic wince as we listened for noises in the house. After a minute of silence, we found the courage to sneak out of the laundry and work our way upstairs. I didn't know what compelled us to start with the upstairs—most likely it was the fact that the stairs were right there—but I was glad we did. Because behind the first door we found Micah...bound and bleeding.

twenty-seven

"Micah," Libby choked out as she tripped into the room. His head shot up, his eyes wide and vehement. Blood had dripped from the laceration on his forehead, marking his face with dark, red smears. It had dried and caked into his short black hair. If his limbs hadn't been secured to the arms and legs of an office chair with coarse rope, he could have been mistaken for a madman killer.

Libby went to work on freeing his feet, while I gently pulled his gag free. "Micah, what happened?" I whispered.

With a grimace he licked his lips, his mouth sore

from the gag. "Have you got Indie?"

"No, where is she?" I wrestled with the ropes around his wrists, finally pulling one free. He shook the rope off and tenderly checked out his wounded head. He looked groggy and slow. Surely that blow to the head must have knocked him out. I wondered how bad his concussion was.

"We need to get to her." His dark eyes flamed. I focused on undoing the tight knot binding his other wrist.

"Tell us what happened." Libby pulled the ropes free of his feet and sat back.

"We were in the office, about to download the files." Micah pointed at the big mahogany desk on the other side of the room. A laptop was open. The screen danced with rainbow swirls, indicating the computer had been open a while. "Where's the memory stick?"

Micah winced. "Indie must have it. She was just finding the files when I blacked out." Micah touched the back of his head. I peered over his shoulder to see a second wound. "I didn't even hear Liam come into the room. When I came to, I was tied to this chair. Indie was screaming at him to let me go. Liam was rabid. Going ballistic. Screaming at Indie that she was a cheating whore. He grabbed her by the hair and threw her toward the door." Micah's face bunched as he struggled with the words. "I tried to wrestle free and get to her, but then Liam smacked me over the head again." He closed his eyes, looking sick as he fingered the cut on his forehead. "Do you think she's okay?"

"We'll find her, Micah. It'll be okay." I finally tugged the knot free and Micah wriggled out of his bindings, rubbing his chafed wrists. He lurched tall and made an attempt for the door. Two steps in, his legs turned to Jell-O and he had to catch himself against the wall.

Libby and I rushed to his side, propping his arms over our shoulders.

"Damn it," he mumbled. "My head's spinning, man."

"What did he hit you with?"

"I didn't see. Something hard and metal."

I swallowed, praying it wasn't the butt of a gun...or a tire iron. The Burbank newspaper article flashed through my brain.

"Whatever he hit you with was nasty, Micah. You've probably got a concussion," Libby said and then looked at me. "We need to get him to the hospital."

"Not without Indie."

"But Micah—"

"We're not leaving without her." His languid voice was still firm.

"He's right." I shot a look at Libby. "We can't leave Indie behind."

Libby knew I was right, but she was scared...and she had every right to be. Big, strong Micah was a mess and we'd practically have to carry him out of there.

I steadied him against me as we made our way out the door and down the hallway.

"Where do you think she'd be?" I whispered.

Micah methodically took in his surroundings, obviously scrambling for recall. He winced, annoyed that things were blank. "We came up the stairs and went straight to the office," he muttered as he looked down the hallway. "Let's try down here first." He pointed ahead and we struggled our way forward.

"Should we just try every room?" I glanced at Libby.

"I guess so." She made a face, looking as uncertain as I felt.

Leaning away from Micah, I checked the first door I came up to, my nerves rattling against each other as I eased the door open. The room looked tidy and untouched. I quickly shut the door and moved onto the next. It was slow progress with having to drag Micah along with us. I was tempted to suggest he wait for us in the hall, but I knew that would never fly.

We reached the grand central staircase and I toyed with the idea of voicing my suggestion. Micah could wait at the top of the stairs. As soon as we had Indie, we'd collect him and make a beeline for the door. Better yet, he could work his way down the stairs while he was waiting for us. I opened my mouth to suggest that, but then heard a muffled scream. We all did. Our bodies pinged tight as we listened.

Come on, scream again.

Although the noise was one of distress, I begged for a repeat. Surely it was Indie. Any noise she made would help us find her.

"That way," Micah whispered, tipping his head.

Following his gaze, Libby and I walked him down the hallway, listening for another scream. We got lucky, if you can call it that, a minute later when we heard a sharp crack and then a wail.

"In there." Micah's voice was like steel as he pointed to the door at the end of the hallway.

We hustled towards it and I was sure my gut was going to drop out the bottom of my pants by the time I got there. Another crack and this time a whimper.

"You know I don't like doing this, Indie, but you leave me no choice. I expect you to be loyal!" Liam's voice was pulled tight, like a string that was about to snap. "Now tell me what you were doing here with Micah!"

Silence.

"You tell me, Indie, or things are going to get really ugly." His menacing tremor made me want to puke.

I didn't want to open the door and see, but I had to. My fingers were clammy as they wrapped around the knob and I eased the door open.

Poor Indie was on the bed, her wrists tied to the slats of the headboard. She'd been stripped to her underwear and her thighs and torso were covered in red welts from Liam's belt. Her eyes were round with fear, but I didn't miss the acceptance either. She'd endured this before and I wanted to rip Liam's heart out. Looking at Micah's shocked expression, I wasn't the only one.

Liam's eyes were blazing as he raised his belt and

before I could think about it, I yelled, "Liam, stop!"

He froze mid-action, his eyes clearing as if coming out of a haze. His usual mask was not in place, so his malice was there for all of us to see. Libby shrank back from it, while Micah lurched forward.

"You asshole. I'm gonna kill you!" His lunge fell short as Jell-O legs kicked in again. Liam stepped toward him, whipping the belt in his hands. Micah caught it and tore it from his grasp as he fell to his knees. Liam's dark expression rippled with fear. He was taken aback by Micah's strength in spite of his wounded state.

Liam's gaze shot past me as if he were looking for someone. The foreboding that shadowed his expression told me that the person he was hoping would burst through the door to help him wasn't here.

That one look gave me the confidence I needed to step further into the room and reach for Micah.

"Libby, untie Indie."

She jumped to do my bidding, rushing to the bed and keeping her eyes away from Liam. Her hands were trembling as she reached for the ropes.

"She's mine. Don't touch her." Liam's black voice made Libby pause.

"Don't listen to him, Libby," I quickly said.

Liam smothered me with his molten gaze. I tried not to let it unnerve me as I helped Micah stand. He was wrapping the belt around his knuckles, looking ready to smash it into Liam's face.

"Stay calm." I squeezed Micah's elbow before

looking back to Libby. She was still standing by the bed with her arms by her sides, locked in place by Liam's pulsing wrath. "It's okay, Libby. Set Indie free, Liam's not going to touch you."

His eyes shot back to mine, flinching at my confidence.

"You're going to pay for this, Caitlyn. You're making a really big mistake."

I swallowed, fear vibrating up my limbs. "I'm not afraid of you, Liam." Total lie, but I hoped that it would sound convincing enough for him to shed another layer.

He spun away before I could read more, snatching something off the nightstand.

"Liam, no!" Indie sobbed as he turned, aiming a gun straight at me.

I swallowed, taking a step back before I could stop myself.

His eyes grew bright with a powerful smirk.

"You don't want to do this, Liam."

"Yes, I do." His white teeth flashed and he pulled the trigger.

twenty-eight

The shot exploded across the room. Libby and Indie screamed, while Micah let out a wail and fell to the floor beside me, clutching his thigh.

Shit!

I dropped to my knees, quickly assessing Micah's leg. Yanking his hands away, I pulled at the torn fabric and nearly fainted with relief when I saw the bullet had only grazed Micah's leg. The cut looked painful, but it was clear that it was only that, a deep cut. I resisted the urge to search for the bullet that was probably embedded in the armchair behind us.

"You okay?"

Micah nodded, sweat beading his brow as he tried to control his breathing.

I whipped off my light sweater and pressed it against the wound. "Keep pressure on it, we'll get you to the hospital soon."

Indie's sobs filled the room.

"Shut up!" Liam screamed at her. "Don't you cry for him, you cheating whore!" With the back of his hand, he clipped her cheek, dulling her cries.

Libby looked ready to pass out, her white skin stained with tears. I wanted to join the girls, dissolve into a puddle of tears on the floor, but I couldn't. I was the only one capable of handling the situation.

Man, I so didn't want to. I wanted Eric to bust through the door and rescue me. I cursed myself for turning off my phone. What if it'd been him calling?

Closing my eyes, I willed myself not to fall apart. Liam was stronger than me, not to mention he had a gun trained at my head. The only power I could use against him was my ability to see through whatever veneer he had in place.

Could I do it? Could I peel back enough layers to say the right thing and get us out of this? Did I have the guts to not press my lips together and back away like I always did?

Probably not.

But I had to try.

Standing on shaking legs, I raised my hands and took a step toward Liam.

I couldn't talk at first, couldn't make a sound squeeze past the iceberg in my throat. Finally I licked my lips. "Give me the gun, Liam."

"Stay back!" He pointed the pistol at my face.

"Please, Liam" I reached out my hand. "You don't want to do this."

"You don't know shit about me." Most would discern that his voice was quaking with rage, but I saw fear...more than fear. I could taste it. Something deeper, greater, was driving Liam to do this. I was still unsure if it would push him to put a bullet through my brain, but I couldn't back out now. I kept staring at him, willing another layer to fall away, and it did. I saw the guilt and shame and then past that, as another layer fell away, the hurt, the abandonment...the desperation.

A pity for him began to stir within and I was sure my expression folded to match it. "You don't want to kill me, Liam. I know you don't."

His eyes flashed, the shame and guilt pressing forward, followed swiftly by self-loathing, and suddenly I knew. It all came clear as I studied his transparent expression.

"You've seen someone die before, haven't you? Watched the life leak out of their eyes."

"Shut up!" The gun shook in his hands, his blue eyes wild.

"The smell of the blood as it poured from his head. The whisper of his last breath."

"Shut the hell up! I will shoot you!" he screamed.

"You want to go through that again? You want to be responsible for someone else's death?"

He blanched, the gun trembling in his hand. "It wasn't me!"

"Yes it was, Liam. You hit that man when you were trying to steal his car, didn't you? Smashed him on the head with a tire iron and then you ran."

Liam's lips pinched tight as all his emotions swirled together like a tornado. His voice was quaking as he yelled, "He was threatening my brother. He had a gun to his head. He was going to kill him. I had no choice!"

I so needed to calm things down. Liam's finger was still on the trigger and if the gun accidentally went off, I was dead.

"I get that. You were protecting your brother."

"Mason was the one who finished him off." Liam licked his lips, glancing at Indie as if seeking her approval somehow. He didn't want her looking at him like he was a murderer. "I didn't want to." His lips wobbled. "It wasn't my idea, but Mason said we had to or the guy would ID us and we'd get arrested. I can't go to jail."

"You don't have to go to jail." Liam spun back around to face me. "You were just doing what you were told. That makes sense. You love your brother. He's all you've got, right?"

Liam nodded, the relief starting to spread. The gun was still aimed at me, but at least Liam's hands had stopped shaking. I inched a little closer to him.

"I know you're a good person, Liam."

LIE!

"You've just been doing what you were told. I know you don't want to hurt Indie or anybody else. But it's all you've ever known, isn't it?"

I had no idea where that line of thinking came from, but I suddenly saw it—a flash of a little boy cowering in the corner. The sick fear on his pasty white face, his bright blue eyes round with terror.

"Shut up." Liam closed his eyes.

"Who used to beat you, Liam? Was it your dad?"

He didn't want to answer me, but couldn't help a small head shake.

"Your mom," I said it softly.

"Get out of my head," he whispered through clenched teeth.

"You hated her, didn't you? You were pleased when she died. You were free to live however you wanted."

Liam's lips pinched together. His eyes were open again, but he wouldn't look at me. "You and Mason got to live the life you deserved, but then it all fell apart, didn't it? Mason killed...again...trying to protect you."

"He didn't kill her! She fell down the stairs! It was an accident. If she hadn't been trying to chase us, she wouldn't have tripped."

"It wasn't your fault."

"No! Even the cops said that." His chin rose a little. He felt justified, but then that guilt crested over him once more.

"But the man, the innocent man. What do you think the cops would say about him?" I kept my voice as soft and calm as I could. In all honesty, I didn't know how I was doing it.

Liam's eyebrows dipped together, his lips trembling as he drew in a ragged breath.

"If you shoot me now, what will they say about it?"

His nostrils flared.

"You won't get away with it this time...unless you plan on killing all of us. How will you hide the evidence this time? Where will you run? How will you live? Start up another cheating ring, get the rich kids to finance your life again?"

"You don't know shit!" The words jerked out of his mouth. "You rich bitches with your charmed life. You have no idea what it's like. We did what we had to. We've never had the luxury of choice!"

"I know that Mason's been making all the decisions for you guys. You don't want to be this way...and you don't have to, Liam. You have a choice." I swallowed, praying this would work. I didn't know how much longer I could keep going with this conversation. His gun hadn't dipped or wavered once. Emotionally, he was at the point of breaking, but could I do it? I stepped toward him; the barrel of the gun was now only two inches from my face. "You can shoot me. You can watch my blood splatter across the room."

He flinched.

"And then you'll need to kill Micah." I pointed to the

floor. "And Libby." I pointed across the room. "And Indie," I whispered her name, knowing it would tug at his heartstrings. He loved her. That much was clear. It was a warped love, but it was still real.

"Do you want see the life leak out of her beautiful eyes? Do you want to see blood matting her hair? You'll have to carry her limp body out of here. You won't just want to leave her, will you?"

Liam couldn't take his eyes off Indie. His gaze traveled the length of her body, his eyes welling with tears.

"Don't be responsible for any more deaths, Liam. It's time to become the person you want to be. Mason can't control you anymore."

The air went still around us. I had nothing left to say, no more words to win him over. I'd seen Liam down to his core. He was a gaping wound to my eyes and I had nothing left to heal it.

The wait was excruciating. I couldn't take my eyes off Liam as I monitored his emotions. He couldn't take his eyes off Indie. She kept her gaze steady, her expression tender. She didn't feel any warmth or love toward him, but she was smart enough to put on a show.

Finally, the gun dipped. I wanted to cry with relief as I stepped forward and gently unhooked it from his hand. Shame, guilt, longing, agony were pulsing from Liam's face. "I'm sorry," he whispered to his girlfriend.

She shook her head, her eyes glistening with tears.

I nodded at Libby to untie Indie. I wasn't sure how

long the miracle would last.

"Caity," Micah said. "The gun."

I was about to frown and ask why, but I read his expression and there was nothing sinister within it. He was still pissed at Liam and he wanted to kill him, but I saw honor outweigh that emotion, so I slid the gun across the floor. Micah caught it in his hand and unloaded it, making sure to empty the bullet from the chamber as well. He gave Liam a molten glare as he pocketed the bullets and tucked the gun into his jeans.

Liam stumbled back on wobbly legs and fell into a chair. Dropping his head into his hands, he let out a hiccuping wail then began sobbing like a little kid.

I wasn't quite sure what to do. My first instinct was to comfort him, but that was stupid. I needed to get Micah and Indie to the hospital. Libby wrestled with the last of the ropes. Indie eased off the bed, wincing in pain. Reaching for her dress, she pulled it on, biting her lips against a wail.

"Let's go," she mouthed, her eyes still rich with fear.

I was obviously missing something.

twenty-nine

I raced to Micah and helped him up. He leaned against me as we hobbled out of the room. Indie closed the door behind us and came around the other side of Micah.

"I'm sorry." She clung to his side. "I'm sorry."

He kissed the top of her head and tenderly squeezed her shoulder. "It's okay. I'm fine."

"We have to get out of here." Indie's quivering voice pushed us down the hallway. "He does this sometimes. Falls apart, and when he revives, it's...it's terrifying." She shook her head and whispered, "Mason," then walked forward before I had a chance to ask her what she meant.

We got to the top of the stairs and were about to descend when Indie pulled us to a stop. "The memory stick." She yanked it out of her dress pocket, rubbing her thumb over the smooth plastic.

"What? Are you insane? You told us we had to get out of here," Libby whisper-barked. "What about Mason? You just said his name, it must be important."

"Exactly. Mason. We need some kind of insurance...against both of them. They're petrified of going to prison. If we have this evidence, it'll protect us," Indie whispered urgently.

"I want to get out of here. We have to get Micah to the hospital." Libby argued back, pointing at our bleeding friend.

Indie's face crumpled, tears spilling from her eyes. After a quick read, I saw everyone was on the edge of losing it. I snatched the stick off Indie before I could think better of it.

"You guys go. I'll get the files and meet you at the hospital."

"What? No. We have to stay together." Micah shook his head and winced.

"I'll be fine." I touched his arm. "You, on the other hand, look like shit, so would you please just get out of here?" I turned to Libby. "You drive Micah's car. Mine's still at the beach. I'll be five minutes behind you."

They all stood still at the top of the stairs, hesitating.

"Go, you guys!" I nudged Libby to turn around. She

reluctantly trotted down the stairs and I turned my pointed gaze to Indie. "Take care of him."

Indie nodded. "The files are in a folder marked Business. Just grab the whole thing."

"Okay." I gripped the stick in my hand and took off toward the office, hoping Liam would remain a sobbing mess in his room and hoping that Indie, Libby and Micah would make it out of the house without Mason showing up.

The front door slammed and I breathed a sigh of relief as I nudged the office door open with my shoulder. The stick nearly fell out of my hands as I sped to the computer and tried to jam it into the USB drive. Bringing the screen to life, I quickly found the folder Indie was talking about and dragged it onto the memory stick icon. I tapped my finger as I impatiently waited for the blue line to inch across the screen. The files were copying at a snail's pace!

The massive painted portrait of Indie and Maverick Swanson stared at me as I drummed my fingers on the desk. The opulent office was unnerving for some reason. I knew it had nothing to do with the decor and everything to do with the fact that I was fully freaking out. What if Liam came out of his room? What if he had another gun stashed in the house somewhere?

I was near sweating blood as my imagination took flight...and then my insides spasmed as I heard a voice holler up the stairs.

"Liam!" The front door slammed shut. "Liam! Where

are you, man?"

My head spun as I tried to control my erratic breathing.

Mason.

It had to be.

The blue line inched across the screen. The copy was sixty percent through. Why the hell was it taking so long?

"Liam! You home?"

The voice came up the stairs. I held my breath as I listened for footsteps, willing them *not* to turn left toward me. My heart was thrumming out an uneven rhythm as I watched the door, convinced it would open any second and I'd be faced with Liam's murdering brother. I wished I could remember what he looked like. My brain scrambled for the grainy image of his face, but I couldn't find it.

I thought I heard footsteps moving away from me and turned back to the computer just as it dinged, indicating the end of the download. I yanked the stick free and shoved it into my pocket.

With my breathing on hold, I crept toward the door and eased it open. It took what felt like an eternity to find the guts to peek into the hallway, but I finally forced my head out. It was clear. Sucking in a breath, I slowly pulled the door wide enough to squeeze through, praying it wouldn't creak. I was just turning for the back stairs Libby and I came up when I heard the shouting.

"You idiot! Where are they now?"

"I don't know, man," Liam wailed.

"Well, what were they doing here? What'd they want?"

"I just saw Indie and Micah and wanted to kill him...and punish her. I thought they were having an affair! My girl was cheating on me!"

"I don't give a shit about your girl, Liam. You're pathetic! What was Caitlyn doing here?"

"How do you know she was here?"

I heard a sharp slap. "Focus, Liam! What did she want?"

There was a long pause and I couldn't move...until I heard Liam gasp and shout, "The computer! Shit! The files!"

I bolted, nearly stumbling down the stairs as I made a beeline for the laundry room. I threw myself out of it, pushing open the fence and sprinting down the driveway. I didn't want to look back. I hoped they were still in the office, fussing over the computer.

Turning left, I took off down the street, willing my legs to move faster as I hurtled down the hill. My Mini was waiting for me, still looking out across the peaceful water. I scrambled for my keys, nearly ripping my jean pocket as I yanked them free. Fumbling them in my hands, I dropped them on the ground and scraped my knuckles as I collected them back up and shoved the key into the lock.

My insides were shuddering as my trembling fingers shoved the key into the ignition and turned.

Click. No rev, no life, no engine.

"What? No, no please." I gripped the wheel, near hysterical as I turned the key for a second time.

Again with the click.

Yanking my phone from my back pocket, I pressed the ON button and waited expectantly for my screen to come to life. Instead I got an empty battery symbol.

"Not now! Please! No!"

I threw the phone onto the passenger seat and thumped the wheel, resting my head against my hands. I wanted to dissolve into tears. My harrowing afternoon was catching up to me like a bullet train. I needed to get to the hospital. I needed to get away. I wanted Eric. I wanted to be able to talk to him and ask him to come and help me, but I couldn't. I was alone and the thought was terrifying.

Breaths punched out of me fast and erratic as I tried the key again, but to no avail. My car was dead.

A black car pulled up beside me, making me jerk. I glanced over at the driver who gave me a friendly smile as he slammed his door shut. He was in shorts and a T-shirt, obviously ready for an afternoon run in the sand. He wasn't a buff-looking gym guy, more of an athletic build, lean and muscly. It made me think of Eric, which just brought tears to my eyes. Reaching for my phone, I rubbed my thumb over the screen and tried it one more time. It was an idiot move. I knew the battery was dead, but I was desperate.

Tears glistened in my eyes as I laid the phone back

down and pushed the door open. I guessed my only other option was to walk.

"Uh, excuse me?" The jogger looked ready to jump down to the sand and start his run. "Are you all right?"

I gave him a glum smile. "Car trouble." I shrugged.

"Can I help at all?" He stepped toward me, his blue gaze friendly and warm. "I have a phone in my car if you want to call someone or I can take a look if you want me to." He grinned. "I'm not a mechanic or anything, but I know a few things."

I couldn't help smiling at his sweet expression. I was about to nod, open my door and pop the hood. I was about to let the guy help me, but then I saw the flash. I'd been too caught up in my angst to notice it at first. But it was there.

I ripped off his mask and saw the rancor, the intent to kill.

The blue eyes suddenly looked familiar.

Oh, shit! I was staring at Liam's brother, Mason.

thirty

My eyes bulged before I could stop them and Mason must have noticed, because he grabbed my wrist as I started to step back.

His grip was strong and unrelenting. He yanked me close.

So close I could feel his breath on my face.

"Give me the memory stick," he whispered.

As much as it terrified me, I looked into his eyes, trying to peel back layers and get to his core like I did with Liam. Maybe I could unnerve him as well.

But all I saw was evil. This guy was going to hurt me and he was going to enjoy doing it.

"I don't know what you're talking about." My voice pitched.

His grip tightened. "I know you took something from my computer and I want it back."

I shook my head.

His free hand clamped around the back of my neck, painfully digging into my flesh. His blue eyes flashed bright and angry. "I warned you that if you didn't back off, I'd introduce you to a new kind of pain. I wasn't kidding."

Shit. Shit, he really wasn't.

My chin trembled as I fought the tears.

"Give me the memory stick and I'll let you off easy."

I winced as his fingers dug in. I wanted to give in. I wanted to rip the stick from my pocket and place it in his hands, but I couldn't. Not after Indie had been beaten and Micah had been shot. How could I let them suffer and then just ruin it all by giving into my fear?

I pressed my lips together and shook my head.

"You're making a mistake, Caitlyn."

His malicious grin made my flight reflex kick in big time. My knee came up, just the way it used to when Toby was being a jackass and trying to wrestle with me. Seth taught me how to do it. I didn't connect as soundly as I wanted to, but it was enough to make Mason buckle and loosen his grip.

I turned and sprinted. Why I chose the sand, I would never know. I should have run up the street, raced for someone's house and banged on the door, but no—I chose the lumpy, uneven surface to make my escape on.

Terror had turned my brain to putty. I pumped my arms and begged my legs to keep moving. My ankle turned in the soft sand, but I managed to collect myself before falling. Taking a quick peek over my shoulder, I saw Mason gaining on me. Damn, he was fast.

I wailed as I scrambled away from him and tried to find a steady rhythm again, but before I could really get started, his arms were around my waist and he pulled me to the ground. I landed with a thud, sand shooting up my nose and into my mouth. I spat it out as Mason flipped me over and drove a punch into my left cheek.

Pain shot through my head and I cried out.

"You stubborn bitch. Give me that damn stick!"

His hand came around my throat, his thumb pinching into the side of my neck as he pressed his weight down on me. My air supply cut off immediately and the edges of my vision turned blurry as Mason's free hand roamed my body, hunting for the memory stick. I wriggled beneath him, trying to buck him off, but my limbs were growing weaker by the second.

As my world grew black, I was faced with the reality that my life was about to end. Oddly enough, my first thought was that I had let the strange, homeless man down. He never should have picked me. Regret made me want to fight back, but it was too late. I didn't have the energy for fight or flight.

I was done.

And then everything changed.

Mason's weight lifted off me in an instance. My body spasmed with coughs as I rolled to my side and fought for air. Peeking my eyes open, I spotted the reason for my sudden release.

Eric.

He had thrown Mason off me and was now diving after him, pushing him to the ground and pummelling him with his rage-infused fists.

Mason fought back, slapping at Eric and trying to get a punch in, but it was pointless, Eric was in full control and he wasn't giving Mason an inch.

"Eric." I rasped, holding my aching throat. "Eric, stop! You'll kill him!"

I didn't want Eric saddled with a murder charge.

I crawled across the sand with the intent of pulling Eric off Mason, but he had obviously heard my weak warning.

He grabbed Mason's shirt and yanked him up. Blood was streaming from the lean guy's face, his nose looked crooked and his blue eyes were glazed. He seemed small and pathetic next to Eric. I peeled off his mask as Eric gripped him with shaking limbs that were only just in control. He was terrified of my Hercules... and he should be.

I didn't need to read Eric to see his rage. It was pulsing out of him as he whispered between clenched teeth, "If you ever hurt my girl again, I'm going to kill you."

With his mask off, I saw straight through Mason's nonplussed glare. Eric shoved him away. Mason stumbled to the ground and glanced at me one last time before scrambling across the sand and racing back to his car.

"He believed you."

"That's because I meant it."

I tried not to let Eric's tight voice unnerve me as I stood from the sand on shaky legs, watching Mason trip and stumble to his car. My gaze then drifted to Eric who was turning toward me, his expression stone cold.

I didn't know what to say to him. He looked pissed. Crossing my arms, I dropped my gaze to the sand, breathing through my nose in an attempt to rein in my spasming stomach. Sobs were itching to break free. I blinked at tears and finally looked back up at him.

His expression had softened a little. "Come here," he whispered.

I gratefully stepped forward, hoping for a warm embrace. Instead he held me at arm's length, inspecting my neck. His brow creased with concern as he gently ran his thumb over my tender flesh. His expression buckled as he touched my bruised cheek. "You promised me you'd stay out of trouble."

"I had to go and help Micah and Indie, I couldn't just leave them."

He scowled.

"I called you. You didn't answer," I ended with a mumble.

"Which is why I called you back as soon as I heard your message. And what do you do?" He threw his hands up. "You hung up on me."

I was beginning to think that pissed was an understatement. He looked livid. I couldn't help reading him and saw that it was just fear talking, but it didn't make any difference. His fear was being manifested as anger and there wasn't much I could do about it.

"I didn't want anyone to hear the phone," I muttered, knowing instantly it was the wrong thing to say. Eric's pointed glare screamed the obvious. I had snuck into a situation that in my gut I knew was dangerous. I should have stepped outside and taken the call...or at least called him back. I should have waited for him.

But it was too late. I couldn't change the past.

"I'm sorry," I whispered.

He shook his head and looked away, making the silence between us awkward and deafening.

Finally, I sighed and rubbed my forehead. "Can you drive me to the hospital, please? I want to check up on Micah."

Eric's concerned gaze shot to me. "Is he okay?"

"He got..." I swallowed, hating the truth and the fact that I had to tell it. "Shot." The word barely made it out of my mouth. It was so small and tiny, but Eric still heard it. His skin blanched, his usually calm gaze going wild for a moment.

"Who had the gun?"

"Liam. I...I managed to talk it out of his hands. We were safe. It was okay."

"Safe?" Eric scoffed. "Yeah, sounds really safe, Caitlyn!" He spun away and started walking for his car.

"Please don't be mad with me." I chased after him, grabbing his arm.

He jerked to a stop and glared down at me. His stance was intimidating and flaring with anger, but his expression was rippling with anguish.

"You don't get it." He shook his head. "You have no idea how much I've come to care for you in such a short space of time. Do you have any idea how much that freaks the hell out of me?" He ran a hand through his hair, licking his bottom lip. He breathed a couple of times, obviously wrestling with his surging emotions, trying to bring them into check. "I nearly lost you today. If I'd been five minutes later, Caity." His hazel eyes caught me and I couldn't look away. I just had to stare into his troubled gaze. Tears glistened in my eyes as he kept going. "What if I hadn't cleared your message right away? What if I hadn't seen Stella as I drove past school and demanded to know where Indie's house was? What if she hadn't told me? What if I hadn't seen you running for your life along the beach? What if I'd driven here another way?"

"But you didn't." I interrupted before he could come up with another what if. They were killing me.

He shook his head. "I don't think you appreciate how close you came to dying today." His annoyed look returned as he glanced over his shoulder at our cars. "Come on, I'll take you to the hospital."

He didn't reach for my hand, just strode across the sand ahead of me. I crossed my arms and scurried after him, feeling like I'd just run a marathon and crossed the line with nothing to show for it. I gripped my arms in an attempt to stop the shaking and ward off the feeling of desolation.

thirty-one

Eric fixed my car in silence. I hovered behind him as he plugged something back in, then wiped his hands on his butt and closed the hood.

"He disconnected your spark plugs."

"How do you know stuff about cars?"

Eric squinted against the sun, avoiding eye contact. "I don't know that much. Gramps just taught me a few basics."

"Do you think Mason disabled it before coming up to the house?"

"That's my guess. He obviously recognized your car and planned to catch you here." Eric swallowed and swiped a hand under his nose. With a sniff, he flicked his head toward his car. "I'll follow you to the hospital."

"Okay." I wanted to reach out and touch him, make some kind of connection, but he strode away before I could. Fighting tears, I started the engine and backed out of the small parking lot.

Fifteen minutes later we were pulling into the nearest hospital. Eric took my hand as we walked toward the emergency room, but there was no warmth in his touch. I hated it. He was there, but he wasn't, and all I wanted to do was fall into his arms and cry like a little girl who'd scraped her knee.

In spite of the fact I'd just survived death and still had protective evidence in my pocket, I felt like my world was about to shatter into a thousand tiny pieces. And it had nothing to do with Indie or Liam, and everything to do with the guy holding my hand, but not looking at me.

Eric had to ask three different nurses before we found the others. Libby was on the phone in tears. I picked up two sentences of her conversation and realized she was talking to her mom. I gave her a weak smile, which she returned before pointing to a blue pulled curtain to my right.

I crept toward it and was about to pull it back when Indie's willowy voice stopped me.

"Are you sure you're going to be okay?"

"I'll be fine. It's just a scratch." I peeked around the curtain and saw Micah gather her fingers into his. His head was neatly bandaged and I spied a white patch of gauze through his ripped jeans.

Micah's large, dark thumb rubbed over Indie's white hand. The contrast of their skin was stunning next to each other. They were a beautiful couple. I knew most would think it too soon to assume such a thing, but I could see behind their masks and in their hearts they already belonged together. Micah confirmed my thinking when a soft smile pushed at his lips. "You don't have to be afraid anymore, Indie. I won't let Liam near you again." He ran his finger along her hairline, freeing her face from a few loose strands.

She gave him a shaky grin. "I know." Then she nibbled her lip, looking nervous. "Thank you for being there for me."

"I always have."

Her smile grew. "I know."

"I should have stepped up sooner." His lips pinched into a tight line of regret.

"I should have let you." She squeezed his hand. "I used to daydream that you would come and rescue me...and you'd carry me away to safety." Their eyes locked in an intense gaze and her pale orbs were practically glowing when she whispered, "I still remember the day you walked into school for the first time. You were so tall and strong and intimidating, but there was something about you. You gave me this small smile. Not on your lips, it was in your eyes and I knew right away."

"Knew what?"

She shrugged, her face blooming with color. "That I was going to fall in love with you."

His white teeth appeared, unable to hide behind the beaming grin on his face. "Me too." He chuckled. "I never believed in love at first sight. Thought it was bullshit...until the day I saw you."

She reached for his face, placing her small white hand on his cheek and running her thumb over his lips. I held my breath, unable to look away as she leaned forward and gave him the sweetest kiss I'd ever seen. Blinking at tears, I pulled back and turned to face Eric. But he wasn't behind me. He had moved to stand by Libby who was now off the phone and explaining everything to him in a flurry of hand movements. His expression was dark yet filled with concern.

I stepped toward them to hear what Libby was saying.

"So, Mom's calling the police and Micah's parents for me, and they're gonna meet us here." Libby sniffed. I whipped off her mask and saw a surprising strength beneath the surface. In spite of her quivers and the wobble in her voice, she was determined to bring the Donovan boys to justice.

Eric nodded at her. "Do you think the files will be enough?"

"Indie told me on the way here that there are more than just files in that folder. It's got photos of some things they've done to us." Libby blinked. "Video footage of one of my friends getting beaten and another girl who was forced to..." she swallowed. "They recorded it. They used it to keep them in line and warn the rest of us." She looked to the ground, ashamed.

I touched Libby's shoulder. "You have nothing to be ashamed of. You were the victim here. It's guys like Liam and Mason and Carter who have to go down for this." Libby looked at me, surprised that I'd read her so well. Eric shot me a look that told me we weren't seeing the same thing on Libby's face. I popped her mask back on and forced a smile. "You're brave and your actions today will put an end to this."

"I should have spoken out weeks ago. I could have saved Indie and others so much pain if I'd just had the courage to say something."

I squeezed her shoulder. "You had the courage to act today and it's not too late. Indie and Micah are..." I grinned. "They're gonna be fine. And so will everyone else." I dug the memory stick from my pocket and passed it to her.

She took it with a relieved smile. "I'm going to see Mr. Van der Belt tonight."

"Do you want me to come?" I hoped she'd say no. I didn't think I could cope.

"No, it's okay. Mom and Dad are both coming with me. I told her enough on the phone. She's a counsellor. She's good with handling this kind of thing." Libby looked to the floor.

"So all we need to figure out now is what to do with

Indie." I sighed.

"She can't go back home." Libby shook her head.

"Most definitely." Eric crossed his arms. I couldn't help thinking how sweet it was that Eric had stepped up, introduced himself to Libby, and slotted himself into the situation. His forthright behavior provided a sense of safety, even in spite of his terse tone. "We don't know if those guys will retaliate."

"They won't." I looked up at him. "You should have seen the look on his face after you threatened him. He was petrified, Eric."

"Threatened?" Libby frowned and, as if seeing me for the first time, her eyes went wide. "Did Liam hurt you? Did he find you in the house?"

"No." I bit my bottom lip. "I ran into Mason down by my car. Eric arrived just in time." I touched my throat.

"Oh my gosh." Libby's breaths went all quivery.

"It's okay, Libby. I'm all right, everything's fine."

"We shouldn't have left you." She touched her forehead, looking ready to break down.

"Libby." I shook her shoulder. "It's over. I'm fine and he's not going to touch me again. Mason Donovan might be a psycho, but he's just as scared as his brother of being caught. I think the Donovan boys have gone into hiding. We won't be seeing them again."

"You might think that, but you don't know that for sure." Eric's jaw clenched.

I turned from his anger and focused back on Libby. "Indie can come home with me."

"No way." Eric's voice was steely. "Your parents are in Hawaii. You're not going back to stay in an empty house."

"Indie needs to be somewhere that she feels safe. Staying with strangers is not going to provide that for her."

"Staying in an empty house with you isn't either."

I let out a frustrated sigh. "Fine, what would you have us do then?"

Shoving his hands in his pockets, he drew in what I could only assume was a calming breath. "Go and stay with someone?"

"Like you?"

"No, you're right about Indie staying with a strange guy. She's never even met me. And besides, I wouldn't willingly inflict my mother on anybody." He frowned. "I think you should call your brother."

My nose wrinkled before I could stop it. "He's still a stranger to Indie."

"With a family and wife and young kids who present no threat to her."

"I don't want to stay at his place."

"Call your sister then."

I made a face. "I'd rather deal with an irritated Seth in a pristine house than a clucking Layla in her chaos."

"Whatever. Just call one of them." He pulled out his phone and passed it to me. I hated the cold, indifferent expression on his face. Unfriendly Eric was back in town and I dreaded what that meant for me. I tentatively took the phone and walked away from them, reluctantly dialing Seth's number.

To say he was shocked by my revelation was an understatement. Much to his credit, he did listen without interrupting too many times and even agreed to let me take Indie home to my place. He'd bring Julia and the girls to stay with me until Mom and Dad got back.

Oh joy!

I hung up the phone battling a mixture of relief, exhaustion, and dread.

The dread part was winning and I stayed in my private corner for a second to gather myself. Seth agreed to come to my place, but on the condition that I called Mom and Dad. He also said Indie could stay with us as long as she needed, on the condition that she call her dad. She wouldn't want to. I knew it already and I shuddered at the thought of having to tell her.

But selfishly, the thing I was dreading most about my immediate future was facing Eric again. I had crossed a line, broken my promise to stay safe and I think it was the end of us. Something so sweet and amazing, which had only just begun, was about to end and there was nothing I could do about it.

thirty-two

The police were already chatting with Libby and Eric when I got off the phone with Seth. We were forced to stick around for another hour, answering copious questions. Poor Indie had to strip and have photos of her wounds taken. She asked me to sit in the room with her and I have to say, she was pretty damn tolerant throughout the process. Thankfully the police were merciful enough not to make us go down to the station, instead saying they'd be by with more questions if needed.

Eric walked Indie and I out to my car shortly after Micah's parents arrived. We walked to the car in somber silence. The day was far from over.

Eric followed us back to my place, but didn't stick around. Julia's car was already in the drive when I pulled up in my Mini. Eric didn't even get out of his car, just put down the window and told me he'd give me a call later. I waved goodbye in stunted silence, fighting off tears as if my life depended on it.

Indie gave me a sympathetic smile. "Your boyfriend?"

"I'm not sure." I shrugged, my eyes glistening. Her eyes welled up and soon both our lips were wobbling. I stepped around the car and drew her into my arms, careful not to squeeze her too tight. We spent the next few minutes softly crying into each other's shoulders.

Seth pulled up and ushered us inside. He was gentle and sweet with Indie, using his calm, fatherly voice. Julia, a pure-gold lady, hugged us both tightly, making Indie yelp. She took one peek down the back of Indie's dress and ordered her up to the bath. The anguished look she shot me was telling. She would care for Indie as if she were her own daughter; that much was obvious. She'd already set up a spare mattress on the floor in my room, assuming Indie would want the company throughout the night.

My nieces, Kimber and Serena, were on their best behavior, playing quietly in the sunken lounge and only sneaking curious peeks occasionally.

Julia's bath thing worked; Indie sat down to dinner looking refreshed and a touch less fragile. Neither of us could eat much with the dreaded phone calls impending, plus our meal was interrupted by the police.

Seth held my hand and Julia wrapped her arm around Indie as we both cried our way through more details. Behind Indie's mask was a plethora of emotions. I didn't miss the guilt. A part of her still felt bound to Liam and she was ashamed to fink on him. That emotion kept bouncing off a deep relief, which then bounced off regret and beneath those layers, I saw the lost child she was fighting not to be. Her mother left her when they were young and her father had always been a busy man. She and Maverick had been raised by nannies and housekeepers. It was hardly a stable environment and probably explained why she'd fallen for Liam's charms and then found herself trapped within his dark snare.

I squeezed Seth's hand, flooded with gratitude. In spite of being the young squirt and often feeling disconnected from them, I came from a family who loved me and would drop everything to help me.

Seth made me call Mom and Dad as soon as the police left. I chose to speak to Dad first. He always coped with bad news better than Mom. It took a lot of convincing, and in the end it was Seth who insisted they not cut their trip short. I hung up feeling shattered and on the verge of collapse, but we still had Indie's call to go.

"Just do it." I sat on the bed beside her, taking her hand. "As soon as you're done, we'll call Micah and you can tell him everything. I know talking to him makes you feel better."

I didn't actually know it. I assumed it, because talking to Eric always made me feel a million times better. I bit my lip, wondering if I'd ever get to talk to him again. I collected my charging phone and checked the screen as Indie dialed her dad. It was blank. No texts. No calls.

"Hey Dad, it's Indie." Her voice was soft and fragile. I rubbed her back. "I know you don't have long to talk, but I have to tell you something... No, actually, it's about Liam." Her voice disappeared, drowned by a waterfall of tears.

"Indie? What's wrong, honey?" I could hear his muffled voice through the phone. Indie covered her mouth with her hand, unable to say the words as her father continued to repeat her name, sounding more and more worried.

In the end, I gently took the phone from her grasp. "Hello, Mr. Swanson?"

"Who's this?"

"It's Caitlyn Davis, sir. I'm a friend of Indie's, from school."

"Okay, what the hell is going on, Caitlyn?" His voice was calm and firm. I looked to Indie, swallowed and began talking. I told him everything. It was the third time I'd done it that day so I was able to add in extra details where needed. It was probably my best retelling of the events yet. I knew it was brutal, but I didn't skip a thing, even the stuff about Liam punishing her. Wanting to end with something positive, I finished with how Indie was in love with Micah and what a good guy he was. Man, if I'd been Indie, I would have been dying, but she was too busy crying to really notice.

"She's safe, sir. The police are looking for Liam and Mason now. And she can stay with us as long as she needs."

The movie producer's voice was quaking when he replied, "Thank you, Caitlyn. Tell my daughter I'll be home by Wednesday."

"Okay."

"Has Maverick been told?"

"No, I don't think so."

"Please leave it that way. He's very protective of his sister and I want to be the one to tell him."

I glanced at Indie; her tears were finally ebbing as she mopped at her face with a thick wad of Kleenex. I pointed to the phone and she shook her head, so I finished up the call for her.

Dropping the phone onto the bed, I sunk down beside my friend.

"He's coming home."

"Really?" She looked confused. "He never leaves a project."

"Well, he's leaving this one for you." Her sweet smile was fractured and I knew she still had a long way to go, but at least she wasn't alone anymore. "Want to call Micah?" She nodded and reached for the phone.

I quietly left her to it. Sneaking into the hallway, I leaned against the door. The girls were in bed and I could hear Julia and Seth chatting in Seth's old room down the hall.

And once again the loneliness rounded over me. Sliding down to my butt, I clutched my legs and rested my chin on my knees. My mind wandered to the homeless stranger. I couldn't help wondering if he'd felt that way.

The sense of isolation was suffocating. The urge to get up and run was strong, but my legs were tired and my body was done for the day. My only choice was to face it, accept the new reality I'd been given and try not to die in the process.

Leaning my head back against the wood, I felt the tears rise once more and wondered how I possibly had any left. They weren't hiccuping sobs though. They were soft and silent, my soul mourning for one more loss I knew awaited me.

thirty-three

The next day at school was weird. People kept staring at me, no doubt checking out the shiner on my left cheek. Micah limped into school and a second wave of gossip surged through the student body. I saw faces, heard whispers. People knew something huge had gone down the day before.

I gripped my books to my chest as I made my way to class. Indie had chosen to stay home with Julia for the day. Her belt wounds were still really tender and she was too fragile to face anyone. Micah had promised to go see her after school.

Julia had offered me the day off too, but I was

restless and felt like school would be a good distraction.

Man, was I an idiot.

I still hadn't heard from Eric and even though I despised looking at a blank phone screen, I couldn't help bringing the device with me and checking it every two seconds. Another idiot move, because it remained blank. Eric was obviously still pissed.

I couldn't concentrate through Algebra. My mind was a splintered mess. People kept looking at me, wondering. The whispers as I passed from Algebra to English Lit grew with intensity.

Where was Liam?

Why was Indie not at school?

What had happened to the all-powerful Micah?

I sat with him in the back of class. We didn't talk, just gave each other knowing looks that said it all. I could see he wanted to get to Indie, and the only reason he came to school was to convince his parents that he was well enough for an after school date.

The vibe in the school grew with intensity as the day progressed and it wasn't until I walked into the cafeteria at lunchtime that it all came clear. I saw Libby sitting with her old friends. She looked worn and a little fragile, but her smile was genuine. She squeezed Andy's forearm before waving me over to the table. I approached slowly, glancing over my shoulder to see my old group of friends glaring at me. Chase's dark gaze was intense. I ripped off his mask and spotted the guilty fear, his regret. I whipped my eyes to Stella and saw the same thing.

Wait a second.

Turning back to Libby, I scanned her friends, whipping off masks as I went and I saw it—bright, sunny relief.

"No way." I slid into the seat beside Libby.

She nodded with a grin. "I was there for two hours last night. We went through all the files with Mr. Van der Belt. Everyone's name was on there. All the people who were paying for work to be done...all the students doing the work. The videos, the photos...they even had a target list."

"A target list?"

"Yeah, people they were keeping a special eye on— either to recruit or sell to...or eliminate." Her gaze fluttered to the table.

I sighed. "I was on the elimination list, wasn't I?"

She nodded.

"What did Mr. Van say?"

"He was really good about it. Told me he was going to deal with it discreetly."

I peeked over my shoulder at the defeated group around Stella. "Do you know how?"

Libby followed my gaze and shrugged. "Not sure exactly, but I'm guessing a bunch of those guys are going to be attending summer school."

I didn't know what brought it on, but giggles rushed so quickly up my system, they burst from my mouth— loud and clear. I covered my lips, my shoulders quivering with mirth...and then Libby joined me. Within a minute the two of us were a laughing, crying mess. I wrapped my arms around her chubby frame and clung tight.

She squeezed me back and for the first time in forever, I felt like I was hugging a true friend. One that didn't need me, one that didn't want to use me...one that just wanted to hang out with me exactly as I was.

thirty-four

Micah followed me home. I introduced him to Julia and Seth who eyed him with surprise, obviously both jolted by his towering persona. As I watched Indie shuffle into the room, I guessed I understood their feelings. They were a contrast in so many ways, but when he spun to face her and her eyes lit with that smile, it felt so right. He gathered her in his arms, whispering something soft and delicate in her ear. I turned away, wanting to give them some privacy. Julia kept gazing at them with a mushy look on her face. I couldn't help a grin.

"You guys can go hang out in my room if you want

or there's the back deck." I pointed down the hallway. It was hardly as nice as our large front deck, but it was private.

Micah nodded his thanks and walked Indie down the hall.

I turned back to Julia and chuckled at her.

"What?" She gently slapped my arm. "They are just all kinds of cute together."

"I know." I opened the fridge and grabbed a bottle of water. "I heard them talking yesterday. They're one of those love at first sight couples." I unscrewed the cap and took a swig of liquid before leaning against the bench. "So they have been pining for each other for months. Now they finally get to be together." I couldn't help a wistful sigh, wishing the same for me. A hard knot formed in my belly and I tried to get rid of it with a few gulps of water.

It didn't work.

Julia finished slicing up some apple for her girls, arranging it neatly on a plate and letting Seth steal a slice before walking it down to the sunken lounge. She came back, munching her own slice, before leaning against the counter and smiling at me.

"How about you, Caity? Any man in the picture?"

It took every ounce of willpower not to dissolve into a blubbering mess. My lips pinched tight and I forced a complacent smile. "I don't know." I shrugged. "He's pretty annoyed at me for getting into trouble yesterday and I'm...I'm not sure where we stand. He said he was going to call me, but..." I pulled out my phone. The screen was still blank. I slid my thumb over it, like I had a hundred times that day, just to check. But my message box was empty. Empty and ominous.

"Well, you should call him." Julia moved to the counter and started packing away apple remains.

"I'm scared if I do, it'll be the excuse he's been waiting for to break up with me."

"It's been less than twenty-four hours, would you relax?" Seth glanced up from his computer screen and received a solid glare from his wife. "What?"

"How did you ever manage to woo me?" She rolled her eyes.

He just grinned and winked, which set her cheeks blooming. I looked away with a scowl.

"It's not that Chase loser, is it?" Seth took a swig from his beer.

"No, we broke up." I scratched my forehead.

Man, that felt like a millennia ago. Thank God I didn't have to deal with him anymore.

"So, who's the new guy?" Julia rinsed out the dishcloth and wiped it over the chopping board.

I was starting to feel super uncomfortable having the conversation, especially with Seth sitting right there, but I shrugged and stupidly kept talking. "His name's Eric. He's a freshman at UCLA."

"Wait. Eric from next door?" Seth's brow furrowed as he placed his beer back on the counter. His blue eyes bore into mine. I swallowed. My brother's eyes narrowed. "So when his car was in our drive last weekend, he was actually here, wasn't he?"

Oh shit! Crap! Um...

"You know what." I cleared my throat. "I think Julia's right. I should go and find him. Talk this out." I looked to Julia, panic no doubt cresting over my features.

Her lips pressed together as she fought a giggle.

"Caitlyn."

I ignored Seth's firm tone as I yanked the keys from my pocket and made a beeline for the front door. I wasn't sure if I'd lose my nerve while driving to the UCLA campus, but it didn't matter. Anywhere but home with Seth was preferable in that moment.

Julia's laughter finally broke free as I reached the front door. "Chill out, Seth. She's not twelve. You remember what we were like when we first got together."

"That's what worries me."

Julia giggled again. "Honey, she's not your daughter, so you don't have to worry. In fact Kimber's only eight, so you don't have to worry about this kind of thing for a least another eight or nine years."

"Or twenty," Seth mumbled.

I grinned as I shut the door behind me.

When I spun around my smile disappeared. It was replaced with an open mouthed 'oh' that I couldn't seem to get rid of. It stayed in place until Eric reached the bottom of our front steps.

"Hey." He didn't smile, doing nothing to ease my

tattered nerves.

"Hi." I stood frozen on the landing.

He shoved one hand into his jean pocket while running the other through his dark locks. "We need to talk."

"Okay." I swallowed.

"Walk with me?" He held out his hand and I nervously took it. His grip was a little warmer and tighter than the day before, which was encouraging, but not enough to still my erratic heartbeat. Maybe it was the calm before the storm.

We walked the streets in silence, Eric keeping his gaze high and steady. I wanted to read him so bad and was tempted when I gazed up at his still expression. I started to peel off his mask a couple of times before catching myself. My willpower was crumbling by the second and I was about to give in when he started talking.

"The thing is, Caity. I um..." He stopped in the middle of the street, scratching his bottom lip. I stood beside him, anxiety making my head pound. Eventually he sighed and locked his gaze with mine. "I've been let down a lot by people I care about. I find it really hard to trust, you know?" He pursed his lips, struggling over the confession. "Dad walked out on me and Mom when I was five. He stuck around, sort of. Following up one broken promise after another...and then he just disappeared altogether. Stopped calling. Stopped trying." Eric sighed. "Then my stepdad came along and he was great. I really liked him, but Mom drove him nuts to the point where he couldn't cope anymore." He let out a disgusted snort. "After that it was a string of Mom's boyfriends, always trying so hard to be nice to me and the girls in an attempt to please my mom. As soon they got what they wanted from her, they'd vanish." His grin was hard and cynical, but eventually started to soften.

I wanted to reach for him, hold him, but was scared my touch would pull him out of his confession like trance. I held my ground, waiting.

"The only person who's been true to their word is Gramps...and you."

He touched my cheek, his expression finally the soft one reserved only for a select few.

"Me?" I frowned in confusion. "But I...I totally let you down."

"No, you didn't, Caity." His thumb caressed my cheekbone. "You called me, just like I asked you to. And if you hadn't, I never would have searched for Indie's house and I never would have seen you running for your life along the beach. I couldn't have been there for you if you hadn't called."

I glanced away from his sweet expression, feeling slightly undeserving of it. "I shouldn't have hung up on you."

He snickered. "Yeah, nearly broke my phone over that one." He cleared his throat. "But I understand why you did. I'm sorry I was so pissed yesterday. I was just scared." His voice nearly broke as he was talking, making me want to cry all over again. The fact that his anger was manifested by a fear of losing me was an overwhelming relief. I drew in a shaky breath as Eric brought his other hand up to rest against my cheek, gently forcing me to look at him.

His smile was sad. "You've got this super power and I'm the only one that knows, right?"

I nodded. "You and Micah. Oh, and I guess your friend from college."

He sighed. "So only a trusted few."

I nodded again.

"Well maybe you could just try not using it then."

Huh, that was a change. Hadn't he been the one telling me not to deny the world my gift? Yesterday really spooked him big time.

I wanted to nod fervently. I wanted to please him.

But I couldn't.

My forehead creased as I tried to form the right words. "It's not like I want this ability, Eric. I mean, you've helped me learn to control it, but..." I pressed my lips together. "I never expected to see the Indie and Liam thing. I wasn't searching for it at all, but I saw it and I'll probably see other stuff in the future too. How can I turn away? I can't... If someone's hurting, I can't just turn my back on that, especially if I think I can help." My forehead was a wrinkled mess as I begged him to accept what I'd said.

His smile finally softened one degree more as his

eyes gleamed with tenderness. He shook his head with a soft snicker. "That homeless guy was right. You're a good soul, Caity. And damn it, that just makes me love you more."

My heart jolted, my lips parting in surprise. "You love me?"

"Little bit." His nose wrinkled.

I couldn't help a smile. It blossomed on my face like a spring flower opening up to the sunlight. Gripping his wrists, I whispered, "So you didn't come over to break up with me then...even though we're not officially boyfriend and girlfriend yet?" I blushed.

He tipped his head, a smile hiding on the edges of his serious expression. "As long as you promise to call me every time you get yourself into shit, then no, I'm not breaking up with you...my girlfriend."

My insides sizzled with giddy excitement.

"Well, as long as you answer your phone, we should be sweet." My cheeky grin was met with an unamused glare. I winced. "Too soon?"

"Little bit." His eyebrows rose and I giggled.

"Well maybe we should just cut this conversation short by kissing or something."

His golden smile appeared, the one I could sink into on a daily basis. He moved toward me and pressed it against my willing lips, filling me with a secure warmth that shunted all my fears aside. I wrapped my arms around his neck as his hands moved to my waist, pulling me close and holding me against him so the world couldn't touch me.

epilogue

The sun was hot and luscious as I made my way across the grass and down to the sand. Eric was bobbing on his surfboard out in the water, his torso wet, shiny and delicious. I paused in the sand, watching his strong arms paddle through the water and his lean body jump into position on the board. I couldn't take my eyes off the way his muscles curved and moved as he carved up the wave.

Damn, he was hot. And he was mine. Still.

It had been two months since the Liam incident. The Donovan boys had disappeared off the face of the earth. As each week passed, I stopped looking over my shoulder a little less. I didn't know what had become of them and I didn't know if they would one day resurface, but I think I'd read them right and I couldn't help pitying them just a little. They were scared little kids who had never had the chance to grow up right. I feared for the people in their future, but it could no longer be my problem.

I couldn't carry that. Just like I couldn't carry the world. The whole incident had really put me off people-reading, not that I was that into it in the first place. I still did it without meaning to sometimes, but I had decided that unless I saw something dire, I wasn't going to act. The world could survive without my meddling for a while.

My senior year at Pali High was drawing to an end and I had made it through unscathed. I couldn't say the same for everybody. Thankfully with Liam no longer ruling the school, all problems seemed minor. But Stella and I would never be friends again, that much was clear. In fact I lost all my old friends. Chase and Stella made sure I was completely shut out. What they failed to notice was that I didn't care. Libby had quickly become a close friend and since Indie was back in town, we were hanging out with her and Micah a bunch, too.

Stella and most of her sad-ass, cheating friends were finishing their senior year on a major downer. She was running off to Europe for the summer with a private tutor. I'd heard she'd planned to catch up on all the repeated work she had to do while checking out

Tuscany. She'd probably work her way through Italy and end up on some Spanish beach by the end of the summer. I no longer cared.

The people I did care about, however, were doing great.

Libby, free from the demanding workload, had ended up flying through her last couple of months. Thanks to her, we aced our Biology assignment. She got into Princeton, just the way she'd wanted to and would be graduating with one of the highest GPAs in the school. She was hanging around L.A. for the summer and we were planning on catching up as much as we could.

Indie had spent the rest of her year on set with her father. She really didn't want to go, but he'd insisted. She'd had a tutor to get her through and when I saw her a few days earlier, she'd managed enough credits. She was going to graduate. She and Micah were still loved up to the max and she'd managed to convince her father to let her attend U.C. Berkeley, which was where Micah had scored his basketball scholarship. Things were looking good for both of them.

And me. I was pretty happy too.

Eric made his way out of the water, a big grin on his face as he ran up the beach toward me. Dropping his surfboard to the ground, he collected me in his arms and laughed at my squeals as his wet body soaked my clothing.

"Thanks for that." I kept my hands on his damp

shoulders.

"Anytime." He nuzzled my neck, making my skin tingle. "What are you doing here? I thought I was meeting you later."

"I know. I just wanted to show you something." I pulled the acceptance letter from my back pocket and tapped it against his chest.

Grabbing his towel, he dried his hands and carefully unfolded the paper. His curiosity morphed to pleasure and he leaned forward to kiss me. "Congratulations."

"Thanks." I nodded. "I've heard U.C.L.A. is a good school."

"It is." He grinned. "I know a couple of people who already go there. One in particular, who is very keen to show you around...keep you out of trouble." He winked.

"Hey, I've lasted two months without trouble." My grin faded. We both knew it was only a matter of time. I shoved the letter back into my pocket and tried not to let that thought bother me. "I figured that this was probably the best school for me. It'll be good to have certain people nearby, you know with all the trouble I supposedly get myself into."

"Supposedly. Mmhh." He stepped forward, gliding his arm around my back. "I sure hope you know someone who can keep you safe, Caitlyn Davis." His eyes danced.

I shrugged, biting back my smile. "I'm pretty tight with Hercules, so I should be sweet."

He captured my grin with his lips, his tongue dancing

with mine as he lifted me off the sand. Eric was right; I wouldn't be able to stay out of trouble forever. There were too many screwed up people in the world and I'd be drawn to help another sooner or later, but with him by my side, I knew for sure that I could handle it.

****

Or can she?

Keep reading to find out more about the trouble Caitlyn will get into in Two Faced (Masks #2).

dear reader...

Caitlyn's new ability is a life changer and she's going to need Eric more than ever as she enters the world of college.

But can Eric handle what Caity sees next?

When she spots something sinister about a person he's always looked up to, Eric is thrown into turmoil. His trust in people will be put to the ultimate test as he tries to decide if dating someone who can see behind people's masks is something he can handle.

Can Caity and Eric survive their first year at UCLA together?

Find out in Two-Faced.

xx
Melissa

acknowledgements

Thank you so much for everyone who has contributed to this project. I'd like to give special thanks to a few key people.

Margery from Evatopia Press - it was so fantastic working with you on the initial drafts.

Emily - the new cover rocks my socks! Thank you so much for your creativity and talent.

Cassie, Beth and Brenda - as always, your feedback is top notch and so vital in making sure my book is a strong story that people will enjoy.

Kristin - thank you for your extra help at the end with proofing this book. You caught so many little mistakes I'd missed and I'm so grateful for your keen eye.

Rachael - thanks for being the world's best assistant.

Songbirds & Playmakers - thanks for all your support. I love posting in the group each day and interacting with you.

My readers - I wouldn't be doing this if it weren't for

you. Thank you so much for reading my work and then taking the time to tell me about it.

My boys - Jake and Brody - thanks for always making me laugh. You are my cheeky monkeys and I adore you.

My family - your constant love, support and faith in me is so appreciated. I love you all so much.

My inspiration - thanks for another great story idea. I love the characters in this series, thanks for always fueling my imagination.

CPSIA information can be obtained
at www.ICGtesting.com
Printed in the USA
BVHW032136240621
610431BV00005B/99